The Briggar Stone

JAMES PARSONS

First paperback edition 2024

Anuci Press edition 2024

www.anuci-press.com

CoverDesign by Adrian Medina

https://fabledbeastdesign.wordpress.com

ISBN 979-8-9905033-3-5 (paperback)

ISBN 979-8-9905033-4-2(ebook)

Oh, had his powerful destiny ordained

Me some inferior Angel, I had stood

Then happy; no unbounded hope had raised

Ambition. Yet why not? some other Power

As great might have aspired, and me, though mean,

Drawn to his part; but other Powers as great

Fell not, but stand unshaken, from within

Or from without, to all temptations armed.

Hadst thou the same free will and power to stand?

65, Book IV

Milton Paradise Lost

For the tiniest angel, with amethyst eyes,

and hair spun like gold, 'fore the alter did rise

Pronouncing these words in disguised tone

'o impious imp, be ye turned to stone!

1891 R.L. Stevenson

Chapter One

The Briggar stone was a strange and mystical local relic. Up and down the country there were many similar large rocks with often not entirely defined reason for being where they were placed. Briggar was more unusual than most in that it seemed at times to defy gravity and perception in the ways in which it arched and leaned directly over the river as it stood right on one side of it. It should have fallen in easily long ago but somehow it remained huge in bulk at almost ten foot in height and around four foot wide. There had been at least a dozen main theories to the reason for it being there, some though it stood as a marker used by the Romans or other waring groups in times since Cromwell and civil disputes, many of course believed it to be of Pagan origin or part of a building or temple even of some other faith. Some of those historians mused that it may be the last part of a whole building or temple once there but since destroyed or ruined by attacks or nature, the rest possibly deep under the riverbed out of view. To the local townsfolk they had a few simple but satisfying enough rumours about what it had been put there for, what it signified. Many believed it probably as either druids using it to worship the elements or some basic marker of land limits from feudal lords of some centuries before. Some did however seek to believe more dramatic but still unfounded notions such as it being a temple to a god or goddess, offerings given there, holy men and women came to the riverside to baptise, pray and a regular bloody struggle beside the temple could be witnessed before it was knocked down to the ground by a new king. These ideas came extrapolated or optimistically interpreted from excavated old notes and poems and stories recorded in extremely old local history books and journals in the town library or the bookshelves of a few families.

The day had passed quick though unremarkably for Jackson in his office rooms down the low west end of the town. He took one last brief break early evening and noticed out of a window entrance hall a familiar man passed along with a dog at his side. He heard the quiet argument followed by a burst of laughter and stepped out onto the street to catch the man. Once outside Jackson stepped around passersby but the man was gone down some street or alley all too fast. The left his employees working away until they had finished their designated work as he walked to his car while the sky above darkened. The hour was late, and dusk came down when Jackson walked alone down the side lane to reach the Briggar stone. His new disciples would be waiting for guidance. The barking was there, dogs being walked by locals as usual along the riverside. He saw more lately, those small pug types were gaining popularity and some larger ones too. He wondered what breed the ones he heard could be, the barking sounded so defined and almost like language as it snapped out across the way. The rows of tall trees masked the view of them as he walked on. He heard talk, some conversation behind the trees. Some heated argument, between the barking. Were the voices ones he knew personally? Was the owner talking to the dog like it was a person? People did do that with their pets, as pointless as it seemed. No wait...it was someone arguing with the animal. Barking returned but the barks were words. They surely were. Was that right? No, it must be a couple with their dogs, trying to agree about some personal matter.

The trees parted and he came out to the wide-open grass lands beside the river, metres ahead the Briggar stone on the riverside. He turned back when he thought he heard his name called. The arguing couple could not be seen but two large overgrown dogs stood on their back legs, forelegs against each other as if they were fighting like deer or ram. They separated as if they knew they had been caught in the act, stopped for a moment before they rushed away back through the dense trees. He shrugged and walked on, came to stand before the stone. He looked down and checked the time on his watch, looked out and saw Pete and Sally approach. Over on the far right one of the large dogs stood and stared right at him before it bounded away. He stepped ahead and touched the rugged surface of the giant ancient stone which stood over the flowing river. The sound soothed his mind, dispelled his troubled thoughts as ever. His name came like a bark, torn through the silence from behind.

He swung around to see Pete with a friendly patient smile, Samantha to his left.

'That's right. I'm here now. Hello both of you. You look well. Are you feeling blessed to stand here beside the stone at the riverside with me?'

'Yes, we do, we are blessed,' Pete replied.

'We are, yes, we're blessed,' Samantha added.

Jackson kept one hand against the stone and with the other he reached out and touched Pete 'Tell me now, what's different?' he asked.

They looked at him and at the stone before the river.

'I...no...I...see better. I see more' Pete said and took away his glasses. He tried them on and off once again. 'My sight, it's like it was when I was younger, so much clearer again. Oh, my word...oh...' he peered down at the flowing water of the river down before them. He spun around to look back at the town, the buildings, the trees lined up on the perimeter and back to Jackson 'My sight is perfect. You've healed my sight,'

'Not I but the stone. And Samantha, what have you experienced lately?' Jackson asked. He offered a warm and persuasive smile to her.

'I have seen something, a place. It was the same as what Pete described last time. This place had a serene light and wonder. Hard to describe but it was peaceful but exciting at the same time. I wanted to be there but was sacred to get there as well,' She turned and looked at Pete who stepped around as he looked at his surroundings with an ecstatic wonder and glee.

'Will that last?'

'We shall see,' Jackson replied calmly.

'Okay. Are we ill?' she asked.

Jackson laughed pleasantly 'No, believe me you really are healthy, more than most people in our town. Now Pete, what you've experienced remember it was not me but the stone and what it represents, what it connects us to. You must promise to listen to me, anything to protect Briggar stone and the connection it provides. You promise?'

'Absolutely, anything at all'

'That's good. Now please, sit and pray here. You are not judged here as you were at your previous places of worship, those hypocritical churches with their rituals but lack of belief. The same goes for you Samantha. More of what you want may just arrive' he told them. He stood with them, walked calmly around them, and looked from the town back to the ancient stone behind him. They finished their quiet prayers and stood.

'Good. Same time again when next I call. Keep well and keep your faith,' he instructed with his calm sincerity. He sent them on their way and as they walked back into town, he drove back in his large four by four over the stone trail and muddy lane to the roads ahead. As the car moved along, he heard the yelping howls of dogs like words of warning somewhere among the trees.

Chapter Two

Mae had been working long and hard hours but that was what had got her to this point of success with the independent company and contracts with major brands coming in. She could not slow down anytime yet she believed. It was there now, the perfect design. Her hand had put it all in place, the inspiration had finally arrived from somewhere somehow. It had not felt as if had come from her, her own intuition, her mind but from some other place. However, it had come to be there for her to see on the screen didn't matter, it was there ready to be cut and sized up and sent to the company who had been waiting. Relief washed over her when she sat back in her large armchair and heard the voice.

'Outside...' the voice from the corridor whispered.

Mae looked out of the studio room window to the shuffling, gruff noise down below. Her fingers gripped the window frame tight on seeing the animal. It was almost the size of a horse, but the shape of the body and head did show it to be a kind of dog. It must have been the largest dog she had possibly ever witnessed if indeed it was some form of canine. As it twisted and turned, she thought for a second she had been mistaken and witnessed a horse but the head of it came back around plain to enough. Lee had not been lying to them or playing any kind of practical joke this time. This creature was unbelievably huge she thought as she watched it roam and sniff down at the lower side wall and grass around. It stalked around below its nose rustled in the fallen leaves and grass, but its paws made an echoing crunch and crack over twigs and debris down there. It tilted its head up toward the window and Mae jerked back behind the curtain afraid. There was something in the strange canine face of the dog which expressed some kind of familiarity she thought. It did not entirely scare her. After a few minutes she decided to make her way down and step outside.

She began to wonder how late she should work and if the thing would be down there and waiting to attack her. What kind of dog was that? Where had I come from? Had it simply been in her mind? Had Lee simply put the idea of the large dog there? She had seen the paw prints and heard it down below the window. It had seemed so very real to her earlier. She thought she might ask Jackson to collect her if it returned but she did not want to talk about the dog as she would seem paranoid and unstable. She worked on until eight at night, some Sousie and the Banshees keeping her motivated on the stereo while she worked on the design project.

The dog was gone when she stepped around in the dried mud outside the studio and saw the curiously large paw prints behind the studio in the muddy ground and grass and turned to walk in the other direction. She felt the need to look the dog in those eyes which she believed she already knew and had some human quality to them. She walked for near fifteen minutes alone with the sound of sparrows and some other distant dog with its owners somewhere along to beside the river which stretched along behind the grass fields behind the studio side of town. She peered down at the running water of the river a few feet from her. It did bring a calm to her mind, the flow hypnotic, ebb and silent reflection of the sky and clouds over her. She saw the Briggar stone somehow aligned right next to the design studio and decided to return, compelled to walked toward it instinctively.

Mae turned away and walked back inside the studio, slammed the door shut behind her and moved to her own room in a sprint. When she returned, she found a message from Jackson on her phone which sat on her desk.

'Hey babe, you doing good today?' it read.

She thought briefly and replied.

'Good yh. Had a walk just now to clear my head. Productive day so far. Thnx'

She heard the rustle in the equipment room and with her right hand gripped on the door frame she leaned in. She saw the three mannequins still halfway inside the room with their collective blank heads void of expression, only a thin strip of daylight cast over them through the curtains. They stood faceless once more, simply manufactured torso with fabric designs pinned over them.

'I'm losing it. You lot aren't helping' she told them 'Kathrine, you'd actually laugh if you saw me today.'

She turned back and entered her own room, sat back at the desk, and opened the monitor screen and new design work to simply stare with satisfaction and relief some more.

'Thank you' Mae whispered to whatever had moved and led her hand to illustrate such designs after the feeling had been stirring within her knowingly for so long, waiting to be put down to be seen.

There was breathing over her shoulder.

'Help you...help me...hell...hello' the voice rasped from behind the mannequins under shadow. A caring, familiar voice of a close dear friend which she believed she would never ever hear again in her life-time.

She spun around. The layers of shadows cast by cabinets and old equipment she could see the basic silhouette of a thin emaciated and dirt smeared figure in a ragged dress which stood opposite her. The face while obscured by shadow she had known and loved deeply, and the hands came out forward with some light cast over them. She could see broken nails and layers of mud and torn and tattered cuffs around the wrists, blood, and earth all along the arms and legs as if the person had pulled themselves up from a hole in the ground. The figure moved a couple of steps, and before her she saw a person, she had believed dead who looked back at her, withered smile, tattered clothes and bruised and raw flesh under the bright narrow slice of light which shone through from the side of them.

'Katherine?' Mae asked quietly, her voice dry and fearful. She knew that voice, it lived in her memories, in her mind. The name slipped through her lips without thinking how she was possibly seeing the person before her. Katherine had been declared dead after having been missing along with her parents after weeks of police searching the town and wider areas. She had gone from them, gone from Jen and Issy; three years gone. They had attended the funeral, mourned her, said their goodbyes and with difficulty managed to move on with their lives.

'Hell…hello Mae…,' Katherine said with a dry damaged throat through chapped and blistered familiar lips. The mouth made a smile toward Mae who simply cried and froze where she stood. Katherine looked to her with a trembling pale face from behind the mannequins in the corner of the room 'I am pleased…this is what…you want?'

Mae took a step toward her as she fixed on the dirt smeared thin arms and the battered hands. Katherine moved back into the shadows of the room.

'Katherine, where have you been. There was a funeral, we all thought you had...'

'I... moved...away...my family...' Katherine responded slowly. The words fell out like broken pieces of jigsaw into thick muddied waters.

'Are you hurt? Your hands and arms, have you been in some kind of accident?' Mae asked. She stopped where she stood as she realised Katherine did not wish to be touched or seen in full view just yet.

'Do you need some help, some medical attention, are you hurt?'

'...not hurt...'

'Okay even just...a shower, bath? The restroom is down the corridor there' Mae suggested and pointed to the corridor outside the room.

'I helped you; you help me...' was the simple and quiet response.

'You...were you...did you move my hand as I drew?'

Katherine gave a slow speechless nod of her head.

'Right. Thank you, it means a lot. You're unblocked my creative lull. It looks fantastic, the design. Kind of familiar but not. There is so much in it all, the imagery is bold and simple but detailed and striking. Do you want something to eat or drink?'

There was a silent moment before Katherine spoke again.

'Help you. From here' she said with one hand outstretched.

'Aren't you with your family?'

'Hide me Mae...'

'Can you tell me what's happened, why? You can stay at my flat...'

Katherine simply moved back into shadows, let out a sigh and rubbed her hands against her head rhythmically.

'Alright, stay in here for now if it's what you want. I'll bring some water, food, painkillers. I won't tell my colleagues you're in here. I will come and check on you later.'

Mae walked to the left and took a hold of the drawstring to open the blind and let in daylight. A sudden moan came from the shadows, from Katherine.

'Oh. I'll leave the curtains, no problem' Mae responded.

She closed the door and walked out down to the kitchen room as Lee came along with a smile.

'Things are looking now then, aren't they?' he said.

'What? Oh yeah that's right. Hey, don't come into my room for the rest of the day. I need to focus and make calls and emails, do checks on the design. Tell Beth too, okay?' she told him.

'Right yeah, okay. Not a problem. I'll look at the next briefs we had lined up and start my ideas' and he entered his room door closed behind him.

She returned with the things needed moments later and led Katherine into her own room with discretion. She sat back down to look over the new design. She ran tests over the clothing templates and rearranged the sizes of parts of it. She could hear Katherine behind her, feel her presence over her shoulders as she worked. It was strange but she appreciated it however Katherine wanted to be there with her. After half and hour or more Mae stopped and thought out loud.

'I feel like it's been there in me for a long time, since before we put together this design studio, since...since our college days maybe. There it is. These are the designs, the images, the clothes I had to get down from my mind. They'll be made and worn. They will. Thank you. I'm glad you're back. Don't hide over there' Mae said, 'You don't need to.'

Katherine remained cloaked in shadows of the room between and within, uneasy, hidden but content to stare back at her.

'Okay, well when you feel you can, come out and be with me. You're sticking around, are you? You want a drink, coffee, whisky? Okay when you want.'

'Here, yes, for you' the thin voice of Katherine replied.

'Good, I'm pleased. Good to have you back. You've been missed you know that?' Mae said as she looked back at her old friend with wonder.

She took her smartphone on her left side and casually messaged Beth to tell her an old friend had dropped by and was with her in her room but not to disturb them anytime soon until she gave them a heads up. When early evening came around before six o'clock, Mae walked out to the corridor and met Beth and Lee by the staircase.

'Who's your friend?' Beth asked quietly 'She's still here?'

'Yes, she's been away awhile, and she's sort of shy. I'll see her out soon. You guys get going now if you want. Thanks for your documents, we'll discuss them properly tomorrow' Mae told them and saw them off before she walked back to her own room.

The evening had arrived, and the room was total darkness, only the small lights from her computer and smartphone glowed red and green to remind her of the layout.

'Katherine are you in here?' she called. No response came as she walked in a flicked on the small table lamp on her desk.

A croaked rasp of a word erupted in the dark, all corners of the room finally illuminated if dimly.

Mae looked all around the room before her and there was no trace of Katherine in the room. She spun around and stepped to the doorway, looked out into the corridor.

'Katherine?' she called.

'Help Mae...help...me...' the voice of Katherine spoke from downstairs.

'You're down there already. Okay, well wait for me. I'll just grab my things,' Mae called. She rushed back a moment later with her bag on shoulder and files under her left arm as she quickly made her way down the stairs. The front door to the studio was wide open, the chill breeze entered inside. Mae did not find Katherine there and so walked outside.

She looked from left to right, the many tall trees and overgrown wild bushes and thick clumps of grass confronted her sight initially until she did make out the thin shape of Katherine behind the trees, a shoulder and part of her face visible.

'Katherine, aren't you coming to my flat or are you, are you going your family?' Mae asked.

'Tomorrow' Katherine replied quietly.

'Back tomorrow?' Mae asked 'Okay then. See you here again early if you are sure.'

Katherine instantly disappeared somehow between and beyond the trees and so Mae turned her back and walked into town.

The smartphone Mae held buzzed, and she saw a message from Beth-

'Don't stay too long. I'm leaving now. See you tomorrow.'

'Are you leaving now? Wait a while. There's that dog and strange man outside. Lee was telling the truth 'She messaged back.

Mae called her 'I'm outside by the entrance. I don't see...'

She caught sight of the back of a male figure which moved away up the side road which led out of town toward the old tyre factory. He was gone seconds later but she heard the faint barks echo through the darkening night around her.

Chapter Three

Mae came through the pub doors and straight away noticed her long-time old friends Jen and Issy sat on a low sofa by the side wall in the pub. They cheered and raised glasses at her as she came across to hug them. More time had passed than usual between their regular meeting every couple of weeks. She had hardly noticed until the events at the design studio had made her need to meet with them face to face as soon as she could. She felt her whole body shake and she rubbed her hands together and clenched her handbag as she moved through to be with them. Could they see the genuine surprise and confusion and joy in her eyes and face? Would these two close old friends believe anything she might decide to tell them about the return of their departed and believed deceased friend Katherine?

'Good evening you silly gals, it's been too long. What was going on?' She said, squeezing each with arms linked, a dig in the ribs of each. She sat between them her hands ceaselessly fiddling with her handbag nervously. She was aware of doing it but could not easily stop her fingers fidgeting. She took a deep breath and force the smile wider and offered it to each of them.

'Bloody hell Mae. Chill your arse. What's going on with you though?' Issy asked, sensing the out of character nervousness.

'Me, nothing too wild,' Mae replied as she sat back and tried to relax 'The day job, better than ever. How about both of you. I get that impression as well.'

They each nodded, smiling back.

'That's great, and that big client design project-it's done, is it?' Issy asked.

Mae glanced at her, mouth agape as time seemed to freeze around them.

'Yes. Yes...I need to tell you both that...the final design has come around and its amazing. It was like I wasn't evening doing myself. It was someone else, like I had help. It looks great, they want it and want more I seems' she told them.

'That's fantastic. Must be such a relief' Issy responded 'We knew it was moving slow and an important client. Hey, my team with the council youth project, it's finally all going super-nova. All on course as hoped before we stepped out after being foolish students with the endless hangovers. Full-time hours at the youth centre direction team, solid role now personally, making good progress. Got my own little team set up and give space to grow my team.'

Mae nodded with a nervous smile 'Nice one mate. Jen girl, how about the film stuff now, where's it at?'

Jen smiled 'Yeah, only last week we connected with the guys who made the award-winning short with that actor, the tall funky girl with the mad eyes who is working with Nolan, they say. I'm going to do some small things with them in a few weeks hopefully if they like my current work on the local history culture vlog thing going on. The sponsor might leave us if we don't get a boost in viral viewing figures soon, so the heat is on but it's good.'

They clinked their glasses together triumphantly, smiling and laughing.

'Alright so let's have a couple more am I right?' Issy said with a joyful wail as she stood patting her friends on the shoulders.

Around thirty minutes later when Issy went to the toilet Mae leaned close to Jen.

'Listen, there are some things that aren't how they should be.'

'Oh. Ah, you're not getting any is that it?'

'No, I've got Jackson still but...maybe he's been overworking way too much. Deadlines beating me down but...'

'What is it, what's up? You seem anxious for real.'

'You ever think you don't hear things right or see things that you know aren't there but see them anyway?'

Jen tilted her head and reached to touch Mae's hands on the table 'Mae, you doing any drugs to cope with the workload?'

Mae looked around the pub, scratched her neck and moved her long hair around her neck and shoulders as she looked down at the table before them.

'I remember our friend Katherine. I mean, I...do you ever think you see her? Or feel her around you?'

'Yeah, of course. The memories don't leave. I miss her.'

Mae stared straight down at their hands on the table 'Do you think, if we had difficult feelings or memories connected to her or someone close who's passed away, we might let ourselves think they are around us in a very real way?'

'Are you okay?'

'Yes. Yes, I'm really good, work's good, I'm good I...' she looked down as she continued '...I am sure she was at my studio. She helped with my work and was there and we spoke. Then later, she went away.'

She looked up and saw Jen unsure how to react, a slight smile restrained by a cautious raised eyebrow and hand out to touch her own over the table.

'You do think you're feeling okay?'

'Yes. I'm not taking the piss and I'm not going...she was there.'

Jen kept the hand and Mae's hand but leaned back as she looked away for a moment. When she looked back at Mae it was with an expression of tense doubt and discomfort. Issy strolled back to join them, grinning at each, and slapping them on the legs as she sat back beside Mae.

'What've I missed girls?'

Jen remained silent and let Mae respond.

'Just talking bollocks about Netflix and shows. Where are you heading with the vlog reporting films next week then?' Mae asked and the time was for Jen to talk.

'We're talking about Katherine. You see...' she looked at Mae as she continued 'Mae has seen her.'

Issy glanced at both with a cynical smile for a moment until she could tell they were in no way playing with her.

'That's not funny' she said quietly. Jen shrugged and turned to glance at Mae who sat with her head low.

'You saw her?' Issy asked.

'She was at my studio. Gone now' Mae quietly told her. Jen gave a look to be reasonable.

'You work too hard' Issy said simply 'Take some time off now the client is happy.'

Mae slowly looked up to her 'We've believed she was dead or missing.'

'We did, yes' Jen agreed and rubbed her hand gently as she kept her eyes on Issy.

'Ghosts are bullshit' Issy scoffed as she choked up and a tear rolled down her left cheek.

'She is back, but not meant to be. She's been with her parents. They are looking for her' Mae continued.

'We went to the funeral. And her parents and then they left town. She...' Jen began until the words became too difficult to release.

'She's alive, is that what you're saying?' Issy asked.

Jen flashed wide eyes at her with a stern expression.

'She is. But she's...different, maybe ill or not in great shape.'

'You say, they're looking for her? Like she's escaped? Did they take her away?' Issy asked.

'The family moved, back to some other property she said. She doesn't want to be found, not yet.'

Jen spoke next 'We left her to rot. We shouldn't have done that.'

Issy placed her palms flat on the table and breath out 'I didn't. She just closed in on herself. She was too shy, too self-absorbed. We couldn't do too much. She'd didn't help herself enough.'

'People can always help others' Issy added.

Mae shook her head 'Not always. Not her'

'Some people don't know how to get help or open up, that's not their fault. Doesn't make them wrong or idiots. We left her' Jen said.

'So where is she now?' Issy asked.

'I think she's gone to the old place they lived or...well I said she could come to my place so she might turn up there. I offered but she didn't turn up. I think they might come around looking and she knows that.'

'Where was that old family house? Do you two remember?' Issy asked. Jen and Mae looked at her blank. They looked at each other as they each tried to understand what Mae had told them.

'I remember Katherine told me how she used to go near the river, along the riverbank, watch the water flowing, coming here from elsewhere. It fascinated her,' Jen said 'There was almost some kind of accident where she fell in but was pulled out as she blacked out. Her parents didn't think it was a major thing, but she had fallen deep down in the river but lay there under the water and experienced the most otherworldly sights. She believed she saw ghosts, phantoms, angels, and other things. Sights from times which came later or so she told us. She was such a dream, that amazing imagination.'

Mae nodded 'She's back, been through difficult things. She'll heal. She's the same person we knew. Same great imagination I can tell you that. My new project has become something fantastic, better than I could have put down. She led my hand, brough it out of me.'

'Issy, I am telling you both the truth' Mae said quietly.

'Alright. Where is she? Do we tell police or social services now?' Issy responded.

'She'll be back. Probably to my studio. I just had to tell both of you in person. I'm not ill. She is back in town. She is alive, our dear sweet friend is alive' Mae said with a look of subdued joy.

'Okay, we believe you, you know we do don't we Issy?' Jen said and looked across for the right reply.

Issy sniffed and gave a nod 'We do. We'll watch out for her parents. Let us know when she is back. Maybe we can come see her. I would like to see her again.'

'Same here. We will' Jen added. 'This is it. Mae, let us know if she returns. We'll come meet both of you right?' Jen said as they began to walk in separate directions at the top of her street.

'Yes, I'll message you. I'll be in touch. See you soon' Mae told them. They hugged her and consumed another couple of drinks, talked about films and holiday plans before they stood together and left the pub around ten thirty. They walked up the street together and Jen and Issy watched Mae go her separate way and wondered why their old friend had come to visit her first and just what had she been through over the last three years while missing and presumed dead to this world.

<h1>Chapter Four</h1>

When she was certain that the morning had arrived, light emerging through the curtains Mae left her bedroom to make coffee quietly in the kitchen. There was trouble in her mind, conflicted questions about what she had been dreaming while asleep and awake recently. Her phone soon drummed a vibration on the kitchen table with a message. The name of Jackson appeared on screen. He had given her such exciting new experiences in life and in bed over the last year or more. It had not been a constant thing, not a steady relationship or even a real announced thing but each time they came together was a thrilling experience and to ignore his message was a real challenge. She was not in the greatest headspace but to speak or be with him could bring warm safety and comfort even if it was only for show. Even a satisfying good fuck might help in the short term she thought.

'Hello there, you well?' she asked while she tried to mask any uneasy distraction in voice.

'Good now I hear you. I'd like your time if that's alright. I'll be in town today, I've a work meeting but later on...feel like meeting up?' he said.

She paused, unsure of what her plans should be. The troubling sights and the encounter of what she believed to be Katherine yesterday had changed everything ahead at this point.

'You there Mae?'

'Yeah. Some things have happened, been busy in a different way. Can't easily explain.'

'Then don't. Or tell me later when it feels better. So, feel like meeting later in the day?'

'I have great things to tell you about the project at work, it all came together out of the blue, I just put it all together on the computer and...'

'And what?'

'Some surprising things happened. I should be more relaxed than I am but...you can't always know what the day will bring can you?'

'That is true. So, tell me about it later. See you around five or six tonight' he told her and ended the call. She made her coffee and walked around her flat feeling like she was being watched while that made no sense.

As Lee walked up the road to the studio with his coffee mug in hand and whistled, he stumbled and straightened up. He peered down to see he had put his left foot into a very large hole, more like a footprint in the earth. There was another a couple of steps on, two more after and then they were harder to observe. They seemed to lead out and around the side of the ground floor of the design studio and to the wide overgrown open grass land beside. Behind which connected out the roads and parks and the riverside. He frowned, shrugged, and walked back toward the front entrance. That was when he noticed some bizarre much smeared up against the front door frame. It was smeared up around his own eye level and appeared like some crude mix of mucus, blood, and dirt. It disgusted him. He quickly found his keys, fumbled with the lock, and walked inside. As he stood making their coffees in the staffroom Beth and Mae walked in together chatting freely.

'Morning you two. See that nasty smeared shit up on the side of the front door outside?' he asked.

'Come on Lee, use the toilet like us women. Hope you'll clean it later' Beth said with a roar of laughter and a huge grin on show.

'What, no it wasn't me. Not this time. It was like a big turd was wiped down the door side with like, bloody bits all in with it. Some animal has done that or…it could be some kind of warning from someone' he guessed.

'A warning from who?' Mae asked as she took up her coffee from him and moved back to share a cynical look with Beth.

'No, there's that bloke. That huge dog outside, the bloke with the big dog the other day…' Mae said.

'What he'd wipe his own dog's shit up the front door?' Beth asked.

They looked at each other in disbelief.

'Lee, please just clean it off in a while yeah?' Mae said.

They walked from the staff canteen to their room entrances and left Lee mouth open before he huffed in frustration.

Beth stood beside Mae and leaned close to her 'I did think I heard those dog sounds yesterday evening before I left. Should we call some-one?'

Mae straightened 'Oh really? Did you see him?'

'No, just heard them as I was tidying things up. They were gone when I went outside.'

'I'll keep an eye out later in the day. Might be some strays around near us.'

'Is your old friend coming in again today?' Beth asked before she turned into her room.

'I...I can't be sure. She might be in the area today. I'll find out later' Mae told her as she entered her room with the that same thought in mind. She looked around the room at the wide desk, the old sofa, the cabinets, and smaller tables. She hoped to be greeted by Katherine. Until that happened, she sat down and opened her computer to start work on the other new projects lined up.

Over an hour later out at the front entrance of the studio grounds by the gate stood the man in his early fifties at least. He had a sly smile as if he always had more than enough secrets to bargain with. He nodded and finished with his cigar, flicked it to the ground. The slender large dog by his side looked up at him and then joined him in staring at the design studio before them.

'This is where Mae works, look what she's achieved. I bet she's made some people proud' he said as he looked up at the windows and out at the sides. The dog snuffled and roamed around by his shoes at the fallen autumn leaves and wet grass. He walked by the front entrance casually, glanced over at the doors and up at the windows. He nodded to himself as he scratched his hands, licked his dry lips.

'Can I help?' a voice asked behind him. He turned to see Lee stood grinning at him. There was a bucket of soapy hot water and some old rags as Lee took a break from cleaning up the filth smeared up the side of the entrance door. 'We design to quality fashion at request, bespoke. Dresses, jackets, shirts, things in quantity for occasions with design brief or we offed examples. You need anything like that? Maybe for special events, large parties, weddings and more. You look interested with the building. Have you been around recently? Think I might have seen you...'

The man gave a nod 'I know the town, how it used to be, the land, the old origins of the buildings such as this one here.'

'You know about bags for your dog shit too?' Lee enquired with a look of sarcasm.

'I know what matters. You know the history of where you work? What shaped the town you live in?'

'You know what this used to be?'

'That's right. The name is Ron. I know we have an iron monger which became a small pie shop which went bust after a few decades. Family business. Good when things last through a family like that isn't it?' through generations?'

Lee looked the man up and down, viewed his long coat, respectable shirt, and trousers beneath, good shoes, leather or imitation with nice buckles and heels. The man was clean shaved with grey at the sides, hair smart peppered grey slightly but still thick enough. The eyes had some fierce emotion in their dark hue which focused on him. He looked at the dog, which was quiet enough and looked a loyal sort, but it looked like it could move fast and savage when ordered to do so. It did have a mouth full of impressively sharp teeth it displayed while silent which made him keep a distance.

'Well Ron, some people don't have to worry so much about a job, some just step into the shoes of your old man or parents, learn the trade. Doesn't happen too much now though. My family lost a business, but I was only just born then. Easy times aren't around for most of us these days.'

'Oh, what was the family business?'

'They made wooden things-furniture and toys and things. Not normal carpentry stuff so they went bust. Retail Park opened up out on the main road between here and the next main town, big companies grew bigger, stronger competition, coming in killing off the small businesses. Sad but way of the world I suppose.'

'Wooden things...yes, so your name is Lee Tillborough, is it?'

'That's us, yes. You remember it?'

'I certainly do. I remember your grandfather, even his father I think, good men.'

'Really? Shit, how old are you?'

'Older than I look, but I was younger back then. This town could do with something like that business again, I think. You never thought of doing something like that?'

'Maybe had it in the back of my mind, to keep the family name going. But who'd pay for it all? I'm doing this work at the studio here now so that's not an option for a few reasons anyway.'

'What do you do, what's your part in all of it here?'

'Not a lot of designing right now unfortunately, for me at least. Mostly just a dog's body, fetching things, sending things, cleaning the place. Being using and taken for granted too often if I'm honest with you.'

'And how long will that continue?'

'Not forever, Mae's going to give me more opportunities to add my own things on the next project.'

'You can believe that you think?'

Lee gave a look of brief embarrassment 'I have to really.'

Ron looked around the street and the design studio front. He patted his dog on the head and looked back at Lee. 'I know many places in town, many businesses, how they're doing, which ones look to be set for big things, the ones which have something special. I know them and how they're doing financially, which need input and help or more creative flair. You might want to hear about them sometime, they might want to know about you, what you could offer if given the chance.'

Lee looked around, up at the first-floor window. He saw Beth and Mae in the canteen making coffee, laughing about something together. He looked back at Ron.

'That's your dog yeah?'

'Certainly is. Faithful bitch follows me everywhere. Sometimes that can be a pain, but a man needs a companion so. But you're thinking about my words, aren't you?'

'Yes, okay. Let's meet for a drink and you can tell me more. You've got me interested, Ron' he said. Ron suggested by the tallest tree at the end of the street next day at five in the evening and it was agreed.

Mae sat before her computer monitor, the files of the fantastic new pattern design spread out on the screen, and she sat back with a confident smile, let out a sigh.

'Katherine, you're here, aren't you?' she called quietly. The blinds were closed, only the slighted strips of light shone into the room. After a silent moment, a reply come through the room from the overlap of shadows 'I've missed you. I've thought about you a lot,'

Mae turned around in her chair, slow so as not to frighten, or startle her 'Have you been alright, are you hurt?'

'I...can't say...too much. Remember...my stories I told?'

'Of course. Your imagination was so vivid. All the animals and creatures, the places, and things you described and drew back then.'

'Look at your design now' Katherine suggested.

Mae turned to the computer monitor, looked at the way the dress designs had quickly evolved with the new intricate patterns. Shapes and forms became clearer from among and within the lines and contours.

'Oh wait...figures...people...creatures. It's kind of like a storyboard. Wait, are they some of those things?'

Katherine simply smiled and backed into the shadows 'Hide me, I am here. Keep me here...' she whispered. Mae stood afraid but pleased to see her friend. 'You left us, that's what everyone thought. Do you want to tell me about it, why you went away? I would like to know' Mae said.

Silence greeted her.

'I think something has happened and you have been affected by it,' Mae stated 'I think your parents have something and should be held to account. I want to help you, like you're helping me.'

'Hide me, help me...' she heard again. Katherine moved around within the shadows of the studio room behind the mannequins. She seemed made of flesh and bone as before, seemed whole in a physical sense but something about her did seem different, not the same as before, even something to be wary of perhaps Mae thought. Katherine stepped back deeper within the shadows beside the long purple curtains.

'Don't come near. Let me stay,' Katherine whispered from behind the mannequins.

Mae did not understand why her friend had returned now, at this time and was speaking some riddles. Why could she not tell her what her parents had done?

'I was not supposed to return. It had been long enough...' Katherine continued.

Katherine merged into the shadows, only her eyes visible. Mae stepped forward and moved closer to the curtains which contained her. She stood and reached out between the mannequins to touch her, to comfort her old friend. The deep shadows of the room consumed her.

'I need you. I am here for you. Hide me'

'You know I will. I won't tell. Stay there'

Mae stepped back from the dark corner and mannequins to her desk and turned back to her work. She desperately wanted to call the police or social services but if Katherine did not want that she would hold back from it, at least for a while until the truth was what had happened was clearer.

It was midday when Mae stepped out to the corner café to pick up her tuna wrap and made her way back. As she approached the gate to the design studio, she came to find Ron there, smile on his face, no dog. He came toward Mae.

'We know each other, right? You know my daughter' he said with an affable smile and a tilt of his head as he rubbed his hands. She noticed him pick at his chipped fingernails with some visible irritation briefly while he looked at her.

Mae was taken aback. She had not seen this man since before Katherine had passed away. Four years had almost passed. He was supposed to be dead or that was what they had all assumed before Katherine went from them a short while later when she decided to look for them and failed to find them. Mae had spoken to this familiar man many times, sat with him and his wife while she had visited Katherine before or after college. He had always seemed like a charming father, better than her own in some ways. But he stood before her, and she could only wonder what he had done to his daughter, and she had to hold back an immediate outburst if she was to help her friend in any way. Something about his eyes and his thin wet lips made her feel nauseous, repulsed deep inside.

'You...where have you been?' she asked, the words difficult to speak as she was simply in shock to see him before her.

'We travelled away, to see family. You look well' he said as his eyes moved up to look at the studio behind her.' This is where you work? Fashion wasn't it, at college?'

'Yes...yes, it's a small studio. Some others and me. Your wife, is she back as well?'

He nodded with his smile curled up yet sour, his eyes contained some hint of dissatisfaction and withheld emotion.

'Yes, we are in town now' he said as he stepped closer and gave more urgent and vulnerable expression 'Have you seen our Katherine around recently?'

There it was. The link, the name and the question connecting them, her old dear friend, and his daughter. Could she tell him that Katherine was up in her design room? Would he storm up there and pull her away, back to some place of torment and abuse? Would it be best to be honest to him, her father who had always seems such a kind and decent man?

She looked him up and down and replied 'I don't think I have, no. Did she return with you?'

'She came back first, but yes we're all here' he replied as he continued to fidget with his broken nails and bruised hands 'It may not be for too long, a short return probably. You think you might have seen her; you don't seem entirely sure you haven't?'

'I mean, I've seen traces of her, my memories when I've been around town. That's what I mean. You know, we all thought she...and you and your wife...'

He gave a solemn nod 'Alright, that will do. Be careful around. Last time we were here there were some big dogs sniffing near this area, strays but they could be unpredictable so watch out for them.'

'Yes, I might have seen some. I agree, we've called the local authorities actually.'

'Right, might not make any difference...'

'So, look I have to get going. I hope you find her, tell her to drop by here soon if you can, I would really love to see her again.'

He changed his expression to a slight narrow sneer as if accused of some shameful act or ridiculed. 'She is around somewhere. I hope you see her.'

'You have a phone number I can contact you on?'

He took out a small notepad and quickly scrawl a number, tore the page away and passed it to her.

'Here. I will call back around. You may see my wife first.'

'Okay. Good to see you and hope to see all three of you soon.'

She watched him walked out of the studio grounds casually as he gave a wave before he turned off up the side street into town and she felt the hair on her neck prickled and she shivered before she moved quickly up to her room. The day moved along quick for all three of them in the studio and Lee was first to pick up his belongings and say his goodbye.

'Hey, it's been wild. Gotta go, see you losers tomorrow yeah?' he called down the corridor as he rushed down the stairs and out of the studio. He walked to the end of the street and looked around. Ron was nowhere in sight, and he started to think the guy had been taking the piss. He moved his shoulder bag, kicked the dirt, and began to walk into town when a shadow came over his own on the paving stones.

'Hello again. Been a productive day, has it?' Ron asked as he stood and offered a wink.

Lee turned to see him 'Oh, I suppose so. Where you want to go, get a drink somewhere near?'

They took a walk in the evening out toward some pubs, but Ron kept them going further along.

'Not going for a drink just yet?' Lee asked.

'Let's keep walking, I'll show you a couple of places of interest. So Lee Tollborough, that family name, yes, I do remember your grandfathers, saw them making those chairs and children's toys. Skilled men, shame, real shame it ended. You know, I think I remember when that retail place opened up. There was a couple of council businessmen cleared the way, some talk they received dirty money, bribes against local interest, cleared the way when a few businesses were not keen. They pissed off a few hard-working family businesses including your own. In a way, ruined your life. Two men in particular, one even still alive I believe. Works just up the road ahead, semi-retired but still makes an appearance. He owns a few properties which are sitting doing nothing. Would be good to see a special wood craft shop open around here again don't' you think?'

'Would he allow that?'

'I think he owes it to your family and you. I think he'll allow it-if you want a place for your projects, your expression, your skills, and designs.'

'Are we going to talk to this bloke?'

'I'll have a word. You think you like the idea?'

'I...I do like it, yes.'

Ron soon let him return to the studio with a head full of questions. Lee return and joined Beth and Mae as they each continued to look over the next two projects individually and send initial sketches and thoughts between each other over WhatsApp and email. The moved along somehow faster than most and soon enough Lee and Beth left the studio and Mae was left to lock up alone. She stood in her room and looked around her.

'You still in here Katherine?' she called. No reply came.

She lowered head, closed the blinds, turned off the desk lights, tidied her things on the desk and left the doors open as she checked the windows and stood by the entrance doors for a moment. She eventually decided Katherine must have left before she had noticed and so began to leave the studio alone.

The evening came and Mae changed her clothes in her flat with some upbeat music around her, tunes which usually lifted her spirits but that was a problem on this day. She looked for one of the dress tops Jackson had seemed to find a turn on a couple of times, combined it with shimmering skirt and tights, matching heels. The smell of the river emanated out from the bathroom, the sound of the river woman muttering somewhere in the flat around her. It was hard to keep her out, trying to block her presence. She clicked the volume of the music up louder and hummed along at the same time, forcing a smile as she looked through her clothes. She tried to ignore it all but found it too difficult.

Shadows warped around the room; the voice whispered into her ear. The shape on the wall to her right moved close. The silhouette moved and a human form stepped out from within shadow. In the hall the figure of Katherine watched her.

'Oh shit. You scared me. Katherine? You followed me here? Great, that's good you just startled me' She uttered quietly. 'I am going out, there's food in the fridge. Help yourself. I'll return later.'

As she stood in the kitchen, a juddering rumble shook through and around her, a framed poster fell from the wall ahead, a pot plant hit the floor and she stepped back, clenched the kitchen top behind her until the sensation ended abruptly. She waited and called out.

'Katherine? Are you alright?'

'Outside...' the quite respond came from down by her bed, Katherine hunched low. Mae stepped over and peered down beside the curtain to the street outside. She saw the large dog bound along around as it sniffed and nudged at some discarded takeaway box and leaves by some bushes.

'Fucking big dog that' Mae said. She turned back to look Katherine. There was no movement, no sound anywhere in the apartment.

'Katherine? Still here?' she called. It was just her and so she sat down to the television with a bowl of ham and cheese pasta and a familiar reality tv show. Once Mae fell into sleep Katherine floated down from the ceiling where she had hung. She glided down to rest beside Mae while she slept. As they lay side by side, patches of pastel light spread over them, and the tendrils slithered out from Katherine and pierced the warm flesh of Mae at her neck and arms through the night.

Chapter Five

Morning came and Mae sat up in her bed. Her bones ached and she stumbled more than usual as she shuffled to the bathroom. She soon got dressed and had a quick breakfast of coffee and toast before she rushed out to the design studio. She decided to get the bus as she felt a weakening fatigue slow her down. She had not found Katherine in her flat but guess she would turn up at some point in the day. Half an hour later Mae arrived at the studio, greeted Lee and Beth and once she checked on their individual progress with the new design patterns, she sat to check over her emails alone. Within his studio room Lee was sat at his computer desk as he idly tried colour and fabric variations on his project designs. Some movement of light over his right shoulder distracted him.

'Oh, you're actually making me a tea for a change are you, Beth?' he called and turned in his swivel chair. She was not behind him or in the room. He did see some part of a face, eyes and mouth half obscured in shadow to the left of the corner of the room. The light from outside stretched and clouds gave shadows weight in the room. On a mirrored cabinet if there had been a face, it was gone from viewing him.

'Fucking weird. We need more people here, going stir crazy just us' he mumbled 'Hey Beth, coffee time yeah?' he called out into the hall. A moment later she peered into the room agitated to check in.

'If you say so. That mean you're brewing up?' she asked.

'Well...fine' he huffed and stood with a shake of his head before he shuffled to the kitchen room to fill the kettle.

Before lunch came around Mae joined Beth for the next caffeine boost and a chat.

'You seen those dogs out in the long grass outside the studio?' Beth asked while they stood together in the kitchen with the kettle on the boil.

Mae gave a nod 'Still hanging around, are they? I think I've noticed them around town.'

'I like dogs, but I don't think we need strays shitting around outside the front entrance of the studio. It'll give the wrong vibe and I don't want to shovel shit every morning, do you?'

'God no'

'I saw one, but it was kind of smaller than what Lee mentioned but it was some crossbred thing, dirty looking.'

'I guess it's a long-term issue. We should message the council or some pest control agency in the area.'

'The one Lee saw was much larger according to him, like really big. The way he described it but the same the way it looked.'

'So what, they're a pack, a family' Mae considered before they returned to their individual rooms with hot drinks.

'There's been a man with them, or that's what Lee said. He hasn't mentioned them again' Beth said as they walked out with their coffees and departed to their own rooms.

After lunch Beth stood out front and walked around in the late sunlight as she sucked on her vape stick. She moved around the right side of the building lost in her thoughts of design and visuals as Ron stepped into the grounds silently from the left side of the building. The shape of the landscape around him bent, a wide ripple tremored over the ground around the design studio and the perspective and placement of the studio and the town and everything around it seemed to jolt and grind in place while Ron came and stepped inside the open door to studio. He moved in quick and quiet with a glance up the staircase and around the hall downstairs. He licked his dry lips and scratched his bruised and dirtied hands as he decided where to begin. He moved up the stairs swift and with intention. A few steps and he moved through the doorway of Mae's room. He surveyed the walls with their many posters of famous artworks and clothes designs and photographs from over the decades. His eyes came to land on the main desk at the side wall, the notepads and stack of recent sketches piled on from the last couple of days. From behind him he was confronted by Mae.

'Hello again. What are you doing here?' she asked and tried remaining polite. While she did know him and understood his concern to find his daughter, she still did not appreciate any person simply wandering into the studio uninvited.

'Thought I would come to check up with you, ask if you had seen our Katherine yet?' he replied as he gazed around the room behind her.

'No, I have not. I'm sorry and Ron I must ask that you leave. I've important client coming by soon. It's a professional working environment you see, they will not be impressed to see anyone who doesn't work here. That just how it is. I'm sorry, do you understand?' She told him. She watched his dried lips and the wringing of his strangely bruised hands, the scratching of his broken fingernails one over another as he looked around the studio.

'I think so. Yes, oh yes. You haven't seen my Katherine around the area at all?' He asked as he stepped closer toward her into the room. Mae picked up her phone from beside her and a scalpel knife from her design tools in the other hand low by her side.

'Don't fear, Mae. Katherine has been confused, not in her best self lately you see. She should not be out, away from home. We need her back.'

'She's not at your home, you're sure of that?'

'She is not, no' he said with look on his face which somehow appeared forced and even mocking.

'Fair enough,' he replied and glanced at building around him 'So this business is doing well, is it?'

'We think so. In fact, just this week I've produced some work that's the best in a long time for a very important client. If they like what we've offered them, it could open up some potentially very big work overseas and with household names. The design didn't come together until this week. Felt like it was waiting inside me and somehow it was released, drawn out of me finally. Like it was guided through my hands to the computer with help. It was so strange' She felt proud of the work and could not stop herself talking about it but when she realised what she was say to him she managed to hold back anymore information.

'Oh, well that sounds good. Look, I heard there might be some strange bloke, well a few people doing some sort of religious thing out of town down by the river, just over behind the studio there and along it somewhere. Be careful if you walk down there, maybe don't go that way for a good while. If anyone like that tries to talk to you about some kind of faith or worship or something'

'Oh, some religious nut? First, I've heard of them. I don't think I'd be easily led into that kind of thing. I'm basically an atheist. Are they pagan or something more sinister?'

'Not really sure but there's been talk. Been spotted near the big old Briggar stone on the riverside, so keep away I suggest. You will, won't you?'

'Right, okay if you really insist.'

He smiled with a nod of relief as he turned and looked over the rest of the room leisurely with quiet interest. She coughed a little and moved near the door to prompt his leaving.

'Like I was saying Ron, this important client is arriving...'

Some scuffled bark was heard way down the hall, and he turned to look. A sudden scowl etched across his smug face as he turned to the sound. She stepped away from him, scalpel gripped tight. She dialled local police on her phone with her other hand, raised it to her ear.

'Hello, yes could you send someone to Visions studio, Markely Place crescent of outside town centre, by the riverside. My friend is missing, and her parents are looking for her' she said in a low voice as she watched him step from the room and make his way down the stairs. He stormed off out of the studio before he heard her call end. She followed quickly down to see him leave and walk away from the studio grounds; a large filthy dog bounded away ahead of him up the street. Between the overgrown trees she lost sight of him. Seconds later she caught sight of the dog down by the riverbank joined by another the same breed, no owner anywhere near them.

'Mae...hello...Mae?' she heard.

She turned to see Beth was stumbling a few yards over to the edge of her out on the wide grass area to the roadside as cars rushed past. Mae went out and caught her, pulled her back toward the studio.

'Come with me, come back in now' Mae urged as they moved back inside.

They walked back in, door slammed behind them. Among the mannequins in the dark corner of the Mae's room Katherine moved out, her body and robe broke apart, all atoms and cells divided as she morphed through the wall and emerged on the other side. She glided down to the ground as she came together as one and slunk out away into town.

Chapter Six

Out far near the woods and riverside Ron stood by a tree and looked back toward the back end of the area where Jen and her friends had reached, a mile or so from him. The dog came out beside him. It stretched out and fell to the ground as night descended over them. It stared up at him, fanged teeth, and long legs as it shook out, growled, and changed its form under the shade of the tall trees around them. It lost the canine form to become a series of bizarre animal hybrids-part cat or puma, some kind of boar or sow and eventually it stretched out and stood tall with long naked female legs and waist with an upper torso of bear or some clawed beast. The face was clearly that of Lily. She smiled at Ron, her arms stretched out, fingers spread, arms covered with thick fur as her legs stepped to him.

'I wish to be more than a dog as we move around our town' she breathed 'Don't you?'

He shook his head. 'No, too much. It is a glorious wonder as ever but choose a form and go with it. We are dogs, shouldn't confuse things and ourselves' he declared. 'This is exactly the time to be what-ever takes our fancy, whatever, however. It's been far too long, and we are capable. They are not watching us now. Come, we're supposed to be looking for our daughter' he said and led her as she returned to the form of dog out across the overgrown field at the side of town with a glance back at the design studio before he moved on. They moved through the field and into the woods beyond it for a while. After a while of looking and standing under the trees the dog stood and looked at him.

'You want to go back?' he asked. It seemed to nod, and the mouth opened as it knelt, shook and its body shivered as it stood and bounded away from him. He nodded and checked his watch.

'Pub time, that's right' he said and turned to walk into town. He watched as the dog bounded away alone and he hoped it would retain that form while out among the locals.

Minutes later in local pub Milton's Bridge he entered and found Jackson stood at the bar. They smiled and gave a cursory nod at each other. Jackson paid for a couple of beers, and they moved across to sit at a table down in a far corner.

'Well look at you, back in town. Can be for too long, can it?' Jackson stated as he stood proud and waiting. They shook hands before Ron released a sudden burst of stilted laughter.

'Oh no, a brief visit, you know us. I like to check in on things, on you as well. We do wonder about you' Ron replied.

'That means a lot. You are coping back there, aren't you? You aren't missing much remember.'

Ron laughed and investigated his pint of local ale, unsure to drink much more of it.

They listened to the vintage rock tune which played out from the speakers above them.

'So, it's all going very well for you this way of living in town now?' Ron asked.

He drank back even though it was hard to keep down.

'It's very relaxing and fulfilling. I'm appreciated as you would expect but for respectable work in this day and age, civilised times around us, more than before at lease. It's not that I have to do it this way, you know that, but it feels better this time. I see why they want things this way, why they strive against the odds for success in good suits, powerful cars, and large bank accounts.'

'When they see no gods, they want to be one, that we have observed in many different ways' Ron agreed. He scratched away spots of dried blood on his long dirt crusted fingernails.

'It is not simply Nietzsche's lazy soundbite but a desire for respect and achievement.'

Ron waved his bruised hands around and pointed out of the side window with one jagged long nail on his forefinger 'Can't last forever though, can it? How will they remember you this time?'

'It doesn't have to be about that. Do think beyond what you've known from the past, however far back you believe that goes and in whatever manner you believe it to have happened.'

'Jackson, we are pleased for you, really, we are. Making the money, growing the business as you do with your team of employees, it's respectable and something to be commended, yes indeed.'

Jackson watched Ron scrape his broken and chipped nails over the tabletop restlessly 'But...'

'But do you want to have something else with it?'

'No, no time for that. I'll leave that to you and your lady. I'm far too busy, you know that. You enjoy your own ways. Do it the right way, not too much mess and chaos'?

Ron coughed, held up hands of clawed fingers, bared fanged teeth suddenly and steered his fetid black tongue out around his chapped lips with a false smile before he pulled it back inside.

'We're doing it our way, oh yes but it might need some help and extra set of hands and don't want you to get the idea that you're excluded or left out of it on purpose. You hear me?'

Jackson looked around 'Don't be a show off. Put it away, you fool. I hear you. You can find me, you know that. You do not need me for a long time. Drink up, toast to our different but successful ways of passing our time. Drink up'

'You might see us in the next few days, we're around, I like said checking in, we like to visit. Remember they used to say we should feed the dancing dogs by the riverside and if we didn't...they would come for us, drink our blood?' Ron said.

Jackson drank some more before he replied. He gave a quiet laugh 'Oh that's some good local folklore. Few centuries back. Seen those dogs, have you?'

'Seen a few dogs around.'

'I'm sure. But we're not superstitious, are we?'

'Should we be?'

Jackson straightened his tie and his jacket, gave a cough. 'Tell Lily hello from me of course' Jackson told him.

'Oh of course. Don't work too hard at the office' Ron said with a wink as he stood and left the pub. He looked out down the street and remembered his next appointment was due in less than half an hour and he moved briskly along.

Out beside the gates to the design studio Ron met Lee and they walked toward the fields together. They walked through a narrow row of trees and came out where Lee was sure that part of town looked different to how he usually knew it to be.

'Which way have we come? Is this out near the doctor surgery and Chinese takeaway?' Lee asked as he looked around them.

'No, I mean if you walked another way, yes. Are you feeling lost?' Ron asked. As he watched him, he restrained a puckish smile.

''Course not' Lee replied but he stood silent a moment as he gazed up at row of very old strange carved tall posts. They resembled totem poles but were of a Celtic or pagan style over them.

'They're familiar, aren't they? Been here centuries' Ron said. Lee nodded slowly while not entirely convinced.

'Oh, yeah, always thought they looked weird but got used to them. Almost forgot they were there.'

In truth, he believed he had never set eyes upon them while he had lived all his life in the town. What was going on around him? Was he experiencing some mental problems?

'I know a good few parts of town that many folks overlook or forget about easily. It's a real shame. You'd almost think some parts had disappeared altogether' Ron told him 'These tall posts are incredibly old. Any idea how old?'

'Are they medieval or Victorian or even older?'

'Good guesses. Think much further back. Seventeen hundreds if not earlier. They hold such history, markings which point to local tragedies or victories in feudal or civil wars or religious or spiritual clashes over times.'

'How are they still standing? Have they been renovated or treated with varnish or something surely?'

Ron shrugged 'I believe not. See they hold those small but deep held metal points and parts driven in at certain points up and down them?'

'They look pretty dangerous, surely they should have been taken out or made safer for people in town passing by' Lee suggested.

Ron took one of his long and jagged fingernails and scratched it down the side of the post near to him. 'Tell me Lee, have you heard of the burning angel's legend?'

'Nope, don't think I have. What is it?'

'Moonlight witch trials?'

Lee gave a blank look in return 'You making these up?'

Ron sniffed, tilted his head, let out a resigned sigh. 'Never mind'

Lee turned and stepped away as he spoke. 'I know about those child killers up the road, decades ago. Fucking sick and horrible as hell that stuff'

'Yes, true. Different thing but you're right.'

'Doesn't it matter for tourists, history teachers?'

'For you. Identity. Local fear, local lore. Sets us apart. How about The Dog Dancers of Briggar Street. The locals with faith survived. The ones asking too many questions, committing too many sins were the victims of these devices and these rituals. They brough it upon themselves. All a part of the law and order of the times' Ron explained to Lee.

Ron seemed to laugh a little as he stepped to the nearest of around a half dozen spread metres apart up the inside quiet walkway. He touched one of the sharp metal ridges, rubbed it with his fingertips, moved his fingers to his lips, licked them with a thoughtful nod of approval.

'Yes, such history. Like the history which directed the path of your family fortunes for example. We will be changing all of that.'

Lee moved closer to the tall wooden totem posts stood between two of them. Ron clasped a hand tight over his, looked him in the eyes and grinned.

'Now keep all of this in mind. You never know when these old tales may come in handy' he said and pressed down with gradually increased force as he continued to watch him.

'Hey, hey that bloody hurts' Lee blurted out as he pulled his hand away. He checked his palm and found a tear almost an inch long with fresh blood which trickled down his arm.

'What the hell Ron?'

'It will help you remember what's important, I hope. See you soon my friend' Ron told him, and he stepped away around the near corner. Lee rushed to follow but when he stepped up the next street could not see him anyway.

'Ron' he called up the street. He looked down at his right palm and clenched it to hold back the blood until he could dress it.

Under the large, framed oil painting reproductions sat at the wide oak desk Mr Cownlow frown as he flipped through the pages of his diary book and looked up to his laptop database to reference meetings and cross off those done. He chortled to himself and leaned back as he took out the small tin of miniature cigars from his jacket pocket and tapped one on the desk as he glanced over at the framed photograph of his wife and children. The light flickered and grew from over his shoulder, and he spun around curious to know the source. The cigar fell from his hand and his mouth gaped open when he witnessed the luminescent large form which gravitated above the floor. It shone like bright sunlight, a crackling and warm orange hue around the burning white of it. It formed a human female figure, and he could just make out the shape of a face with close eyes. The arms came out toward him.

'What...are you?' he asked.

The effusive and glowing bright white figure in the air before him was Katherine but she neither saw him nor spoke. He moved down closer to him and cupped his face with her blistering opalescent white hands. She held his face as his eyes widened in amazement.

'A real angel? Oh my god. Fucking hell, oh god, forgive me, forgive my family. Tell me please...' he began. She clamped tight her hands onto his face and under her ragged fallen robes her chest and stomach peeled and flowered open, the skin recoiled to show a brief glimpse of a cosmic chasm. She pushed down his head and took in his body before he had the opportunity to clutch anything around him. The flesh petals of her body sealed back up and she floated against the back wall where her body deconstructed down and merged inward. A moment later she emerged outside in the forest surrounded by the tallest trees. Her body shone blistering white light once more as she opened, and it dropped Mr Crownlow out onto the autumn leaves and broken branches below as she came down and stood before him. He was unconscious as she pulled him up and dragged him along through a narrow path few were familiar with. His head knocked and bumped against several stones and swollen lumps in the earth as she took him through to the arranged place set up and ready for him. She took up one of his arms and tried it to one aged tree and tied his other to the tree to the right of him. She flayed his chest and legs, his face and head slit with a steady flow of warm blood down his face. She left him unconscious for Ron and Lily and wandered away to the riverside where she washed and cleaned the blood from her hands and arms in her unfocused sleepwalk. She moved away careful not to make any sound as she stepped over grass and ground back toward the studio. She returned and appeared to Mae in shadow of corridors of the studio. Mae smiled up at her and beckoned her quickly into her room.

'Come in, sit down. Speak if you want to, I'll listen. I'm grateful for your help with my designs. I wasn't sure it was you at first.'

'The dogs are out, old times of town' Katherine whispered. Her eyes opened wider as she became aware of her surroundings.

'Yes, we've seen them. It's your father Ron, isn't it?'

'They bark...'

'He did come here but I sent him away. I didn't tell him that I'd seen you, I won't do that. I'll get you help when I figure out what you need You were at my flat weren't you? That's fine, stay as long as you need to.'

'They walk...and talk...' Katherine whispered. She moved back into shadow, her form hunched behind the mannequins.

'I'm not sure you should see Beth or Lee, not yet...' Mae called but Katherine was gone from view. She signed and sat to work on the project at her computer.

Mae tried to forget the strangeness of the day when she joined Jackson for a quite meal in the evening at their favourite Italian restaurant. He seemed jovial and lifted her spirits and they returned to his house before ten. While she flicked through channels on the television he stood in the bathroom, blood trickled from his mouth, his eyes turned white in the mirror as he floated off the floor. He shook and gripped the sink as he pulled himself down to the floor and let out a quite moan.

'Still hungry...' he said quietly.

'You okay in there, love?' Mae called through the closed door.

'Fine, just a nosebleed, that's all. Out in a minute'

He returned shortly for another glass of wine beside her in the lounge.

'Feeling better?'

'I think so. Tell me again about that strange guy you work with?'

'Oh, Lee is a regular oddball, one of those exhausting atten-tion-seekers. His pranks get repetitive and irritating but he's nice really and useful. Today, it's just he was doing something more irritating than usual. Wouldn't let up about the mannequins moving in the storerooms and something outside, someone with wild dogs, the view changing. We warned him to grow up and stop distracting us and wasting the day, we've no time for it every day of the week.'

'Wild dogs and animated mannequins? Pothead isn't he, smokes way too much. Does he smoke it at work during the day or take anything else?'

'Yes, he smokes weed a lot, but I do too. Not all day obviously. No none of us smoke it at work or during the day actually. What, you think we mostly sit around stoned all day long?'

'Of course not. But you creative types, I mean come on. No, I just concerned you may need to put him in line if he continues to mess around like this.'

'I will, don't worry. I put my team in place when I need to.'

The meal finished, they left the restaurant, and she noticed the distraction over his face as they walked to his car outside.

'You feeling alright?' she asked.

'You know me, my mind is thinking ahead as usual. Let's get you back' he responded as he ended his hesitant glance up and down the street around them as the black clouds overhead seemed to bear down upon them.

Chapter Seven

Ron met Lee in the Larson Leg pub sat with a pint and laughter which seemed to shake the walls around them. Lee glanced down to where Ron pushed toward him some typed formal papers.

'Sign this, my young business owner. Either go ahead with it or use the money with your family or simply wait around for a long time at Mae's studio while the months and possibly years pass'

'What's this?' Lee asked and looked at the printed document on the table with the cheque and statement. 'That Crownlow bloke, you spoke to him…and this is what?'

'He and I had a good chat, man to man, decided to make a change and take a chance on a new talent. You. So, sign up quick. It's what you want, no more fetching and waiting your turn.'

Lee smiled and laughed incredulously as he leaned and signed the printed statement, putting his name to a new small business venture in town. With that Lee made his way along back to the studio with an unpleasant smile upon his face. He was soon moving things around on his computer monitor screen when the voice called from the doorway behind him.

'Hey, Lee can you go collect the fabrics and drop off the early designs with markings to Wendy this morning?' Mae said.

'Mm, yeah will do, boss' he muttered as he took up the notes and papers from her.

She watched him leave the room, his tone of voice, more assured than usual.

'You know, I don't get enough chances I don't think, doing my own things. You've promised for a long while I could add my own things to a project. Is that going to happen any time soon?' he asked.

'Hey look, I've told you, it will. Don't get pissy, it's how things are. Things move slow, we can't just do anything anytime. Things have to be right, feel suitable for clients. We've got a promise to fulfil a design brief ever time. We can't just throw any old ideas at a project if we feel like it.'

'Right of course not. I get that.'

'Good, just wait a while longer. The right time will come soon enough, it will.'

'It will, I know that' he replied as he turned around in his chair with a wink and a let out a satisfied laugh to himself.

Lee sat back and lounged at his desk as he scrolled on his smartphone. He glanced up at the files of sketches and material details and sheet of data Mae had asked him to send and check over, a disinterested yawn escaped his mouth. With the agreement that had been made with the councillor in town he could hardly muster any motivation to do as he had been ordered. He believed himself not to be a total jerk and so decided to work another week or at least turn up at the studio before informing Mae that he would be leaving to start his new business with his own shop. She might be slightly bitter or angry that it would seem he had achieved that goal with so much less exhausted effort and time than she had spent trying to get the design studio up and running but that was simply his good like he thought.

He sat back with a satisfied grin, chuckled a little to himself, eyes closed and feet up on his desk.

A word drifted in around him, a familiar name curled around and into his ears. His own name.

'Lee...' he heard.

He opened his eyes, sat up, feet down. Turned his head slowly to glance around to the door behind him. The door was open, but no one stood there. He looked down at his phone and saw a message come up from the councillor about clearing the shop property, an offer of help with it, any time soon he would be happy with. He messaged back while smiling and nodding.

'That's my place' he said quietly with a smirk.

'Lee...' his name breathed out and moving, whispered around his head, in his ears once more.

He sat up, stood from the chair, looked to the door.

'Beth, Mae?' he called. He walked to the door; some shadow tall enough to be a person moved away from the doorway in silence. He rushed over and moved out to the corridor. Nobody out there, no sound or movement.

'You want me to make the coffee right? No that I probably won't always be doing it' he muttered and walked along to the kitchen door. Hand on the handle, pushed it open and the voice whispered behind.

'No shop...' it said. He did not hear it clearly or did not want to think he had. He shook his head and stomped to the kettle, as he flung the door behind him. He expected it to slam against the door frame. He turned around with hesitation. It had closed, no sound at all, no slam to be heard. The kettle clicked on the tabletop, already full of enough water and boiled.

'The fuck...?' he uttered as he twisted around to look at it.

A shape moved within the shadows behind the spare clothes mannequin in the corner.

Did he see a face looking at him? Some evil grimace? There were fashion posters, large alternative fashion clothing prints across the walls, more than half a dozen female faces plastered up, watching him, none of them moving or alive. Something or someone had moved, he was sure of it, had blinked and been looking right at him, observing him. He walked right up to the mannequin and the wall of model faces to his right; their printed static wide eyes stuck on him.

'Hmm, fucking thing' he said and pushed the mannequin bust with some aggression before he turned back to kitchen room. He walked in and tapped his fingers against the tabletop before he took out three mugs and started to pour into each, added the coffee power, milk, sugar.

'No...shop...no...life...' the voice whispered from around him. He heard some of it, the words laboured, cracked yet near him right behind him somehow.

'Beth, don't mess around. Your coffee is coming. Same goes for miss amazing in the next room' he called over his shoulder. A hand touched his left shoulder, and he froze. He dropped the carton of milk, saw it bounce off his trainer and milk splashed out over it and the floor.

'Ah shit' he exclaimed as he jumped back. 'Fuck, fuck' he spat out and turned around.

He saw the face of Katherine, but it had dried out and decayed but it smiled at him with eyes thin slits. Teeth were missing, wide cuts and gouges in the cheeks and flesh turned his stomach, eyes bloodshot stared right into him. He backed away, stumbled out of the room into the corridor. Someone stood at the top of the stairs.

'Hey wait. Beth, that you?' he managed to call. He heard the voice of Beth talking and decreasing as the figure moved away. He rushed along the corridor, looked down the stairs for the top step. She was moving away down below.

'Wait, is someone else in here, wait...' he called out. He looked back. The whispered words drifted to him.

'No...shop...Lee...no...Lee...no...'

'Fuck off' he replied and stumbled down the stairs, almost fell to his hands and knees on the last stair. He looked up. The front door was open as he noticed the person with long hair, a familiar silhouette left the building. He followed on quickly, stepped outside and the person he assumed to be Beth was gone from sight.

'Hey Beth, where are you, where'd you go? Someone's up there, some junkie woman' he said. He walked out toward the front gate of the yard. He peered out down then up the perimeter of the design studio premises. There was no person to be seen in either direction.

'This is stupid' he sighed. He turned around and noticed a shape, a silhouette of someone near his height between trees over by the back fence at the far side of the studio. He waited for a moment and then began to head toward the figure. As the daylight shifted, clouds released sunshine and cleared the shadows from the trees he found the person to be a mannequin bust from the studio.

'So why are you out here?' he asked.

'Lee...' the voice whispered out again. Hands came from behind, pushed and knocked him down. The studio was gone. He was sat on the ground starring ahead at the river. He turned and the studio was no longer behind him or to his side, it was nowhere to be seen. All he could see was only the trees, the overgrown weeds and tall grass with the long winding river further ahead beyond right around like a castle mote. Further out the old stone. The Briggar stone.

'No...shop...no...Lee...' the voice continued; the words shredded but insistent.

'Stop it. Who...who is fucking saying that? Come out' he yelled and stumbled to his feet. A knocked to his head, put him down on the grass again. He shook his head, spat out with a growl, and slowly stood with a dizziness in his head. He was faced with the mannequin, this time it had a head, a face, a grin. That face from inside the studio, that dead, decayed female smile with that face looked back at him. He fell back, turned around, and crawled over the grass, looked around in all directions desperately to hope to see the studio somewhere, anywhere.

'Where is it? Where?' he said as he got to his feet, mud, and shit all over jeans and trainers.

A bark was audible from somewhere. He turned, turned again. He saw the person coming near, the man this time. It was Ron who approached casually, the dog a few feet away, barking still.

'Where...?' Lee gasped. He sniffed around and there he saw the design studio loomed large as before behind him.

'Everything alright, friend?' Ron enquired. The dog peered up at him, tongue licked around and over sharp teeth.

'Well...I fell out here, I came out because I heard...I...someone...' Lee managed.

'You're filthy, got shit on you. Might want to go home, clean up. Take the day off' Ron suggested with a wink and a pat on the shoulder.

'Ah yes. Good idea' Lee agreed.

'Oh, and if you see dogs dance around town, feed them especially by the river. So many forget...'

'I'm cleaning up. Later' and with a brief glance at the studio Lee quickly stumbled out to town.

Deep in the forest far behind the initial trees and hidden behind rows of others, further in Ron and Lily arrived and found Mr Crownlow hung up between the trees as they had wished. Ron laughed and nodded as he stepped around and inspected the unconscious man.

'Ah, she's done well. Perfect, just what we needed' he announced.

'He looks intact, no pieces of him taken from him. Should it be that way?'

'As the old lore goes, yes but this is our time. It is our game to play' he reminded her, and he stepped in close and pulled up the head of Crownlow, peeled open the eyelids.

'You see me now? See us here?' He turned to Lily with disappointment in his features. 'Well, we should get started anyway while he is fresh. Let us not waste time. This is but the first'

She nodded as she watched him take out a razor and cut the wrists and neck of Crownlow. The blood began to pour as they dropped to their knees, threw off their clothes and transformed to their exaggerated large dog forms. Once on all fours with fangs bared, they moved in and licked and sucked his blood with satisfaction and purpose. Once they had had their fill they leapt up and bit and tore into him. They tore away only what was necessary, beyond that they made sure to leave a most harrowing and savaged corpse to be found.

Chapter Eight

Lee stepped inside the empty shop premises which was now his to refurbish in the weeks ahead. His family would be so proud of him, they would finally acknowledge his worth and potential, remember how important they had been to the fabric of the history of the town long ago and could still be. He had no idea of the owner dying or how and would not become aware of it for good while due to Ron clouding minds, turning streets, and distorting time. Ron walked with Lee to the shop property which stood empty on one of the side streets from the high street in town.

'Go on ahead, see what you think can be done with the place. Good to know your family did so much under that roof generations ago. You can get it up and running again, get your family name known and respected once more. After all these bad things, those links to the troubles of more recent times. You will be known for offering joy and good hand-crafted artworks just like old times' Ron suggested with a sly smile.

'Hold on, the troubles? You mean the business deals?'

'I was thinking more of the witch trials and those events your family were linked with. But much of that was simply imaginative gossip, scapegoating and folklore, tales of jealous people and fear as old as the hills and beyond. Anyway, you go in there, start making plans. I'll see you later.'

'You don't want to come in and look around as well?'

'I remember it well enough. I'll wait to see the change soon.'

Ron bid him farewell as he departed to another street, Lily as silent dog at his side. Lee shrugged and with the keys in his hand, opened the front door and stepped inside alone. Ron and Lily moved out of town and in among the forest at the riverside. He undressed as Lily transformed to her human form and he threw down his robe and shirt behind the tree at their right, under the large rocks, the familiar location for storage. Naked, he knelt before her, shook his head, bowed to her. His arms shot out and he coughed, grumbled as he watched on with silent pleasure. He shuddered, and the change of form and nature came. His arms grew the fur, the feathers so rapidly. The beginnings of short wings emerged on his back, just below his shoulder blades. His eyes became black in a blink, and he reached out and quick snatched hold of a fox passing by. He bit down, sank in his fangs, and tore away the head, chewed down into the neck and body of it, sucked on the blood and warm flesh within as it dripped down his chin spattered around onto the grass. Lily did not seem pleased.

'Not the wings, not bird for you. Be savage, powerful, that's how I like you' she reminded him.

He stood tall and wiped the blood from his chin, wide torso and legs bulked in size and a face like some mix of mastiff dog and woodland bear, eyes burning red, and feet stretched out long with toenails like five-inch talons. He stalked forward to the river as Lily watched with an undeniably proud smile. He knelt, drank from the flowing water below. He looked at his beastly visage reflected at him with a mischievous pride.

'Best enjoy yourself while we can' he reminded as she moved to him, and they settled down against a thick heavy fallen tree truck and he mounted her with an unstoppable appetite. She held his hips and pushed him deep into her as he thrust and growled with a primitive hunger.

Katherine left Mae sleeping in the studio having drained from her resting body what she needed. She moved out through the town, through the sky under heavy black clouds to the flat where Lee resided. He remained asleep as she came through the wall into his room. She shone with only a slight shimmer as her body peeled open and she took him up into her and moved out in silence unseen across the town and to the forest. She floated through, found the trees where Crownlow had been tied up and once spat from within her body she began to do the same with Lee. His body fell to the dirt, stomach hit a large stone which made him cough and his eyes flickered open. He turned and looked up and let out a hysterical scream on seeing her above him. She was in her sleeping state and moved slow to catch him as he stumbled among the trees confused, knocked him down, pulled him over the dirt and mud under the low hanging trees. The loud bark echoed out from across the field. She knew the source, dropped Lee to the ground. Katherine loped out between the bushes and brambles, under the low arched tree branches as she pulled along the unconscious body of Lee behind her. She took him under the two of the tallest trees, and cords of flesh shot out fast and wound up from her hands around the trees. Two more flesh cords whipped out and pulled down around the ankles and wrists of Lee who made some low audible moans as he was slowly taken up in the air. She fell to her knees, veins prominent over her place face, eyes returned to view the place around her, Lee strung up in the lower basement deep inside the Briggar stone and ready for the taking. She walked quietly away toward town.

Through the deep trees under nightfall Ron and Lily walked back to Briggar Stone and entered through the door together. Still in his large hybrid man beast form, Ron sniffed the air and stalked down into the basement. His huge inhuman silhouette cast across the walls as he came down to where Lee was bound and held in pained silence. His eyes widened with shock and fear as Ron came near before him. Lee had no idea what he was seeing and shuffled and twisted in desperation. He was beginning to think he had been sent down to Hell but for what reasons he could not be sure. He moaned and struggled within his bindings, moaned behind the gag on his mouth.

'Fear me now?' Ron asked though his ugly dog face with his wide bulked out bear shape body and wet thick tongue moved over fangs still bloodied.

Lee nodded as frantically as he could in agreement, his mouth gagged shut.

'Know what I am?' Ron asked.

Lee shook his head with anxious fear. Ron let out a low chuckle.

'Neither do I' he replied with a terrifying smile full of razor fangs on display. He touched the face of Lee gently, stroked him with quiet fascination and care. Lily came and stood obscured the pitiful shaft of light from above in the dank of the doorway up on the stairs.

'Don't play with him like that. He doesn't deserve that' she suggested.

Ron glared back at her. He quickly scratched down the side of Lee's face before he returned to the stairs and disappeared with her up inside the Briggar temple, Lee left afraid and alone in the dark. Ron stood in the lounge, his wide beast chest heaved in and out as he breathed, long but muscular bear arms by his sides as he walked to Lily as she stood back against the long table beside the window.

'Which memory is this one, which time?' she asked as she gazed out at the town below.

'Fifteen hundred and twelve maybe, you know the one. Bears and devils and the maidens cursed. Did not make it into long legend, memorable myths, didn't serve the town or two-faced rulers how they liked it' he replied as his clawed hand stroked his chin.

'Jackson was brutal that time. A mess if I remember, no organisation, too random.'

'I always liked that one, such imagery.'

'Yes, I remember, that is what you love. You want to bring it back, try it again now?'

'Can't we? Think I see a way to make it work. Different time but the townsfolk are weak and needy, perfect opportunity I'd think. You are free with your own games, which ever you like of course my dear.'

'Be my man, be my beast, my legend' she told him as she stroked his furred animal arms. He stormed around the room, knocked over chairs, screamed and howled in a rage. He rushed to her, inches from her face, his breath heavy and insistent.

'I am beast, I am the best lore never remembered. A success, a creation of use, wonder and purpose, living myth and legend. Not a god but another thing they will never understand. They will respect, they will worship and remember' he growled.

'You are. We are. Be my man right now, for me, for our meal' she asked. There was some slight tremor of fear in her voice, her eyes.

He stepped back slowly, aware he had mare her uncomfortable, turned away. He huffed, growled, and stormed to their room to changed form and into human clothes. She let out a sigh of relief, stepped to the wide window and peered out at the quiet town to think about Katherine, where she was, and she was doing this time.

Chapter Nine

The next morning Mae and Beth were waiting at the design studio rooms, remembering that Lee was usually the first of them to arrive most days. They called him but got no reply.

'So, where's lazy loudmouth today?' Mae asked.

'Haven't seen him. Messaged him and no reply. He did send something cryptic about the old place his family used to own a long time ago. Some idea about it returning.'

'Has he gone there? Where is it?'

'Out across town, I think I remember the name of it...'

'I need him in to process the design segments I sent across. Let's go find the mouthy jerk.'

Beth led her up into town past the library and courts, around the mall and gym. She looked around confused at that point. Mae came out and saw the new street with Beth, looked for Lee.

'Is this new, this street?' Mae asked, 'It looks very old, but I don't think I've noticed it before.'

'Same here. Lee did mention something about it but with his level of bullshit…I didn't believe him but look at it. It looks all old England' she said and the wall up between the first two tall totem posts.

'Must have been local customs thing. Or it is intended to appear old. Could be a tourist thing. They do that, play up old history don't they to bring people in?'

She touched the buckled and marked metal prongs in the wood.

'Look, fuckin' dangerous though. Think I might message the council about these. Way too dangerous really'

'Dogs. Dog shapes carved into them.'

'Could be bears or…I dunno some kind of wild beasts from back in the day. Those ones are stood up. They could be people dressed in furs, cave people worshipping them or God or who knows. And flames around them with that wall or bridge over the side'

'Very mysterious and weird'

Beth moved toward the tall totem posts on the street and held onto a piece of ragged fabric which was hooked into one of the metal prongs.

'This piece of shirt, I've seen that. This is from Lee, his shirt, you know it right?' Beth exclaimed as she touched it. She heard a bark somewhere around her. A shadow moved, hunched but tall, twisted around against the sides of the buildings to her right and ahead of them. She turned quick to see but it was gone. A bark and a strained call of some name. Did the dog bark the name Katherine?

Chapter Ten

With no luck in finding Lee, Mae and Beth returned and continued the day's work at the studio just the two of them. The morning was quiet, more focused, and productive even if his goofy jokes were missing from around them, interrupting their workflow as usual. After lunch Beth walked out to the town for a new vape stick and on walk back was greeted by Lily who appeared in a smart suit dress before her on the street of the studio.

'You work at the design studio am I right?' Lily asked.

'Yes. Can I help you?' Beth replied with a half-smile and quick suck on her kiwi vape stick.

'I am back in town and my daughter's friend is your boss I believe, Mae, isn't it?'

'Yes, Mae, that's right.'

'My name is Lily. Do you know the town well?'

'Yes, I live not far from here. I'm Beth. So, your daughter knows Mae well?'

'They were at college together, close friends. Through those diffi-cult teenage times, puberty, rebellion, hormones, finding one's sense of identity. You have your identity at the studio, do you?'

'Ha, I think so. I work on the projects with Mae. It's a bit give and take, or not too much take honestly, she's the boss alright. So is your daughter around?'

'That's the thing, we're not too sure. My husband and me. We are back to find her. She has problems you see, emotionally, mentally. What's your name, your full name?'

'It's Beth Deakinson'

'Ah, I know that name. Yes, I remember that name in this town. I know local history, generations you see, it all stays in my mind, much more than others remember, even some things not in the records or books.'

'Oh really?'

'Yes. The Deakinsons...a good family over a long time but at one or two points cheated of greater things, respect held back. Do you know that?'

'I'm not sure what you might be talking about. I should be getting back to work...'

'Your family, I know things you would benefit from. You and your career'

'You know my family history? What can you tell me I don't know?'

'Some surprising things, my dear. Are you prepared to hear such things?'

Beth looked around, up at the design studio rooms where Mae was probably setting up work for her.

'I've got a while before I start again. Walk around the block?'

Lily smiled and they stepped back out to the main street and headed around the town. As they walked Lily scratched at her arms and made some strange chewing motion under her lips. Beth noticed how ragged and spilt Lily's nails were.

'The Deakinsons were hard workers I remember. My own grandmother knew your own great grandmother and family. It was after the big fires which ruined many businesses. Your family built their own back up-a shoe cobblers and ring makers-and they helped others do the same.'

'Yes, that does sound a bit familiar.'

'They were respected yes, but that is a century or more after an ill-fated scandal hit them and tragedy struck down almost a dozen of your descendants. Know of that?'

'I don't think so, no. Continue please' Beth said and sucked her vape with interest.

'Before they had any successful business in town, they did whatever they could to get by. They came here from Ireland and Poland. You know that?'

'Yes, I have heard that much. My parents are very proud of where we came from originally.'

'I am sure they are and should be. Alright, I say no word of a lie now, wish not to offend as I speak. Do you want me to go on?'

'Is it all true what you are going to tell me?'

'It really is, yes, the good and the bad.'

Beth stood still a moment. She sucked her vape and considered this woman. She had only met her less than half an hour ago, but she felt that Lily was an honest woman and there was the connection to Mae with her daughter. Her own parents never had seemed to know too much about the family further than two generations back and so she felt it could be important to learn more. She told Lily to keep talking.

'Your ancestors were brave, selfless folk, helped the town in a very desperate time of unholy deaths and summoning.'

'What does that mean?'

'In this land there have been many strange and fantastical events and encounters, beings, and confrontations, some real, others made up or only partially remembered, exaggerated, or mostly forgotten or hidden. Some denounced or denied, covered up or written out of the history books for a variety of reasons. The deaths of your ancestors, many at a time was hidden and replaced by a distorted story which benefitted others in this town.'

'Which others?'

'At least two other specific families. They had their sins and secrets, your family were chosen and put in their place, that was when the rest of the townsfolk were quite pleased to see your family rounded up, tortured, or living for their part in aiding witches and cannibals.'

'Cannibals, in this town and witches, real witches, spells and that stuff?'

'Oh yes, that is a hidden truth of our local past.'

'I've never heard about any of that.'

'You were not intended to. It was eventually erased, changed, and written anew. But the shame and guilt are still believed by some, even if never spoken of aloud. Also, these two families who framed your own.'

'What are their names?'

'Spearsmith and... you want to know?'

'I said yes.'

'Benchstock'

'Hold on now, that's Mae's name. Mae Benchstock'

Lily simply smiled and gave a gentle nod. She teased her own hair, the brown curls down past her shoulders.

'I adore your hair, so feminine, such human colours' she said.

'Okay...thanks' Beth responded, not sure how to interpret the compliment.

'You think I look like womanly enough?' Lily asked.

'I...yes, but these days a woman should dress how she wants to, not feel a need to conform or impress men or women around them, or to age stereotypes. You look great.'

'Thank you, thank you so much' Lily replied with a glaring, satisfied smile as she moved her hair around her shoulders, touched her lips and face self-consciously 'Listen, your own family should be remembered and respected more than they are. The past often seems like it is folded away by others, the important parts discarded in favour of trivial things to attract tourists and money. A town should value and honour the ones who do much to build it up even if long ago.'

'I think I should investigate the past of the town. Maybe go dig around in the library a while' Beth said.

'No need. I hate to tell you, but Mae's descendants covered up the good and important things your own family were doing. They took credit and had your family known as superstitious and thieving immigrants. The hard work and efforts of your family were forgotten in place of suspicion and mistrust for a long time.'

'That can't be right. I would know something, anything...'

'I will bring out some documents and artefacts to you. In the meantime, remain peaceful and bide your time.'

They parted and Beth returned to the studio but could not be near Mae for long and comfortably hold her silence.

'You're back. You want to sit together and look over our own early ideas for the next projects together?' Mae suggested. Beth moved back, turned away.

'No, no I don't feel that's a good idea. I think I'll just continue with it in my room' she replied briskly and walked to her room; door shut immediately behind her. Mae watched her go with quiet surprise and disappointment.

A short while later a buzz jolted Mae upright as she sat before her monitor and glanced down to her smartphone. She picked up and answered.

'This is Mae at Visions studio, can I help?' she said as she noticed the number being their current client. Her heart rattled in her chest with anxiety.

'Hi Mae. Look, the final designs you've sent over-we absolutely adore what your team has put together. We're going with it all. We're just so fascinated by it. It looks very British but also has a cross-continental element and kind of gothic with those figures and pictures structured into the patterns. We love it all. Thank you so much' the client told her.

'Wonderful. That...that really is wonderful. We're so glad you like it.'

'Not just that, no we're linking up with another client in Spain and America and we've shown them the design and they are interested in bringing you into the next season design with their collections and early promotion. If you are interested and free?'

'Yes. We...I will have to discuss it all with my team but that does sound very much something we could be interested in agreeing with.'

'Alright. We will be in touch of course. Speak soon and don't work too hard.'

Mae stepped back, took a long breath, and propped herself beside the workbench. She felt faint and moved to a chair immediately. The call had brought the huge relief in the satisfying news they hoped they would hear but as it came while such unusual things had started to occur around them it all was difficult to digest. She heard Beth in the corridor and called out.

'Hey, they fucking love the design! We're safe and the future has some positive things on the horizon' she said with jubilant joyous laughter.

'Oh, that is so good' Beth responded 'Right, tequila time I time' and she marched down and out to town.

Katherine had made no appearance through the day and after a couple of shots of tequila and a while musing the whereabouts of Lee they separated and went home.

A short while after Mae return to her flat, Jackson arrived, and they cooked together and opened a favourite bottle of South African red wine.

'So, this Lee at work and how he's disappeared, did it seem suspicious in any way? It probably wasn't, not where he was found. Must have been a very sad accident. More common than we like to believe.'

'It was really strange. It is hard to talk about but feel I must. What his brother found, his smartphone just inside the forest outside town, he said looked like......I don't know.'

'I think your thoughts are troubled. I'll stay with you, don't worry, I'll be here tonight. We can talk or drink and go to bed early, zone out with any dumb shows on streaming. You are safe here I promise.'

'I know, I think I believe that. In a strange way, I do actually feel safe, I don't know how or why that makes sense. I don't know if someone did get to Lee for some personal or sick reason....'

'Don't think about it. Let's watch a soap opera and go up to bed soon, eh?' he suggested, and they did just that.

In the dark of night Jackson heard the howls from outside and sat up in bed. He turned and noticed Mae had left her side of the bed and he got up to look for her. Once downstairs he saw her outside from the kitchen window and walked out to meet her in the violet darkness of dawn.

'Mae what are you doing out here, and just in a shirt? It's so cold, come in. Are you okay?'

She was dazed and lost in her mind.

'Jackson, yes, I'm cold. Really cold. Why am I out here?'

'You tell me.'

'I...don't know.'

He took her inside and sat her in the lounge while he fetched a large woolly fleece jumper and she seemed to be finding her senses.

'I'm here with you' she said simply, looking a little unsure.

'Yes, you are. But I'm not angry. You feel, okay?'

'Almost. I don't know...I heard barking. There were those dogs outside my studio...'

'But you couldn't help yourself. Not the only woman who could say that' he told her with a chuckle and a wink as he rubbed her arm. He looked pissed off and seemed to hold some curse words back. She saw him clench his fist and change his expression to a silent anger or infuriation.

'Let's get back to bed. I'll lock the door, follow you up.'

She went up first as he stood in the kitchen and looked out at the sun emerge behind the dark horizon edge of town.

'I hear you' she whispered.

C hapter Eleven

Beth did return to the studio the following morning she viewed Mae a different look, reluctant and cynical.

'Got your vape refill?' Mae asked 'We should get on with work, God knows Lee isn't anywhere or any use today. His brother called me. The police are going to start looking in the next day or so, no sooner.'

'Oh, Right, shit. Doesn't sound good.'

'Maybe he's gone raving at a party somewhere. You know him.'

'Of course, you're right' Beth offered and slowly moved to her own room to be alone as she worked.

When the unusual sounds echoed out from the room where Mae worked later, she ignored them, uninterested in being with this woman who had a family which had done damage to her own. It should not be forgotten or forgiven easily she decided. The sounds were organic and repulsive as Katherine had approached Mae. She could not wait until the night and opened out large and segmented wings woven from heat and light and pulled her close, teeth from within peeled back torso pierced and absorbed blood and energy in quiet but glutinous ways. Soon enough Mae sank back in her desk chair exhausted and tired, a sleep took her away until early evening and the dark came out through the windows. Katherine had long disappeared to another place. Around an hour later Mae came around in her desk chair in the dark room, the light of the small buttons on her computer monitor pierced the dark before her face.

'Beth? Katherine?' she said quietly and pushed herself up where she sat. Head clouded, she stood, she stumbled a little as she walked to the corridor.

'Hello, Beth, Lee?' she called. Shadows shifted and warped, a figure perhaps moved away up the wall or around the staircase beyond.

'Katherine...that you?' she called quietly as she walked ahead.

Beth stepped out from her room, shoulder bag on, sour face.

'Hey Mae, you around?' she called. She noticed a female form moved down the corridor and hear some low whispered words. The feet were off the floor she noticed, and she swallowed hard, stepped back.

'The hell...?' she uttered. She heard Mae talk to someone inside her room. Beth rushed up and knocked at the door until Mae came and opened it with a smile.

'Oh, you're awake. Anyone else in here? Your mysterious friend?' Beth asked as she peered over the shoulder of Mae.

'No, just me now. You want to work together?' Mae replied.

'No, look I finished up my part a while back. Hope you enjoyed your snooze. Dogs are still around outside, probably shitting on our doorstep. I'm off got some research to do. Back tomorrow for more of the same I suppose.'

'Right. What research?'

'Town and family history. The history of our families, old events way back, things forgotten by most people. Seems there are lies and tall tales covering some nasty shit which some people made good lives from. But it ruins other families for generations. Dicks'

'Our families? Yours and mine?'

'Yes, someone told me some things which got me thinking, wondering. Could be a few local secrets and lies, we'll see. It might help with some new design ideas I have, local imagery rural and architectural shapes and more. I might work at home tomorrow, so I'll message you I suppose. Bye' Beth said, and she rushed down the stairs and out. Mae was left to watch her go and feel a sense of attitude or resentment somehow. She shrugged and returned to tidy her work at her desk and call it a day.

C hapter Twelve

While the neighbours slept soundly past midnight Jackson stepped into his back garden and sat in the long wooden bench. He relaxed with a glass of wine and waited. After a few minutes, the shaped came forth through the bushes deep among the shadows. The snout and furred body hunched low and came forward. It held the face Ron which smiled as it came halfway over the grass. Jackson sipped his wine and gave a low wave.

'Good evening, friend. Out on the prowl. Care to sit and enjoy a glass of fine merlot?' he suggested. Ron twisted his head up, blinked and raised his canine body up on the hind legs. He stepped back and stood within the shadows of the bushes and brambles in the garden, his nakedness obscured.

'Not tonight, thank you' Ron replied through canine teeth.

'Listen, be any form you want' Jackson said, 'Be creative, enjoy yourself. Have a ball but keep back in Briggar, keep with her, you and Lily, with her. My trust is with you both' Jackson told him. Jackson took his hand and pulled it into his own lower chest. The surge was instant, it fuelled him. Ron closed his eyes, fainted quietly. He steadied himself.

'For you, for Him, for us' Ron murmured as he urgently pulled away his canine clawed paw.

'That's right. Find her and be this, all of you' Jackson agreed.

'Do you see us? Do you remember all of the ways this town was shaped?'

'Of course. And you were there with me. You will be again. Enjoy this freedom. You are not those things from back then. They are long gone. You take care of Briggar, I appreciate that so much, you know that.'

Ron moved back with a snarl, down on all fours as he pushed away within the back bushes and away from the garden. Jackson finished his glass of wine and return inside the house as he heard a howl echo through the night.

As Katherine moved through the night under shadow and behind trees and through alleyways she focused and depleted her strength to bend and fold the streets through decades and potential to hide Mae. She had seen and heard Ron and Lily come down and start their search for her and so she knew to move quick and take what she needed. Once inside the flat she found Mae asleep, and she moved around her as she touched her shoulders with a praying whisper. The release of desire and imagination within Mae caused a transformation as she stretched her limbs while she lay naked. Her body shivered and pulsed as she became a thing, she had only ever known in her private dreams from college days. Moments later she came up from the bed with her body a taller slim shape of a kind of creature which would not usually exist in the real world. She stood as a kind of bird with her own lower half, her legs but with hooves where her feet had been. Without thinking she rushed at her window, unlatched it, and flew out into the night sky. This was a dream. She had to be dreaming. It must be a way to escape stress and anxiety she tried to tell herself in her mind, but her thoughts and focus were clouded, muddled and pushed back in favour of a basic consciousness intent on simply moving over the town, through the air, between and through clouds but above the familiar rooftops and trees. She moved and soared fast and effortlessly and looked down every few moments. She came to rest in a treetop by the start of the woods and peered down in silence. There she witnessed the large dogs down below, those hellish dogs stood on their hindlegs as they stalked below and spoke in human words to each other. She heard them argue and debate killing townsfolk. Their voices so familiar. As one of them knelt and transformed to human she stumbled in the branches of the trees and knew to fly away just as they looked up. They saw only empty trees above them. Mae woke hours later in bed with a fever and the most lucid out of body dream she had ever experienced. As she clung to the mattress she leaned over and threw up onto the floor.

Mae arrived at the studio and after ten in the morning Beth had still yet to turn in. She messaged her and received only a brief message about looking at town streets. On those streets which seemed somehow new and change in some unexplainable manner Beth was confronted by Lily as she stood by the strange tall posts.

'Have you seen these? Are they new? I can't remember them being right here but when I got close, I noticed how old the wood seems and these metal parts seem kind of dangerous for it to be just out on the street here' Beth commented.

'I am glad I have found you. You feel alright?'

'Yes, well apart from Lee from our studio. He...we think he might have died, even maybe been killed. Police aren't totally sure yet but from what his brother told Mae it doesn't sound accidental.'

'That's terrible to hear. You are okay though?'

'Yes. I've been walking around, looking at places I think I took for granted. I've been thinking about what you were telling me.'

'That is good to know. Listen, Beth, you trust me, do you?'

'I think I have to.'

'What I was telling you about your family and what has been forgotten about them, I shall explain more.'

'Don't you have the documents or old things you were going to show me?'

'I have truth and I have knowledge. It is a burden, has been for a long time. You see, these posts, all of them were around long ago. The people of our town used to leave things on them to ward off dangers. You family did this more than most, they understood more than others to reasons and the rituals,'

'What were they warding off?'

'There were at those times, around three centuries ago and longer, many more wild things roaming the land than we ever see nowadays.'

'You mean like boars and wild cats?'

'There were those yes, but there were also things most people will never believe in now. Those things came around, existed and were not always to be feared. At one time we respected them, their strength and loyalty and we fed them and understood their ways for a while at least. But as humans often do, we eventually wanted to use them or eat them. Your family and a few others continued to respect them. They knew to give offerings to them, to give thanks,'

'That sounds sort of religious or pagan. Are we talking about real creatures?'

'Oh yes. And your family understood them and used these posts, they totems for good while, until the change. After that, your family and the few others were disgraced, ridiculed as science and reasons moved across the land. Some of which was help by Mae's family and others as they build up their businesses and claimed land,'

'I Fucking knew it.'

'Yes, now give me your hand.'

Beth put forward her arm while confused. Lily took it, turn it, and pushed back the sleeve to look at the pale soft flesh. Around them Beth sensed the light change, some shift in perspective of the land the street. The height and shape of the near buildings seemed to warp, bend and buckle as Lily held her arm. She moved her other hand over the cold flesh and Beth continued feel uneasy. The daylight faded, the buildings shrank, some disappeared, and the form of the streets around seemed to shift, open, and rearrange entirely.

'Hold still now, this is important' Lily told her.

'Your grip, it hurts' Beth replied.

'It won't take long. It will be better than what will happen. An offering, Lee had no change.'

'What?' Beth asked. She struggled and tried to pull away her arm. Lily held tight and pulled her beside the tall old wooden post to their right. She clenched the arm and moved it up closer to the old metal points. With one hand she grasped one of them, tugged and revealed and longer spike which came out around seven inches and she moved Beth's exposed arm right up close to the edge of it.

'What are you doing?' Beth exclaimed.

'Just an offering, satiate the dogs. Keep them loyal.'

Beth tugged and kicked out at Lily, who fell back to the ground and cursed. Beth ran out as she held her arm, dashed up a narrow side alley and fled. She ran for another seven minutes until she came out to see the riverside ahead of her. She knew the design studio must be near and turn around where she stood but simply could not see it in any direction.

'Where the fuck am I?' Beth gasped in awed confusion.

The trees behind the design studio had buckled inward, arched toward each other, and began to knit together their branches. Mae looked out of the window from the first floor, fascinated by the how they seemed to have changed position so much. They could not have moved so differently in the space of a day, that must be impossible she thought. Strong winds could have damaged them, snapped or split them but she was sure the day had been calm and quite so far. She knew they had not been that way yesterday and to move so much, so low and close together in such a short time as twenty-four hours or less was surely unreal. How could they do that? Someone could have pulled the branches lower and inward but that would take such strength and possibly ropes or intricate devices or with assistance from cars or trucks which would have been seen or heard already by her or someone else who surely would have mentioned such an event. In some way it did look better to her, some part of her was pleased to see the trees bowed together low and unusual like that. She had the desire to go outside and touch the warped buckled branches, the trees but she did not leave the studio. Some feeling told her to remain inside. There was one of the large dogs, it moved silently through the grass and below the warped and buckled trees. It came to stop and peered up around. Did it look up right at her? It turned where it stood, looked at the trees around and over it, the ones further out which stood straight and tall. It gave a loud short bark, watched and those trees began to bend low and warp like the others. Mae stood amazed but fearful. She rubbed her eyes, shook her head as she watched the change below, the dog seeming to initiate it with a sole loud bark. She shook her head in slow disbelief.

She saw the mannequins out on the grass around the studio below. Had they just now appeared or been there all day?

'Katherine, are you here?' she called and turned around.

Between and behind the trees Katherine moved in silence as Beth walked on ahead unaware. She followed the noises she thought had been the cries of a small child. The trees and woods soon folded and bent in around her, confused and misled her as she walked further in. With distant barking of dogs somewhere around them, Katherine came out, wrapped an arm around Beth and the wing tightened over them, the sharp teeth sunk into the side of her, and she fell unconscious. Once on the ground, Katherine dragged Beth along through the trees, over mud, shit, and dirt to where the ropes had been set up earlier. In only a short time she hung her up. She stood and looked down at her membranous pastel wings under her arms before they snapped back out of existence, and she walked away to leave Beth to the fate which was due for her. she killed Beth with strange, mutated tendrils and teeth from within her arms, under wings.

The trees rustled and seemed to move under and between the deep tall shadows all around Mae as she moved in among them. Mae stepped out ahead aware that she was outside the design studio but somehow the shape and size of the surroundings seemed reformed. She felt sick, faint and stumbled. A sound, a shout or moan. Some whisper of words familiar, a chant of caution or accusation. She spun around light-headed and thought she caught sight of Katherine as she glided past her over the crumpled leaf covered ground, blood caked over her arms, eyes rolled back in her head as she pulled a body behind her. Who was that body? What was she seeing? Mae fell to her left knee, looked around her, towering trees surrounded her like a cage. Her heart rattled in her chest as she covered her eyes and face. Did she black out? She opened her eyes, peered through the trees, and tangled brambles ahead of her.

'Beth, are you out here? Come back to the studio please, Beth' she called.

A clear bark echoed from somewhere beyond the trees around her.

She spun around and there before her she viewed the body of Beth tied and strung up between trees. Two feet to the right Lee was strung in the same horrendous manner, lifeless and torn, battered and bloodied. Beth seemed to jerk, kick out and finally drop with movement ceasing seconds later. The large dogs howled and spoke her name. They stood on their hind legs, and one faced her.

'Nothing for the dogs, Mae?' it spoke with a face which had features she could almost recognise as it grinned at her.

She clamped her hands over her mouth and stumbled back, screamed, and threw up beside her feet. She fell, unable to take her gaze away at first until she found the nerve to run back in what she hoped was the way she had come. Through streamed tears and convulsed breathing somehow, she made it back into the studio moments later. She got inside, bolted the door behind her and rushed up to her studio room, collapsed into her large chair. She heard Katherine call behind her. She walked out to the corridor; she saw the familiar silhouette down by the staircase. She clutched her smartphone in her hands, sobbed for while and cursed out loud as she stood and looked out of the window down to see the Briggar stone by the riverside and the woods to the left of it.

'Mae, come here, help me...' she heard from down the corridor.

'Of course, I owe you. Katherine, dogs out there, one spoke to me when I saw things...I think I saw...' she began to say and followed. In a brief moment she was pulled aside into the next room, under shadows. Long wide wings opened out and covered her, cloaked her with warmth as tendrils plunged into her neck and her ribcage. She fell into a helpless sleep while as she whimpered through a pain she knew from some time before. When she woke Katherine was gone, if she had ever been there in the studio at all. She stood lightheaded and clumsily walked through the corridor, out down to the gates outside on the street and made a call to Issy through hysterical tears and sobbing. She remembered the sight of Beth and Lee strung up in the trees. As her stomach began to twist and flip within, she frantically pulled out her smartphone.

'Issy, I'm coming to your place' Mae said hysterically over the phoneline.

'What's happened, you sound distressed.'

'Beth, she...they're dead, somehow. In the trees behind my studio, hung up there, Beth...and...and...'

'Your work colleague Beth, shit. Oh god. Are police there?'

'Phoned them, they're coming to my studio now.'

'You're safe, are you?'

The police came and took a statement while other officers had gone along to the woods and in less than twenty minutes, they could not find the bodies of Beth or Lee. They made sure Mae was stable and waited with her until Issy came and drove her home. Issy led her in quickly, made tea and sat her down.

'This is a horrible week. A real nightmare. You should not have experienced any of this. We're all here for you-myself, Jen, and Jackson of course. So, the police took your statement and all that back there?'

'Yeah, I gave a statement, or they at least listened to my garbled sobbing words and tried to make some sense of it. They think I'm mad, think I'm lying to them. I did see them like that. Really, I did. God, Issy, fucked up things are happening around us. I just...why Issy, why and way it has happened?'

'I have no idea. Don't try to understand it. Lie down, try to calm your head. I'm here and Jackson is coming around soon. We need to be with the police though, get protection, I think.'

'What I saw near, Beth in the trees. It was the dogs, but bigger, big as people, on their back legs and that stone, the Briggar stone in between it all. They spoke, one spoke my name. I swear and Katherine was there, she did something, she had a body there, had blood on her. Beth and Lee cut open and all bloodied and dirty, as if dragged back up from the river. What they did to them...it was horrific, just fucking...like...like a sacrifice before me, up in the trees...'

'Sit down, breathe, just breathe and lie down.'

'Phone Jen. Speak to her. Check with her'

Issy did not think it the most important thing but agreed due to the state of Mae.

'Jen, listen it's me and Mae. A horrible thing has happened. Her friend Beth at work has died, plus the guy Lee, it seems they went the same way. You there?'

'Yes. Shit, where are you two?'

'We're at Mae's place'

'Is Mae okay?'

'She's doing well, I'm with her.'

'Can I speak with her?'

'It's on speaker'

'Hey Mae. I'm so sorry bout what's happened.'

'It's not your fault but it is freaking us out in a serious way. There is something more to it.'

'I'm stuck out by the motorway other side of the city. Stay there with Issy, don't go outside. Are police involved?'

'Yes, they're doing their thing, all that stuff. And after my work friends...Jen, have you seen or heard strange things where you are, have you seen Katherine?'

'Issy, leave it. Just watch some tv with Mae, a movie or something. Calm her. Both of you try to calm yourselves, you'll be safe with authorities in the area on alert.'

'Can you just come over?'

'Jackson is coming soon. Thank you both, I don't know what to think about any of this' Mae told them as Issy hugged her. The knock came and Jackson was there with them.

'I'll leave you two together but Mae, call me anytime tonight or whenever. Jackson, keep by her yeah?'

'Of course, thank you Issy. Speak soon'

As Jackson walked back to his apartment from the off-licence with his bag of wine and bread the loud bark to his right turned his head. He looked across the desolate overgrown field and threw the thick rows of trees and made out the two figures moved in repetitive form. There was some chant or praise spoken. They dropped to their knees, became silent, scampered away between bushes and overgrowth like feral beasts. Something swung and shifted between the low branches of the many deep trees. Two large dogs came to where the people had been moments before. They stood below the shape which hung low.

'Well done, been so long' he whispered and continued back to his apartment to greet Mae soon enough. He read a message on his phone and once in his car he drove to get to flat. He picked her up and arrived at his house less than fifteen minutes later. He poured them a glass of wine each and sat her down in the lounge.

'What's happened at your studio, the death of that Lee and Beth, it's so unbelievably unfortunate. I'm here for you, talk to me, hold me, I am here to support you.'

'Thank you, Jackson. You do believe what I've told you I saw?'

'I absolutely do. Believe me though, you have not seen your friend from college. Your friends, Issy and Jennifer, they're good friends I understand that, but I do think they're playing around, maybe they're both going through some challenging times and want to escape or regress into comfortable past memories and times rather than face or confront today and tomorrow.'

'They don't lie to me or play tricks on me.'

'No, not consciously of course not. I just wouldn't want to see you manipulated or pulled in with their insecure emotions and not now this terrible thing has happened at your studio. You may be more fragile and open to it. Give it a while, I will go and talk with at least one of them in a friendly manner.'

'Jackson, you don't have to...'

'I know you've said they don't always listen to you and mess around often.'

'Sometimes maybe'

'You all miss your old friend, but they should not push you to believe she is alive and here. They need to get over their own stumbling blocks in life, their own career challenges. Maybe they're jealous because your career has taken off quicker than theirs have. I suggest you stay away from them for a short while, give them less attention until they get the message. You are all adults now and should behave as such. Anyway, I'm here for you.'

He told her and held her to him, kissed her head.

C**hapter Thirteen**

The business in the town centre took up much of his time but Jackson always had the Briggar stone in the back of his thoughts every day. He had not stepped inside for years but did return to it regularly and more so in the last few months. He remembered that the local townsfolk had their theories as to what the stone was, why it stood there and never fell into the river and the kinds of mysterious mystical or spiritual reasons to it. None of them had ever been correct. Though he knew what lay inside, he also knew being outside with what he knew and could do held plenty of potential. Jackson had created a small secret group of worshippers of Briggar Stone. His most recent worshippers, Peter, and Smantha he poached from local spiritualist and evangelical churches when he observed their frustration and urge for connection to a creator. He introduced them to the stone and some of the rarely spoken of miracles it offered regularly.

On the crisp Thursday morning Peter was walking to Briggar stone by the river beyond town to pray there after having seen and experienced the miracle and healing Jackson had shown him. Peter brought a covered bundle of wrapped dead rabbits and pig hearts from the butchers in town as his offering as Jackson had suggested. He was careful to not be watched as he walked to the stone on the riverside alone. He knelt down at the back of the stone and placed the bundle of rabbits and animal parts around the base of the stone which faced the river as it flowed quietly. He had seen other offerings taken up from Jackson with Samantha and this was the fourth time he had done this act. He did not know where the offerings went only that they seemed to be taken into the stone somehow. Jackson had let him walk around the stone, from one side to the other after making an offering and there had been no sign of any kind of trickery. It had been the stone; the conduit of God and it had strengthened his personal faith more than ever before. He forgot completely about his previous churches, they surely had never known of anything so miraculous or divine. The last one had asked some much of his own personal income whereas Jackson ask of nothing but regular prayer at the stone when requested and these small offerings. To them Jackson was a real and new prophet to be trusted and obeyed. The offerings had been taken and appreciated by the servants of their deity on the otherside Jackson had informed him. It was the most spiritual act he had personally experienced, more than in any of his churches or healing groups with crystals or other artifacts or rituals. The healing Jackson had shown them had changed their minds, renewed their faith and belief, even if not for a specific Christian, Pagan or other God. God was God Jackson told them and He was present in the stone they now believed, and they thanked Jackson gratefully for leading them to its secret. This was God showing His existence, demanding worship and in return for regular and simple offerings He would listen and heal them, protect them. That was what Jackson had told them, and they had believed him easily and would not, could not argue with what they had seen and felt. It was still to remain a secret until Jackson had built up a trustworthy and reliable group of committed believers suited to the respectful worship to take place at Briggar stone.

Peter sat and knelt down, eyes closed and quietly prayed beside the meat animal organs and rabbit bodies wrapped in their sweating blood smeared plastic bags. He prayed for his uncle Richard to be healed of the long-lasting deafness and heart problems which had restricted his life. He dared not look up to the hands which would accept the offerings from within the stone. Samantha knelt beside him and stopped her prayer as she looked up at Jackson.

'What does it mean that the witch woman is out? Has she done something to our God? Will the miracles still happen, will He still hear us or protect us?' she asked.

'She will. It is very probably a test. To those who really know and worship Her, she will do this. The religious are right with that.'

'Is the witch woman the devil?'

'Not at all. She is a sinner, a test, that's all. We must get her back inside the stone. He wants that. We may have to do things we do not understand, but that is faith. You know that right?'

'Yes, I suppose. You seem a little nervous. That makes both of us then' she said.

'Me, nervous? No, it's just a bad habit, addictive. I've others too I'm afraid. I'm only human, aren't I?' he replied with a charming smile.

'So, we're going to say some prayers here by the stone. Heads down now' he reminded them. 'This one is for you now. Remember the way of things' he whispered beside the stone.

The house where Katherine had spent her teenage years did still stand at the far side of town beyond the high street, near the junior school and the old library. Most people did not ever notice her home even while it had stood left to rot and ruin, all kinds of weeds, moss and deep dark mould covered it, some windows cracked and crumbled away with filth and grime. To many or most it did not really stand there at all, many only saw a wide-open concrete piece of land, more than twenty foot wide, believed contained and so left alone. Those who did still see it looked away quickly as they retained the belief that the family who had lived there had experienced some fatal trauma, one or more deaths in some unexplained accident or much worse. She knew where it stood, she waited in her fatigued state, a precious sanctuary if she dared to spend time inside. The door to her was open, tempted her to look inside after more than three years gone. The silence within seemed to judge her, accused her of running away from the life she knew, the purpose she had been given so long ago. It had been a difficult and problematic place to live, her parents Ron and Lily always seemed disconnected and unimpressed with her emotional yearning and at times abusive. The dreams and visions plagued her for a long time once puberty arrived, taken her concentration and focus more than any boys or girls would sexually. The visions waking or in sleep eventually made some focused sense or logic even while fragmented, enough at least to guide her to the river out on the edge of town. There she had stood behind the ancient and mysterious Briggar stone. She had placed her hands upon it and when she had closed her eyes, something knocked her into the river. She had blacked out. Sometime later she had woken inside a strange wide house. Disoriented, she had no idea where it was situated after a warm meal by a fire she looked out of the high window of the lounge and looked down over the town and river below. It made no sense. She was above the Briggar stone inside a house or room which did not exist from the outside and that was as much as her memory would give her at that point. And that was where she had remained for three years.

Jackson stood before the Briggar stone, checked his watch. As he knew not to expect Peter or Samantha since he had asked them to arrive for their next worship time at hours earlier the next day, he knelt right before the stone. When he was certain there was nobody near, he took hold of his neck and carefully pulled at the skin, gave a quick tug up and away on both sides. His face peeled away with easy like some Halloween mask. Underneath no blood was released but his true secret face was unveiled, a luminous glow to the silver and scaled flesh. He closed his eyes and spoke.

'Hear me, Beniah. I believe trouble is near or entering the town. I feel it. I wish to stay where I exist with my human life and occupation but if you do need me...' he began but stopped, uncomfortable with the thoughts he offered up 'Katherine may be out, she may want to be her human self again, but I know you do not want that. Do you? No, you can't. We...you feel distant. Keep Rondalt and Liliath focused please. I am human, an example to others back there. For you. Amen'

He touched his glimmering, sliver face, touched the stone with both palms and his rose up from the ground until he fell back to the grass behind him. His eyes bled as did his palms and he quickly replaced his human face and walked back across the field behind to his car.

Chapter Fourteen

Jen and Issy arrived at the pub early to decide what they should talk about with Mae when she arrived, what might be too difficult and challenging considering what she had experienced in the recent days. They made some decisions and soon after talking drifted back to when the three of them were in college almost four years earlier.

'Do you remember things seemed so different once we started college, a different town and way of living wasn't it?' Issy said.

'Hormones, my dear'

'Right yeah but it was a lot more as well.'

'We did smoke a shit load of weed like, all the time.'

'Speak for yourself'

'But once Katherine met us and then town seemed to be changed, like we saw it in different ways, didn't we?'

'It was the way she described places around us, around town.'

'Don't start all that again. Not now' Issy answered.

'I have that feeling again' Jen responded.

'No, you've just are remembering those times. Her imagination and creative games, like I was thinking of her but just subconsciously.'

'I got lost in town recently. I was leading my team and the young teens, and I got the streets mixed up, all wrong and we were right where I've been a hundred times and more. Felt a right fool.'

'That's easily done, when the daylight changes and your mind is in other places.'

'It was more than that.'

'Was it, really?'

They had another couple of drinks together but they atmosphere was much different than usual.

'I was looking through my college notebooks, the photos I framed of us then when we were messing about being idiots, getting drunk and high, goofing around and daydreaming.'

'Right. Feeling nostalgic?'

'No, I wasn't. They appeared on my desk in my lounge. I don't think I meant to get them out, but they came out and I moved them around in a collage. They were just...there.'

'You're sure?'

Mae walked into the pub and immediately Jen and Issy who were waiting near the entrance came straight up and hugged her one at a time, Issy kissed her on the cheek.

'Come on, we're going to the usual table. I've got our drinks coming' Jen told her, and they moved across to the right side near the windows together. They could see the delicate emotion and tears forming in the eyes of Mae as they sat down with her and watched her with sisterly concern.

'So, take your time, tell us about what's happen. Are you feeling alright?' Issy asked gently.

Mae let out a deep breath, took one in and began.

'Took a few pills, didn't sleep at all. Glad you two are here. I don't know where she is now.'

'Who's that?' Jen asked.

'Katherine. She's out in town and Ron and Lily are looking. I don't think she is well or...we left her to rot. We should not have done that.'

'I didn't. She just closed in on herself. She was too shy, too self-absorbed. We couldn't do too much. She'd didn't help herself enough.'

Mae responded 'It was her family problems and other things. Job centre pestering her for her to quite college all the time. She didn't get the chance to finish her course before her family went missing then...she did...'

They looked at the table in a silent moment together.

'These huge dog things...' said quietly and let out a laugh which startled the other two.

Jen breathed out 'You've seen her, she is...she's back, in some way' she looked at the other two 'That's right isn't it, let's agree on that?'

'We can go find her; we should probably help them. You're probably best taking a few days at home. We'll call in with food, watch crappy movies' Issy suggested.

Mae shook her head slowly 'She's returned, and my colleagues have died. All in a matter of days. The days since she's been back. What if...what I think I've seen, in the forest behind the trees, she was bloody and carried...what if she has brought danger, her family has some real history which has never been totally clear and why they all disappeared. We don't know properly and probably don't need or want to know. Do we tell the police, or do we let her parents find her, take her back to wherever it was they have been living?'

'You're staying with Jackson, are you?' Jen asked.

Mae nodded 'Yeah, either my place or his. Don't look for her or wait a while. She's unstable, they suggested that much and if I did see her in the trees...with the...,'

'I'll call tomorrow' Jen told her and moved closer, rubbed her arms. Issy took Mae's hands and held them.

'We both will. Fuck it, let's have a whisky yeah?' Issy said and she stood to get them in at the bar.

They waited for a taxi and dropped Mae at her flat first. They took her to the door and hugged her good night. They drove away and Mae fell back onto her sofa in the lounge and as sleep took her the barking of a dog echoed out around outside.

In the top floor room of his company building in the town centre, behind locked doors, Jackson stood and gazed at the two pale corpses he had on the floor before him. Over their bodies were dozens of wounds, scars, holes driven by his hand using various implements and devices over the previous days. There was no life in their bodies, no pulse in their veins. He had strangled them, stabbed them, poisoned them and more. This time he torn out their tongues and blinded them, left them until the movements came to an end. He looked down, stretched out his right arm, cast it over them.

'Rise again, each of you' he spoke quietly, eyes closed.

The veins gradually began to pulse, the limbs did twitch, the eyes fluttered open. They stood, stumbled, and looked to him.

'Thank you...' one of them said. They appeared grateful if ignorant of his reasons or how they had been killed this time.

'You are welcome' he told them 'Sit at the table, join me, drink and eat with me.'

They sat in their tattered clothes, drank his wine with him, ate his bread. After half an hour, he grew bored and put them to sleep once more, left the room, locked the door behind him to continue with the business of day with his doting human employees below.

PART 2 – JEN'S ENCOUNTER
Chapter Fifteen

The walk to the rented office rooms was quiet and thankfully the morning sky was dull and overcast. The slight hangover rolled and thumped insider her head as Jen came into the lower side of town alone and passed boarded up shops and takeaways closed until the evening. She tried not to see the posters advertising greasy kebabs and pizzas. Something reflected in the window, and she turned but the other movement directly opposite was a shabby clothed aged council bin man who shuffled along to take out the next one in front of him on his side of the street. She shook her head and continued. There was a dog barking somewhere around her when the sunlight did decide to crack through the heavy clouds above. She kept her eyes squinted and directed low as she soon approached the building. Seconds to fiddle with her key and she was inside and up the stairs. She glanced outside and the Briggar stone was visible behind the buildings opposite. Was it always there to see from that position on the staircase? She pushed open the office room door and switched on the monitor and computer. Two more aspirin washed down with a reliable fresh coffee was helping Jen to great through the morning after the mix of spirits and beers the night before and with that, what Mae had imparted to her and Issy. She rubbed her forehead, the ache dissipated slightly as she looked out of the window to see Briggar stone over the rooftops of the lower side of town. Such a strong and solid object, she wished she could feel more like that as she tried to keep down her simple breakfast of lightly buttered toast and fruit slices. She looked out and remembered Katherine, her old friend. It was genuinely horrible and tragic what had happened to the people Mae worked with and she really hoped Jackson would keep close watch on her but to think Katherine was back. No, Jen couldn't let herself think that Mae had been lying to them, but it had been three years...no sighting, no news, and the belief that perhaps their sweet old friend had left this world. So alright, believe it, the Katherine they knew and loved so fondly, was back in town, somewhere, somehow. Jen gave a brief shake of her head and a laugh. What would she say to her old friend if she met her? Katherine must have returned to her old family home in town. Where was it? Jen simply could not find the name of the street, the number of the house or location in her mind. Too many drinks. She sighed as she moved around the hall and into her small office room, slumped into the beaten padded chair and leaned over to monitor screen to open the recent vlog files and catch up with the progress. She hoped to get on track with the new vlog editing. They had enough to get it done for the end of the week. People were waiting, the youtube channel was more and more popular day by day. It was a little frustrating having to make a start on editing alone, but Billy had not shown up, Cassy was on her way and so she began with her travel coffee mug on the desk beside her, taking a few confident sips. She scrolled through the files of footage shot on the Sunday at the outside art projects workshop in the lower east side of town. She received a sudden message on her phone from Melissa, the art therapy coordinator confirming that she would like them to return on a regular basis. It made Jen smile as it went along with strong confirmed interest with the Brackenkeel music venue people and the significant influencers in London and France they had connected with.

'Good things on their way' she said as she sipped more coffee between clicking on edits on the screen before her and opened more files.

The loud slap, knock and moan came behind her. She spun around in the chair.

'Hello...?' she said, 'Who's in here?'

Cassy stepped in with a hug 'Late night, was it?'

'It was, yes. Had to console my friend. Two people where she works have died. Can't be entirely sure about the circumstances right now but how they ended up seemed to sound fucking nasty as hell.'

'Oh god, I'm sorry. How are you?'

'Hmm, I'm alright. Tired mostly that all. We're letting Billy take the lead again this week anyway aren't we until I get my inspirational shit sorted again. He can take the stress. Those European and international influencers have connected and want good our help with their versions, and they'll take us into their spaces if we have more and better coming to them.'

'Great. I'll make sure Billy brings the actual goods this week. It is a bit weak really, isn't it?'

Jen nodded and sighed 'Still, he's motivated and eager to help.'

Cassy stepped back with a smile on show 'Should we get on with the vlog stuff in the meantime?'

'Yeah, let's do it.'

They pulled up what they had complied so far and ten minutes later Billy walked in to meet them.

'Hey, morning. Any work getting done here or what?'

'Nah, watching creep snuff movies is all.'

'Really? Well, that's a different start to the day.'

'So, are we going to get something less derivative of every other cheeky, forced social vlog out there?' Cassy asked.

'You know we are. We haven't explored everywhere in every way, yet.'

'You say that but...we have, haven't we?' Billy added.

'No, we haven't. I don't remember you finding us anything startling better so far. How about we keep going and eventually we will piece together something the town and maybe people further afield will appreciate okay?'

Cassy put a hand on Billy chest 'Don't be so bitchy, she's had a difficult night. A friend has had serious troubles. Deaths yeah?'

'Oh...right. Sorry Jen. I'm a mouthy bitch.'

Jen spun around in the chair and stood.

'Forget it. Come on, we should get out and do what we do.'

They left the building together, hauled the bags of equipment onto their shoulders and headed to the other east side of town to the side of the forest and fields before the start of the urban side of town. Jen peered in through the park gates. Billy followed with the camera in hand. With the cameras and sound equipment Cassy led Jen and Billy out toward the river and the desolate farm barns and old structures.

'Why are we here, what's to see?' Jen asked without intending to sound sarcastic.

'A local told me about some kind of pagan or witchcraft stuff that happened around this part of town, between the place you've taken us and that stone on the river, Briggar stone. I think I even saw something sort of weird. So, we'll go find local people from the streets around, get them talking about old customs, traditions and how they take that with modern life every day.'

'Weird how?'

'I might have been wrong, trick of the light or my mind wanting to see something but, in the river, and between the old structures, something some people or things, hard to explain really.'

Jen and Cassy gave each other a glance.

'Okay, we'll stay a while and see what's to see' Jen agreed.

The next hour and a half were far too quiet. They wandered along beside the trees and river but no people, no discoveries, nothing of any significance.

'We should go back to the studio. It'll be some freak being a jerk that's all' he suggested.

'Yeah, fine okay' she agreed, and they returned to his car and to the studio shortly after. Once inside, Billy uploaded the new footage on the programme and cut it up and opened the sound and scrolled over the minutes in the editing software. Coming to join him with a couple of coffees Jen sat beside him.

'Can you believe how this is turning out, we're right on the way to being a successful alternative pop culture news channel for the voiceless, the curious, the youth and we're going international. I mean, seriously' she said.

'If we can keep taking turns with the vlog slots. If you have another couple of weeks without much from your side, I'll keep it going with those spoken words things from my cousin and his pals. It's fresh and different enough, right?'

'It is but...' Cassy said but struggled to sound convincing.

'It's just a couple of weeks, I'm gathering new ideas and things from around. There'll be things I find worthy soon enough. I mean, I think some things are somewhere near I can feel something...' Jen replied. She couldn't let Billy have three weeks of his cousin's pals and family in with their insipid and lame tales of cobbled together folk superstition.

'It's down to your interview style, your charisma, and ideas, me and Cassy are the digital minions, and that's perfect. Look at the day's shots with that Don Porter guy. You got him on the question about local music and art queer performance.'

'I thought he'd just say fuck off' she laughed. They watched her walking and questioning Don beside the bridge and riverside. A muddled pained noise dripped out from the speaker next to Jen.

'This sounds awful' she commented.

'What's that? He doesn't want to even think about people who aren't creative or LGBTQ.'

'No, that sound...the gnarly weird sound'

He looked at her.

'Can't hear anything weird.'

'It's still in this speaker near me' she told him.

'Hmm, no I'm not getting anything on my side.'

'Okay, just forget it.'

'Let's get the edit of the week's part's done up to now, it'll give us some perspective' he suggested.

'Okay. I'm going to go put the kettle on' she told him. She walked out to the small, neglected studio kitchen room, put some mugs down, coffee and teabags in, gave a tired sigh to the room.

'Oh shit. No way!' Billy called out. She knocked a mug to the floor, seeing it shatter at her feet.

'Bollocks' she said and turned to look in the direction 'What's up?' she called and quickly rushed back to him. He was pointing at a dog which had done its business behind her in the shot when she was talking about the history of local homeless artists.

'How did we miss that, its hilarious. Sorry, but look at it' he cried with a chuckle as she came and stood behind him.

'Oh, for God's sake, Billy. So funny. Mug of tea here for the school-boy' she said holding it before him.

'Yeah, mhm thanks' he said taking it from her. She shuffled silently back to the kitchen and looked up and caught some ebony figure which faltered past the window below outside. The figure appeared crumpled, a strange, crooked shape. It may have been a homeless person she thought, they did roam around at times. She took up the kettle which had boiled and began to pour water into the two mugs. She thought about who was watching their video reports and why, what it meant to them. With a glance down red was in sight.

'The hell...' she mumbled.

The coffee in her mug was crimson, a deep red filling up. She looked around her, out in the direction of Billy. Looking back to the mugs, she only saw a regular caramel brown coffee and sandy tea this time.

'Your head is in the clouds' she whispered to herself when she did sit with Billy to watch and edit a few segments of footage she sat silent and focused, thoughtful, and contemplative. Thoughts about the town, locations, camera angles and shot to shot editing were in mind when she saw the bizarre person flit past in one shot. Some strange people around town she thought. Was it another homeless person? If it was, they looked extremely lost to themselves. The person was quickly gone, and she focused with Billy back on her interview with local foodbank helpers. As the camera moved in the next shot it caught a figure wrapped in tattered old clothes leaning over who resembled some degraded victim of violent abuse or neglect, long hair matted and greased over hunched shoulders. It turned and looked right into the camera lens. Though the strings of long greased hair, a pair of haunted and familiar hollow eyes peered straight at her. A mouth opened and words shaped in communication.

'Shit Billy...' she said, her voice wavering with fear.

'Hmm, I know the shot lingers too long on you before she speaks to you.'

'What?'

'You and the food bank woman. When she talks about the conservative politician ignoring them for weeks while the little boy and girl had no lunch'

Jen sat with mouth open, shaking and fingers clawing into the desktop before her. She made a low humming sound, did not blink for the longest time. She leaned in close to the screen. Whispered quietly in disbelief.

'Katherine?' Billy noticed this.

'Jen, you feeling okay?' he asked looking at her. The people on screen bustled around and the figure was gone from view. Jen reached and swiped the footage back over the last couple of minutes, but the tattered clothed woman was gone from view.

'Hmmm...no...I...I need to take a break I think' she quietly replied. He took a good look at her pale haunted face.

'I think you're totally right. You want to just go home?'

'Yes. Sleep, I think. I'm exhausted, dizzy or something. That okay with you?'

'You don't look yourself so yeah. You go. Call us later on, let us know how you feel.'

'Yeah, I'll do that' she murmured as she left the room.

In the Buckle Shoe pub on Clatters Road Ron walked in quick past regulars who sat supping their daily pints to where Jackson sat at a table as he checked messages on his phone. He glanced up as he heard the familiar lilting voice.

'There is the man done well, a success story for all to know and learn from' Ron said as he came and sat opposite him.

'You're busy, are you? Up and down the streets?' Jackson asked as two pints arrived for them.

'Oh cheers, you charming devil. Yes, we are, we will not stop. We are on the hunt. She is in my thoughts no end' Ron said with a distinct nod as he took a long drink from his pint glass.

'Would that be Lily or Katherine?'

'Well, both but Katherine is the one to be found. Have you seen her?'

'I have not. I have my business to run and if I have any spare time this week it will be with my girlfriend. She had experienced some very difficult trauma.'

'What would that be?'

'Her work colleagues have died. In a matter of days. Strange indeed. You'd agree?'

'Oh yes, such terrible news. I hope you know how best to support her.'

'That I do Ron. Town still looks familiar enough to you, does it? It's been a while since you've come down.'

'That is true. Three years is nothing really is it. How long did you travel in the past and return?'

'Different times. I hope it does all seem to have remained as it has been since you left us.'

'So far that would seem to be the case, yes. Time will tell.'

'Keep Briggar stone in sight. Keep me in mind too. If you think you need any help...'

'You are in mind, do not doubt that my friend.'

'Oh, I do not' Jackson told him.

'You hear my dog barking lately? it may have been near your place' Ron said casually.

'I hope not. Does it do any tricks these days?' Jackson asked and looked Ron in the face. Ron seemed to quiver, hold back words until he decided on his response. Ron flashed his putrid long black tongue and slapped the side of his glass with it before it recoiled back.

'No tricks, my dogs simply help with finding our Katherine. No tricks' he said.

'Best that way Ron' Jackson agreed. He finished his pint, stood and they left the pub together. They stood side by side and viewed the town which they had witnessed and carried out countless acts of severe trickery and violence. He watched Ron walk away down the road through town with the dog at his side. Always one dog or another he thought.

Chapter Sixteen

The familiar female shape moved on further ahead of Jen, led her out to the smaller town village streets she had neglected for too long. The streets were the old cobblestone of the buildings around and thatched roofs, cryptic marks, and patterns between streets low down on the paths and roads ahead drew her attention as she walked on. There was history, mystery and deeper rich knowledge waiting to be found and told to others with her vlog channel. She knew what she was seeing others would find fascinating as well, she was certain.

'I've ignored all of this, why, why did I forget about this part of town. It's further out but even so...look at it all' Jen stated as she walked on fascinated.

'Witherbale...' a voice whispered inside her ear from nearby, over her shoulder. She turned but found no one near her.

Jen stopped and looked around her as a couple of people passed by on either side of the street 'Katherine...you're there?'

Up ahead on the corner she saw the thin pale figure with haunted eyes. She heard the response as the mouth remained closed 'My parents. Don't say you've seen or spoken to me.'

'Didn't you want to stay with Mae? You've been to her studio haven't you' Jen asked as she carefully moved closer so grateful to set eyes on her old dear friend. It had been true; she was alive and had come to see them.

'Seen her but...want to see you...and Issy.'

Jen came to stop a few feet from Katherine. She could see easily that her friend seemed physically unwell, drained, and clothed in some simple dirt smeared old dress and jacket. If she had not stayed over with Mae, had she been sleeping rough on doorways or behind bushes and walls around town. She could not let Katherine remain like this, especially if it was due to the ways she had been living elsewhere outside of town. 'You can stay with me; I won't ask a lot of questions. Things happened at the studio where Mae works. Do you know?'

'Witherbale' Katherine murmured, her eyes glazed as she rubbed her old, soiled jacket which covered her thin figure within.

'Witherbale...yes...' Jen said. The vague memory of that part of town she did hold was simply that it was already common knowledge, out of fashion, not of interest and had been studied and recorded to death for many times in the past already, there would be no point wasting any of her time. But now she was here, she was feeling foolish. She came out to where the street connected with a wider town space between and three more streets which pointed away up ahead as the daylight came down and bathed the rooftops before her. She peered down at what seemed to look like old rune marks upon some of the stones of the street and down low on the fronts of the buildings beside her.

'Curious for sure...' she said quietly. She looked up and found Katherine gone from view. She walked on eager to find her old friend, she could not lose her so easily.

The side of the forest along the river was rattled with a sharp breeze as Jen walked out to view the rows of trees and the beginning of the further side streets at the back of town to the side of them. She could not hear Billy or Cassy anymore as she took down her shoulder bag and searched inside for the notepad to record what she was seeing and her thoughts. A shadow loomed over her, and she turned to see a man from her past smile down at her.

Ron stepped out and offered a familiar smile 'Jen, was it? I think so yes. Hello' He came forward from behind someone at the front of the small newsagents and café entrances.

'Yes, that's me. You're...you're Katherine's father...Ron' she responded, 'You're back.'

'Have you seen my Katherine around town, we're looking for her' he said as he scratched his nose and neck, his arms and twitched as he stepped closer, straightened, and looked her up and down. He nodded to himself.

She remembered the words of Mae, her confusion and view that they should simply offer their help and support to her parents after what she had encountered.

'I...but you disappeared, and she was looking...we believed you and your wife, well and then Katherine too...you just disappeared. It's been three years' she told him. She took a step back with cautious suspicion.

'We've been away, together. We're back but only for a short while. Katherine is ill, she must be with us, she must return with us' he told her with a concerned frown upon his face which did not seem to have aged much, grey hair receding and some wrinkles around his eyes and mouth with those thin wet lizard lips familiar enough.

'Return to your home, in town?' Jen asked as she stood with her back to a brick wall.

'No, to our...our other place we live now. We moved to our older family home.'

'Oh, wish I had known. I thought she, I had upset her. Maybe I can visit. You say she's ill or sick though?'

'Jen, if you see her, I will come back around here. Or call our number.'

He gave her a scrap of paper in grime smeared fingertips which she took as he went back to rubbing his neck and a curious movement of his chest and shoulders as he watched her.

'Right, thanks I will. We'd been talking, myself and a couple of friends, remembering her lately. I'll look around, watch for her. I have a feeling she will appear.'

'So do I. I will see you soon Jen' he told her with a smile which looked slightly sneering as he turned and disappeared down a side street.

'We need to go to lower side Witherbale road for a shoot. Something...necessary is there, someone to meet' Jen told Billy as they sat in the small editing room later in the afternoon.

'Oh right. Who is it and why?' he asked.

'I can't really say. I know there's something special waiting there for us. Trust me on it'

Billy seemed dejected but nodded 'Okay. I think I know the place. Some shops and a couple of pubs there have shady reputations though. We should be a bit cautious'

'We do need some interviews and footage with more life, some genuine mystery in our reports...'

'Okay then. Tomorrow if you're up for it?'

'Witherbale tomorrow, yes. Whatever it has to show us' she told him.

Lower Witherbale really was a downbeat rundown part of town. People had expressions of anxious aggression, bitterness, and sorrow. There was a sense of fear and hopelessness in the atmosphere around the place. Jen and Billy walked through the main road trying to seem focused and casual, doing their own thing but as the minutes passed, they both felt they did not wish to be there when it got into dark evening time. Somehow both were pleasantly surprised to discover a small indoor market with fascinating stalls where the owners spoke about their proudly made artwork, clothing, sculptures and more.

'How do people miss all this?' Billy said at one point.

'I know, wonderful and inspirational things here. These people are talented and expressing their thoughts and feeling with all these craft things. This shows the area is not just crime and people with addiction lost' she agreed.

They decided to talk to some of the stall holders and film it for an hour and a half or more. A woman called Enid explained things about her mixed ethnic heritage and how it was expressed in her handmade art and clothes, which led them to Jonas, a long-time Iranian refugee in the next stall across and his talk about the underground music and art collective nights after a couple of murders and break-ins to raise money for families.

'This is great positive community work, collective art expression of sadness but also hope' Jen told him as Billy got a few varied shots with his camera in front of them. There were people walking around and past them looking and buying the items for sale on the stalls. Someone walked past and murmured words which took Jen's attention away.

'Waters...red water...Jen...red waters...' she heard curl right into her ears.

She spun around to look for who was saying the words.

'Billy, who said that?'

'Said what?' he asked 'You did. The question about...'

'No. Red waters...who said that?'

She stepped away, walked off alone down the long open walkway looking ahead at the backs of a few people around the spread-out craft stalls. Which one had said her name? The ugly dishevelled shape of a person shuffled up ahead between two others moving along. That soiled old jacket and dress, the bare feet moved away off the ground through and behind the moving bustling crowd.

'Wait there, stop' Jen called out. She moved on faster, gently pushed past the others. The person she thought had been Katherine has disappeared, gone behind the slowly moving crowd. Jen noticed some small memorial beside one stall to her right. The name on the tribute seemed familiar to her mind.

She slowly returned to Billy who stood waiting back at the stall up the corridor.

'You don't know who that person was who just walked past?' she asked Billy.

'No, I've only noticed her once but you're saying you've seen her three times now as we've been editing' he replied.

'I think I have. Was she following us?'

'At three different places right across town? I'm sure I did not see her in person at any of them. This is kind of creepy. You've a trampy stalker' he suggested, trying not to laugh.

She didn't reply but continued to look around them. If Katherine was near, why could she not simply come close and speak to her? Was she afraid of Billy? Did she know Ron and Lily were close by?

They walked slowly back around to where the market streets began. Far behind some dogs barked. When Jen turned, she thought she was Ron stood far across the opposite side of the road, dog by his side and as she blinked, he disappeared away down another street.

C**hapter Seventeen**

Jackson stepped up beside the crooked ancient Briggar stone relic, the monolithic slab on the riverside. Once he had checked no others where around to see, he touched the reverse side which faced the river waters which flowed below. He noticed the face of Katherine reflected up to him and with a scowl, looked away to the stone as it opened inward for him, and he stepped into a place no local alive knew existed. It closed up to the outside world as he stepped into the hall chamber within, the high building ceiling far above hm as he approached the staircase and ascended, the chill around him familiar.

He cursed as he marched up the steps to the main room. Under the flawed yet masterly carved walls stood the imitation Victorian era dining table with dresser cabinets to the left and lounge recliner positioned on the right. Tanks with thick liquid contained numerous unclear aquatic twisting and writhing forms as he walked past. Howls and groans rose up from below the rooms from the lower chambers. He tutted at the familiar sounds.

'Anyone here, hello?' he called out as he stepped around. He noticed a pile of plates and bones pushed down at the end of the long table and he frowned with plain dissatisfaction.

'Not again. This will not do. I will not take blame again. I will not cover up for your failures, damn you' he called, fist clenched and raised. He walked out to the far left to looked to a doorway into a room there. He pushed the door open and stepped in. He crossed the room and stepped to the window to look out and over the town. Out on the long dining table in the main room he immediately noticed items familiar to him. An axe caked in dried blood, a long sword worn and damaged but still deadly, a skull halved down the middle his initials carved into the side. His old trophies and he knew Ron had left them out for him, put the memories and temptation where he could not avoid it. He shook his head and walked away to his own room, down on the left. The old bed and furniture were there, clean and tidy which he was grateful to see. He moved to look down out of the side window. He saw cars in the distance which moved along the roads, people walking across the long path stretched beside the river around the side of town. There was a stench in the room, in the entire building he noticed, some new fetid aroma. The wall before him cracked silently, split just enough to let in some daylight down by his legs.

'See what happens, you know this, you've been warned' he spoke while still alone 'He'll not be pleased with this. You damn fools' he said and walked back out to the main wide room. As he touched the handle on the door by the upper right his smart phone buzzed in his pocket, and he clutched at it. A message from Mae. She was asking if he could pick her up from the studio in a short while. He messaged back and made his way back down the stairs and out across the grass to where his car was parked.

The lower side of Whitherbale offered a curtain of fog to them as they moved in together to find what they needed. Billy strolled out away from Jen and Cassy behind trees to take a piss. He wiped his hands on his jeans and reloaded his vlogging camera with a charged battery, stepped out and looked around the area. Ron came up alongside him.

'You're working with Jen and Cassy aren't you, the local filmmakers, talented visual investigators?' Ron said. Billy smiled back and noticed the dog at the man's side. It seemed some unclear mixed breed and it watched him with interest just like the man.

'Yes, you've met them?' Billy asked.

'Certainly. Are you onto some interesting things right now?'

'Jen thinks so, she's actually more fired up and excited than she's been for a while. We're looking around some area we don't really know, further Witherbale. We'll see what comes of it. You know the area?'

'I do indeed. The name's Ron, this is my faithful dog by my side. We come out sometimes to see how things might have changed. Sometimes we can only change what we know. The more we know, the more we can change our surroundings. Sometimes we have to do that, even if it might seem wrong,'

'I suppose. What can you tell us about town that our viewers might find interesting or unusual Ron?' Billy asked as he stepped around and looked out at the street area around them.

'Let me think...some parts have gained bad reputations, other parts look wonderful even after centuries-from what I've read, yes there are many misunderstandings of our town. Much history has been recorded, documented, remembered sometimes fondly yet other times with shame and regret. There is a picture of this town which has been painted for all which is not entirely honest or truthful. You know about the tragedy of Willingham hospital in the nineteen fifties?' Ron asked.

Billy sucked in his lips and turned his eyes skyward momentarily 'Yes...we looked into the possible use of experimental drugs or medication by military which very possibly created deaths and long term generational illnesses of the twenty eight patients one night in the country yards when they fell from the second floor windows after having attacked each other horrifically, allegedly'

'Yes, such a terrible event. What about the fisher family with their own language who thought they were protecting everyone by leaving rotten fish on doorsteps once one of their children had a vision. It seemed disgusting and offensive until it actually did prevent dogs with rabies getting to the townsfolk, that was nineteen twenties it's believed.'

'We knew most of that. Some we talked to said the family possibly released the dogs and made them rabid because they were ruined financially by new boats and ship work.'

'Always another view of things. Not every one of them always put on record though. There are other tales, events, mysteries, times which are challenging to believe and would sound far too unbelievable I guarantee but which happened anyway.'

'We're listening. Can't say we'll believe everything we read or hear but we'll give it time of day or fifteen minutes at least and a fair hearing.'

'Now, this is our town. It can't surely be as interesting or fascinating as places like London, Norfolk, Scotland, Wales for tales of mystery and wonder, trusted or strange local lore you'd think? It must all be known and heard by now you'd wage. Oh no, many things are hidden, overlooked, ignored, denied, or buried to retain sanity, identity, or respectability before the rest of the nation. There have been things to make you question your past, your family, your beliefs, logic of physics, right and wrong, life and death.'

'Such as – we're recording now.'

'Be wary, you may not like some things you may stumble upon. Some things are hidden for good reason.'

'You know your Katherine had a great imagination. She told Jen all kinds of wild stories full of strange creatures and locations she believed to have existed at some time or in future, maybe even locally near here. Do you know what I'm talking about?'

'I might know some of those things. She did enjoy the classics like Homer, Shakespeare, Tolkien, C.S. Lewis, Angela Carter stories I think.'

'She told us she knew doorways to other places existed, people who swam like fish through the sky, flew like birds, lived underground like insects, people who returned from the dead and other things. You're getting a folklore aren't you, do you mean local folklore like that? Maybe connected to the river, the hills around us, the mills or that big stone, the Briggar stone'

'No, I was thinking of some very disturbing tales believed to be from our town but centuries ago. Cannibalism, sacrifice, horrific tribal games with corpses or the dead from the armies of those who came to plunder and rule here. Hardly any of it is remembered, acknowledged, believed, or whispered but it impacted everything.'

'Wait-we're a cannibal town?'

'Who knows? That and a place of holy banishment and trials. What do you want to believe, what do you need to believe and what do you dare not ever dare believe?'

'We hide truths or forget what could help us here, I don't know. Whatever helps us get through, day to day or whatever is popular.'

'Well, you could be onto something there. Or just a shamed cannibal town which remade itself once the Romans came and science and printed word said otherwise and civilised us all. Do you know about the witches who need their honey?'

'What, no'

'All forgotten and erased. A couple of centuries ago we were supposed to leave honey and local berry cakes for the women believed to be witches on the first Sunday of their menstruations. With the berry cakes and honey the river worm would know they were too weak to protect us. The witches would be mad after the worm had taken local children. If they had been strong enough, they would have used their witch powers. Because our forgetfulness they curse and hate us'

'Never heard any of that. Sounds good and creepy though.'

'It certainly was. I'll see you soon. We must continue to look for Katherine You'll do the same won't you?'

'Yeah, of course. Thanks for all of these...these things to consider.'

'Anything else?'

'Things behind Witherbale, old barns Jen doesn't know. Go there, you find it. You could take the credit, take the lead. She doesn't focus very well, does she? Cassy will find something too, I think. Jen will have to know how to appreciate both of you.'

He watched Ron walk away between trees and inside a side alley with his dog which a glance at him before it too was gone from view. He let out a quiet laugh as he heard Ron talk to the dog. Did he hear a female voice reply to him?

Billy came to meet back up with Jen and Cassy and explain how he had met with Ron and told of some of the interesting history which he had put forward. Jen shook her head, laughed unintentionally 'Hang on, are you actually winding me up here?'

Billy held up his hands 'Isn't that what we want? It sounds so weird or mad but imagine some things like that might be true.'

'Our great, great relatives were cannibals or fish people or something.'

'Or something. Like he says, what if we just can't handle the truth, the real past or don't know what the hell to do with it?'

'Please Jen, don't put your tin-foil hat on. We've been doing so well so far, standing back objectively while making our vlogs. That's our way. We're not going to be one of those sucked in dumb arse shows for ratings and like while fuelling hate, division and bigotry, no way.'

'No of course not, I just mean what he was suggesting and what my Katherine used to tell us about.'

'There are connections, and you know how much she believed in what she was saying or at least how serious she seemed about it all. Some things there...there's something solid, real worth considering, tangible.'

'From his words. He's winding us up. Or he's fucking a frootloop himself.'

'And what would that mean, she being his daughter...'

'Hey no, she wasn't crazy or whatever.'

'You said she had that great imagination.'

'Yes, but she's...'

'What?'

She did not finish her sentence.

'Let's walk around a little, while they leave it for today' they walked on up along the first street of Witherbale considering the shops and businesses around them, the crumbing old architecture which held up memories under pressure to collapse into the dirt forever gone.

Chapter Eighteen

The business Jackson owned in town was named Pallour & Janus had only been going for less than a decade but was strong and profitable with its manufacture and sales or natural wooden garden furniture and ornaments created and sourced locally. Only three were employed besides himself but they worked unbelievably hard and long hours, barley questioned their orders and thanked him daily as if they owned him their lives. In some sense, they did. Employees Stewart, Ian, and Molly, they became sick, absent, and quietly defiant. He had placed increasing pressure on them too quickly, forgetting they were only human. The business began to suddenly suffer. There were things he could do resolve escalating problems, such impressive sudden things but he wished to handle it as any other respected and talented businessman would today. He was sat in his office, chair backed against the wall as he leaned back and considered the recent profit figures and loan amounts and how it balanced against the next few ventures set out ahead. There were some potential problems, and he noticed these things just did not usually mount up some much like this. As much as he would like to lay the blame at the feet of his employees, he could see that he was most likely the cause of these hurdles on the horizon. His mind had been distracted recently, he had experienced regular bouts of discontent and absent-mindedness during his workdays. He had been watching the Briggars stone. He could damn near swear it was on the move. He heard the barking of the dogs; he knew Ron would be entirely straight with him. But he had made that promise last time, they could have their freedom as he could have his. It had been easy enough to off load portions of work onto his secretary Lucy and deputy manager Gail, but he could not continue to do this. He stepped out to the reception area to find Lucy sat looking over dates and stock orders on her computer.

'Lucy, you look like you're working hard there. I like it. Listen, I'm heading out for a while when Gail returns from the meetings I might not be back. Tell her to call or message me. I might see you tomorrow' he told her.

'Oh, alright. No problem, I'll pass that on to her. Good how we can work anywhere these days isn't it? I appreciate you letting me work here and at home' she responded with a loyal smile as she typed an email.

'Yes, it can be useful. See you later' he replied as he left the building. The cool cold midday came against his tense face as he walked out through the town streets, his mind caught up in a few tangled thoughts and feelings. He needed to be out of the office, to walk out away from the daily work to somewhere quiet, natural, and organic. He walked on for almost fifteen minutes until he came near the edge of town, the end of the urban grey buildings and streets and to where the wider fields and neglected arable land opened out. He walked in among the beginnings of some rows of trees more than ten feet tall, the daylight gradually shaded away over him. He closed his eyes, bowed his head, and began to murmur some familiar secret chant only three others had heard him speak aloud.

His feet lifted from the ground, and he moved up slowly between the trees. He spread his arms out and touched those close to his fingertips on either side. His back began to hunch and shift, it buckled and warped under his jacket. He let out a moan as this happened.

He opened his eyes to reveal vivid red pupils which glared out down and around him. He held up his arms as he levitated there alone between the tall trees. With his eyes closed again he smiled to himself.

A dog barked from somewhere not too far away.

He fell, hit the ground below on his knees and cursed. On his hands and knees, he looked around, peered out between the trees. He could not see the things which had made the loud noise. He stood and dusted himself down, heading back into town, around through the upper west streets to his home.

As he walked out of the rows of trees Ron stood with his dog beside him and watched him walk away. Half an hour later he was approaching his front garden and stepped toward the door, keys in his right hand when he heard someone behind. He turned around to see Ron out at the edge of the garden, the dog beside him.

'Slow day at the office today?' Ron asked as he stroked the dog fondly.

'Needed to be with my thoughts outside. Not usually the case. We're busy' Jackson said as he put the key in the lock and turned it, pushed the door open inward.

'Just passing by, walking faithful here as you know' Ron stated.

'Right. See you soon maybe' Jackson said as he entered his home and turned to looked back at him.

'You want to be a legend? Want to be a mystery, to live after death, others to puzzle over your meaning, the enigma of your actions, your truth?' Jackson asked.

'Could be you and her aren't the best at it. We might have learned from your mistakes. We might be doing some of it for the right reasons, pleasing Him or Her up there' Ron countered.

'Still pushing that stale theory at me. Put it to rest. We shape the town, the people, no more and no less.'

'You can't be sure. We feel it, we're from the same place as you and her, we're from both of you. You lost your memories, not us.'

'That is your belief. This is a truly confused game, Ron.'

Jackson looked down, tapped his front door with his finger. He sighed and stepped back out.

'Okay let's take a short walk, shall we?'

They moved out together, dog beside them for the next twenty minutes.

Jackson felt he owed Ron the company and time of day every so often and this was one of those times. It would satisfy him and hopefully send him back on his way. With his curious smile and casual amble Ron eventually stopped out by the side of the old theatre house.

'They do like to play make believe don't they. Do you think it helps with living day to day?' Ron asked as he placed a hand against the wall of the building beside him.

'Some people have died. The design studio on edge of town and some small shop for sale. Hear about it?' Jackson asked as they walked together along the quiet open field behind the town centre.

Ron looked down at his dog, back to town.

'No, I've been too busy. You know that. You know any of them?'

'Not personally, my girlfriend, it's her friends, some of them.'

'I'm sorry to hear that. How is she taking it?'

'I'm there for her, that will help. She is in a state of shock obviously.'

'Right, I expect so. I'm sure you're a good help.'

'Be careful out and around, won't you?'

'We'll try to be' Ron said with a look down at his dog and he patted in on the head with a fond smile.

As they packed up for the day Jen heard footsteps behind her. She turned to see Ron stood with his dog beside him.

'Done for today, are you?' he enquired.

'I think so,'

Ron stepped around and spoke out 'So some things are lore or legends, yes mysteries which you should not buy into I suggest. But Katherine would get very carried away with her thoughts and eventually it was harming her and us as a family.'

'But you disappeared, and she went looking.'

'No, we moved as a family, back out of town to our old family place further afield. No suspicious mystery. Help her by telling us if you see her. Help yourself by sticking to making these video things, nothing more. That will be enough' he suggested.

'We're onto something good, I think. Something different and fascinating in some ways. Any sighting of Katherine?'

'Not just yet. Do message me if she appears before you, please.'

'Of course, I said we would.'

He seemed to view her with only some slight belief in her words.

Jen with Billy and Cassy made their way along side streets of town along Brinkley Road, down Pepper Street. Did Albert Close next? Where was it? They found themselves stood before Shrovely Road. They all felt confused and displaced. Was the daylight tricking their sense of direction? Was it the noise of nearby traffic or some different bus routes and uber cars going past? Jen was sure that seemed wrong. Billy and Cassy did not mention any difference even if they were thinking it and so they walked on together. They saw roads which led out to the south side of town and where Polbert Road cut across, but Griddle Road was visible which did not feel at all right. This did seem how it should be. Ahead she saw the start of Albert Close and sighed. They walked over toward it but somehow the buildings, the windows and doors did not seem familiar to their eyes. It really must be the light and clouds above them Jen thought.

Jen 'Fuck...my camera, the main vlogging camera...where is it?' she called out.

Jen came alone to walk beside the river at the outskirts of town. The sound of crows and church bells echoed around her as she moved closer. Why did she come? Did it make any sense? Who was the obscure figure among the trees behind the hung dead body of Tilda? The words of the songs alluded to the local river. She was a sucker for a story, digging up hidden or buried truth and she could not help but come to look around. She had not told Billy or Cassy she was coming. It seemed better, safer that way. It felt like her responsibility to look around, not theirs. Her face looked back up from the water below, the reflection changed. She looked uglier, disgusting in the moving ripples of the water. Another woman stared back beside her face.

'Fuck off' Jen said and spat out at it.

The song words were around her, those lyrics of fate, warning, history, or guidance.

'Who, why?' she asked. She heard a brief sudden laugh behind her.

Jen walked over the open grass fields which divided estates and council housing streets and blocks of flats from the more affluent houses which looked down over them. There she saw the shape moved between fences, behind tall trees. The face was lit by the fading daylight and lamplight of evening as it came down around them. The shadows opened and closed to reveal the friend she had thought dead and gone from her life for good. She smiled and stepped over toward her.

'No, keep...back...Jen...' the voice said from the shadows between trees.

'It is you isn't it, it's Katherine?' Jen asked.

The feminine thin figure simply nodded. Jen could easily make out the familiar shape of the face, the mouth, shoulders, the same height, same voice. It sounded worn down, dried up, wounded more than in the past. What she could see of the face looked wounded, bruised, or scared but that could be the evening dark of night around them. They walked along meters apart. No, there were clearly bruises and scars on the neck and cheeks of her returned friend.

'What has happened to you? Do you need our help?' Jen said 'Mae told us she believed she had encountered you. You left quick and she said it almost seemed as if she had dreamed it all. But she was right.'

The cobblestone was precarious, but she was happy to walk with her old friend.

'Why back now then?' she asked.

Katherine moved ahead behind rows of towering, tangled trees and the bright sunlight block her figure.

'Right time, I feel it. I missed you and the others' she quietly answered.

'We thought the worst. I mean, everyone just believed...you'd...anyway, thanks for bringing me out to these streets, this part of town. Somehow, I'd missed it all, overlooked it. Don't think I've even seen most of it before or given it much thought. Here's me calling myself some great new media vlogger and I don't really look properly like I should.'

'You're doing well. I am pleased. You'll do even better.'

'I think I will. No, I know I will. I'll get my team back here. I'm sure they'll be surprised and impressed. Thanks Katherine'

'Welcome'

'Where are you staying now, are you back at your parent's house or do you have your own place?'

'I met Mae. She was going to help me but...no...'

'Oh? We yeah, we thought she was talking about you eventually. It didn't work, she wouldn't let you stay at her place? Could be because of her boyfriend. Look, come to my flat, if you need a place for a while. Sound good?'

'Help me, hide me. I am helping you.'

'Yes, I really grateful'

'I have a problem. I have a job...'

'Oh right, that's good. Doing what?'

'You are looking at the town, the land, history here. This part of further Witherbale was scorched by a fire, it left the strangest markings on the ground, revealed large stones below the town centre market square a long time ago, some say a young woman, possibly a witch, with wings and red eyes was seen around the area for days after with dogs around her. She looked as if she had survived the fire, scarred, burnt but very agitated and aggressive. She disappeared as did local men and families who said they encountered her tried to scare her away. She was never seen in the centuries since. Those men were believed to have been adulterers, abusers, fraudulent men deserving their deaths. The singer knows this. She has the vision, the truth' Katherine told Jen. 'Hide me...'

'You can come closer to me.'

'Your address?'

'My flat down Mosslee road, number nineteen'

'I will be there. Later'

'Okay. Keep safe until then. See you later then.'

Katherine disappeared among the overgrown trees and bushes and the daylight rolled further back away as the bruised evening clouds and grey light came down.

Under two hours later the camera reappeared in the evening. They viewed the footage and found things they had not recorded but it was local, and it was shocking and disturbing. Tilda's voice, her singing could be heard as some large things stalked between trees and brambles. The things were the size of people but resembled something made up of a variety of species. Animals, not bears but not far from it. The focus must be zoomed in as far as it goes, she thought. These things look huge, but they look like...like dogs but moved like people?

'What the fuck are we seeing?' Cassy asked, 'Where was this?'

'I...Billy do you know?' Jen asked.

'No idea. Are they dogs or...is this a prank? Were we pranked? Are you pranking me?' he asked and leaned back in his chair and laughed hard. They looked at him and at each other.

'No prank Billy. Lost the camera, found it later and now we're seeing this. It's fucking weird and scares me' Jen told him.

'Should we really go back? I mean, look at these. Are they animals or...it could be people. Look, are they wearing animal fur or masks? It could be you know, Pagan or some kind of folk stuff they're doing.'

'Well, that's exactly what you want isn't it, Jen?' Billy said with a wide smile on show.

'Jen?' Cassy said.

'It is. He's right' Jen agreed 'We'll keep going around Witherbale,' she replied. Billy nodded knowingly as Cassy simply appeared uneasy.

'What's happening to the original plan for this new project, we're getting distracted, or you are' Billy suggested.

'You can't tell me what we've noticed in that area, near Witherbale outside of the town isn't actually really interesting and worth exploring.'

'No there's maybe things a bit further out, but I also don't want to get shot or piss off any gangs or dealers.'

'They're not everywhere Billy. We've got a decent idea where they hang around and that's the other far side of the town. I don't think they're interested in where we might want to make our weird little films.'

'It's not what we planned to do or where we had in mind.'

'Well sometimes you just must go with feelings, intuition, what feels right. It's what some people aren't wanting to see more of. Look at our likes and views shooting up so fast,'

'And some folks enjoy snuff movies and neo-Nazi crap and we're not making anything like that are we, is that next if people want it?'

'Billy, we'll be okay. Tell Cassy the news when you see her. Beyond Witherbale market and on to the Galey crescent roads and farmlands. Something is worth investigating, my friend mentioned it and we think we go with it.'

'I agree with that...'

'I've a strong feeling in my bones. We're going'

He groaned and let out a sigh 'Right, okay. Again, I'll go along with you. God knows what we'll find for our efforts.'

C**hapter Nineteen**

Early afternoon the next day the three of them drove out to the back of Witherbale. The shops built in the seventies and eighties receded and desolate land followed. Soon after some unusual Highrise flats cropped up and streets of smaller buildings which looked cobbled together from leftover parts of walls and roofs. The sky seemed bruised and poisoned above. They stepped out and viewed the place they intended to find new popular online stories to unveil.

'Where do we start?' Billy asked.

'My friend mentioned a pub and a food hall to check. Some locals who know of changes over the years and young people too.'

'What's the pub called?' Cassy asked.

Jen spun around and pointed with a smile 'Harvester's Pride, right before your eyes. Let us get the first drink of the day.'

They walked in with their bags of filming equipment, Billy preparing it quickly. Inside were only a few older people playing darts, snooker, or dominos quietly. At the bar, a woman laughed manically with the barman on the other side. Jen stepped up to engage her.

'Nice atmosphere here. Good to see people laughing and joking for a change. People can be so down and moody these days' she offered.

The woman named Manda turned to her 'Got to laugh to make it through each shitty day my love. Each god-awful day. That or turn tricks to keep the bills paid. You're not turning tricks, are you?' she asked with a rough cackle.

'No, not personally. We're reporters, documentary filmmakers. We're looking for real views, authentic places, and stories of communities -what they do, what they experience good or bad. No glossy made-up rubbish. Bit of history, reality. Real stuff, with some laughs of course. Got that here?'

'Oh, that and more if you can handle it love,'

'Drinking are the three of you?' the barman asked as he scratched his unkempt beard. Jen, Cassy, and Billy ordered drinks and sat alongside the woman in a corner table by the doors beside the deep left of the main room.

'My name's Manda. My family have been here for hundreds of years and more. Worked in the mills and fields, probably did turn tricks at some point. I went and worked out in the city for a while until I had my daughters twenty years back. My man, he died early, bloody sod...'

'Sorry to hear that' Jen said.

'No, he was a right tosser. Cheating piece of shit after he put the ring on my hand. My daughters kept me going when this town fell to shit again when the work all dried up.'

'Where are your daughters now?'

'One did go to the city to work, does computer stuff or something but one stayed back here. She works here cleaning, busking sometimes. Doing that later today actually. Should go see her. She sings magnificent songs, makes them all us, from stuff about local legends and her dreams and what not. Some parts are about the town-good and bad.

She tries to lift people up but warn them as well, bless her. Locals here love her, goes down a treat.'

'That sounds a good idea. Where will we find her?'

'Across the square, behind the kennels and allotments. Tall and pretty, curly hair with a guitar and flute strapped to her.'

'Great. We'll go, won't we?' Jen said as she looked to her two friends for confirmation. They nodded silently but respectfully as they sipped their beers.

The sound of hurt their ears suddenly. Scrapping, clawing from the other side of the pub.

'Fucking 'ell...' Billy said as they noticed a man kneeling down by the back wall and muttering, head bowed as he scratched and chipped the table before him.

'Oi Wilber, stop that, get up and out now. I've told you plenty!' the barman called over.

'I have to! Leave me be! I have to, you know that!' the old man moaned.

'You'll be alright tonight. Get home, go on' the barman yelled and watched the old man stand and shuffle away outside.

'What's that all about?' Jen asked.

'Just a nutty old bastard. Some men go wrong when they got to that age when they're alone. Mind goes all nutty' Manda explained.

'Was he praying?' Billy asked.

'Maybe. He's just lost it, poor sod. So yes, do go see my daughter Tilda. Hurry or you'll miss her. She does cheer folks up around here. Record her, you really should get her up on that interwebs place.'

'Yes, we will' Jen replied as Billy and Cassy tried hard not to laugh.

'You really must' Manda repeated, hand over hers.

'Okay. Anywhere else worth looking at, people of interest?'

'The church has a special character I'd say' the barman suggested 'It's more of a youth and community club base now. You'll see some characters of note there I almost guarantee.'

'Thank you'

Sat huddled together quietly in the corner of the pub Jen look at Billy and Cassy with an inspired smile.

Jen 'There we go. Manda is a real treasure trove of local lore and wisdom. If only we met more like her'

'She's still kind of guarded and reluctant. I thought she was maybe messing with us, exaggerating some things' Billy suggested.

'Nah, no way, I could see the truth in her face, in her eyes. Okay so same as usual. We go with it so far until we smell any obvious bullshit at which point we move on. But I do feel she's letting us in on some very special things here. And how have we never heard of her daughter and her street songs, sounds just what we're after, sounds really good.'

Jen looked at her 'Billy thinks there were witches in our town, this Witherbale area and put on trial, but some put down curses in retaliation.

'Do we think that's what Tilda and her mother are, witches?' Cassy asked.

'Well, they seem to be good witches if they are. What they call white witches aren't they?' Jen replied.

The sound of flute drifted out clear enough as they wandered along the side streets a short while later. They saw a crowd gathered around, some dancing, some jigging and laughing, some weeping joyfully to the live music. The voice came next-ethereal, captivating, and powerful. Rushing through the people Jen and Billy saw who they assumed was Tilda stood with a guitar around her waist, strumming occasionally flute hung from a rope on her neck and a large warm smile as she sung on, seeing the smiles, and clapping around her. The people around and between them seemed overjoyed, enraptured, and possibly hypnotised by the voice and words she sang. The song ended and she spoke to the crowd.

'Thank you everyone. It is so good to see you here, every day, faithful and brave. Its so good to see you here, everyday faithful and brave. Do not fear the mistakes, the things around us we have let come to harm and threaten us. Our wishes and hearts can keep us warm and safe. Sing with me now' she told them before starting a final song.

The final verse instantly struck all three of them and they listen to the end.

'...hounds around us, town of ours, love will hold us high, all around us, known our land, times our spells denied,

Hidden to save us, chose Witherbale words,

Moonshine and hope will not fail,

Bodies and burning under moonlight the dogs did not fail...'

'...Inside the stone to hide and be,

Turn past and street,

Never be free...'

The flute music ended with ecstatic applause and cheering as she bowed, and people eventually parted, continued with their day, and left the open square area behind the pub and shops. Billy caught it all on camera, Cassy had worked the microphones and boom stick. Tilda saw them as she closed her guitar case and bag at her feet.

'Who would you three be then?' she said with a wry smile.

'Hello Tilda, right?' Jen said 'We're reporters on local cultural interest. Customs, arts, music and more. We take it to the masses via social media so that many more can appreciate the rich and beautiful reality of lives and places not everyone gets to know and see.'

'I see. Did you enjoy me music?'

'We did yes, of course. It has such a special charm' Cassy quicky responded.

'That's all for today. Want more then return same time tomorrow. Goodbye now' Tilda told them as she began to walk away.

'Wait' Jen called 'Can we interview you, just a few minutes. Tell us about your songs and inspiration.'

'My inspiration...' she gave a short laugh 'You heard the words. No, I won't be doing that' Tilda said and walked away.

'Your mother suggested we see you. Told us how special you are to her and the community. She was right.'

'Don't listen to her, someone must sing these songs' Tilda replied over her shoulder as she walked.

'What now?' Cassy asked looking at Jen.

'We return tomorrow. Right now, look around a while longer. Did you get her on the camera Billy?'

'Totally. It looked great I think.'

'Okay, put it away. We'll upload it later.'

Jen led them on around a couple of streets and they found the old church serving as youth centre hub. The doors were open, banged loose in the wind. She stepped up, pushed them inward and looked inside.

'Hello?' she called and the other two followed her in. They walked on down a quiet narrow corridor. It looked as thought it had experienced some partial makeover at some point but had been left unfinished, some walls bare, paint work abandoned, tiles missing. There was some sound eventually, a voice further ahead.

'Could be nothing happening until the evenings, like youth activities or whatever' Billy suggested.

'Yes but...it feels like something was happening...' Jen replied as she moved on.

An argument, shouting could be heard further inside. A male and female voice crying and shouting back and forth.

'Maybe we should go' Cassy said nervously.

'No wait, this is real' Jen responded.

'It's some private discussion' Billy countered. She ignored him and walked on carefully toward the heated argument. Cassy and Billy remained where they stood.

'Oh, shit follow me' Jen called quietly, waving back.

The voices stopped suddenly. She turned as she walked around a corner and saw some large stains over the carpeted floor, deep red brown, black markings. The smell was repulsive and fresh. A shadow behind moved around her. The male voice returned.

'Can I help you?'

The man was tall, built muscular, shaved head with cheap glasses, teeth missing as he put out his cigarette against the wall to her left.

'I am with friends. We're documentary filmmakers' Jen told him.

'Good for you. What you doing here right now?'

'We hoped to interview some people, learn about any local cultural activities taking places-music, art, sport. Anything really. Interesting people and stories'

'I see. You're in a good place for it. We do all of that. And more. Come back later, after six. The teens and young people will be around doing all that later. Better than dealing drugs, right?' he told her with a sneering smile.

'Yes, absolutely. After six. Thank you'

As she walked back down the corridor, he called to her.

'You seen the lady in town singing, have you?' he asked.

'Yes, we really liked her' she said turning to him with a smile. He nodded and walked back into the side room he had come from. When she reached Billy and Cassy she scowled.

'Would you have come to find me if I didn't come back?' she asked.

Billy smiled 'Yes. Eventually. So?'

'A guy in there said youth stuff happens after six.'

'So, are we sticking around until then?' Cassy asked. Jen could see the look of anxiety in her face.

'No, let's get the footage of Tilda and the pub up and see how that is received online. We'll return tomorrow.'

Tilda was returning to her home. She had plans to make a large casserole for them with variety of vegetables, mince, and wine as it was her turn to cook. Behind her down the narrow street she heard some small patter of feet. She turned to saw no one around her. A large feral dog came out from a side opening and shifted back quietly. It seemed hesitant as it moved back while it peered up at her.

'I see you' Tilda said and leaned down to smile at it. She though it looked neglected and hungry perhaps. She took a couple of steps toward it. The bark came but it was like nails down stone. The next bark came, and it sounded like words.

'Kath…Kath…ren' it barked. Tilda stood shocked, amazed.

'Stop, stop' it barked out like angry human expression.

'What?' she asked surprised and a little weary. She could have been sure it she heard it speak the words 'stop it.'

That just could not be possible, no way. The ugly dog shivered and dashed back up a side street. Tilda followed and saw it trot up the narrow street, keen to watch where it went. She seemed to feel she had headed into some area of the town centre she was unfamiliar with. That was highly unlikely she thought, she had been all around every street and every alley since she was a young teenager years ago. She knew every turn, every corner but this place did look new to her. She felt confused, possibly lost even. The dog appeared. It barked again in that strange human sound. Barks like speech.

'Stop telling them. Stop it. Stop helping her' it barked in words.

'No, no. How am I hearing this?' Tilda asked.

She backed away as she watched the dog in the alley.

It shivered and out came Katherine's mother Lily from a side street to stand beside the dog and she lunged at Tilda, covered her mouth.

'Got her' the dog said. It seemed to smile with its canine mouth.

Chapter Twenty-One

The drive to the town centre was pleasant for Cassy and Billy, though Jen sat with her thoughts and questions shifting uncomfortably around in her mind like troubles waters. They uploaded the filmed footage and sat down together to see what they had recorded.

'Looks great, its so strange. I mean, it's a small little town but there are so many people around here watching that Tilda singing and they really do look so happy, kind of like religious people. Like shes a prophet or something. There's something else in their eyes. Do you see it?' Jen asked the other two as Billy loaded and syched up the footage and Cassy fed and balanced the sound and media links.

'You going to get her on a talent show on tv are you?' Billy asked.

'Nah, she's gone viral because of us. Be the next Adele' Cassy laughed.

'She won't need it with us' Jen added.

The words of the songs picked her thoughts, made her think about the town, the history of it. Some words and phrases seemed to call to her, to her own memories. Words of the streets, the families, the births and deaths, legends and folktales or something along those lines. Sacred streets with special characters moving along them many decades or centuries ago. Women of wonder and magic, superstition and hope and wisdom over bad times, warnings of despair and dangers. Was Tilda religious, were the lyrics intended to speak to someone like Jen?

Was there some message for her? They were like stories, cautionary tales Jen thought.

'Hey, stop. Play that part back' she told Billy. He pushed it back on the monitor screen, the songs featured words of the streets around the town, people lost, people drowned, a curse, a woman defiant, drowned...in red waters.

'Fuck, that's actually kind of disturbing' she said.

'Yeah, I hadn't noticed that this afternoon. Neither of you did?'

'Nope. It is weird' Jen commented.

'Same here. It just sounds good, her voice and the flute and guitar. The melody...' Cassy added. The decided to take a break, have a couple of beers each and Jen gave them some notes for the next day before they left to each to their day jobs and flats alone.

A couple of hours later Jen checked the social media account with their video footage of Tilda singing and she was surprised at the amount of likes and views. Hundreds and more each minute.

Billy 'So whos' sending these comments below the clips of town?'

Cassy looked closely at the screen 'Someone calling themselves K-32184. They're saying it's not the real town we're showing. The real town is deeper, lower in the dirt and shame, in the water and blood...'

'Damn weird that is'

Jen 'Horseshit. Someone just messing for attention. They'll always be some sad bedroom troll doing their best to get you angry or depressed. Faceless anonymous sad sack. Ignore. Post the next section Billy.'

He did as she asked once he mixed and synched the sound, back music and edits together with help from Cassy.

'Okay I've switched if off, blocked comments. But some were really interested in her words, the places of town she mentions and the kind of weird old folk stuff. Some talked about the strange shapes behind or around her on the clip. Let's opened it tomorrow and see if they're still interested by then.'

Jen left the door open to her flat for a while as she vaped in the hall. The shadow on the wall outside did seem familiar and she smiled.

'If you're there, come in Katherine. I'll leave some soup on the kitchen counter for you in a while. You've got five minutes' she said and when it passed, she closed the door and went to her room. After sitting watching a news channel for an hour while she looked over a few media and cultural studies textbooks she returned to the kitchen. The soup bowl was empty. Hands gently touched her shoulders. She smiled.

'We've been the to further Witherbale side. That spoken word woman Tilda is interesting. We'll get more footage and speak to others there next. People seem to like what we've posted so far. Thank you' she said aloud. She felt sudden sharp piercing of flesh on her neck, arm, and side. She slept instantly. She woke in the morning in her bed, only her in the flat.

Billy worked his shift at the coffee shop, Cassy walked her dogs for money, and they regrouped with Jen. By two o'clock in the afternoon they check the previous vlog and posted the next one.

'So, we've footage of us talking to the locals at the art and free poetry slam night. All good...now up-us talking to Manda in the pub...looks and sounds okay right?'

'Nice work mate. You'll be snatched up away to edit Bond thirty-six soon. Stay with us 'til then.'

They watched the footage and how he had edited it from location to location, Jen to camera, Jen to Manda.

'We're so good. So, we'll start a real company for proper films and full-length documentaries, won't we?' Cassy asked hopefully. She often did.

Jen heard someone repeat the comment she had seen on the screen.

'Just forget it. We'll keep going' she said.

Cassy and Billy looked at each other and nodded. It was repeated and Jen snapped.

'Shut up. Come on, let's finish up titles and go home.'

'We didn't say anything else' Cassy responded.

'You didn't?'

They shook their heads silently.

'Alright, well anyway let's do this and get done.'

The footage of Tilda was shot well by Billy, Jen and Cassy noticed the pride on his face as he edited and uploaded as they walked into the room with mugs of hot tea.

'The footage is not the best, but I've cleaned it up a bit. No, look there's some weird person moving around behind her' Jen commented and pointed at the footage of Tilda. The shabby thin figure lurched behind and around Tilda on screen through the crowd when she was filmed singing her songs.

'I didn't see that person at the time' she said.

'I was recording, and you were walking around trying to get nearer to her for when she stopped so you could talk to her. I was focused on her really' Billy reasoned 'who do you mean?'

Jen stared hard at but lost sight of the unusual thin and dirty figure she had noticed, gone among the cheering crowd and Tilda.

'Holy fuck' she let out. She checked the people and accounts liking and giving it support but it was vague, many anonymous accounts. It did not mean they were fake necessarily, but it was a lot of interest and so quickly. She messaged Billy. He was just as surprised as her.

'You just never know. But her voice was wonderful' he told her.

'You're more distracted lately. Is it you're friend with the trauma?' Cassy enquired.

'You see yes, my friend experienced some terrible news at her work-place the other day, but we lost a close friend three years ago too,' Jen responded 'Or we thought we did. Our friend had such a deep and vivid imagination, she would tell us about the most amazing and unusual creatures and worlds, the kind no other would even begin to think about. When we had some shitty night, partner, or family troubles she would tell us a story or make some drawing or painting which would take us away somewhere, take our mind away from the difficult real times of every day.'

'So where is this friend?' Billy asked.

'I can't exactly say. She is around and I am grateful for that right now.'

'Tell us one of her stories, please' Cassy suggested.

'Well...one in my mind right now is about a woman who would appear near the river of this town. Some say she came up from the river from many miles away or even from deep down in the sea. Some say she was part fish.'

'Like a mermaid?'

'No, more like an eel or deadly sea creature but she came upon the land as a woman and seek out men who abused or murdered local women. Sadly, it was killed by a group of such hateful men it was believed. But years after some say they did see her in the river or some large fish with a woman's face which pulled people down and away into our local waters...'

'Okay that is freaky.'

'Fucking weird. But cool. She made that up?' Billy asked.

'Maybe she did, maybe...maybe it came to her as a vision from the past.'

'Really?'

Jen simply looked at him with a frank smile and raised eyebrow.

'Okay then…I'm getting some beer. Anyone want some?'

Billy and Cassy begin to feel uncomfortable at how parts seem to be what they are seeing and hearing…

He returned minutes later and viewed the next batched of new footage with them.

'I don't know if I saw some weird woman in the footage but the dog thing…' he said 'it was watching us, it had really strange eyes and face, not like a regular dog, the proportions were sort of…human. You didn't see it?'

Jen looked at him 'No, not properly. A glimpse maybe. I'm too busy doing my thing interviewing and looking for the interesting people and places. Cassy?'

'Well maybe. The dog thing I mean. The scruffy woman, I don't know. Kind of weird, wasn't it? We're losing focus here a bit I think.'

'Yes, you're right. Billy, forget dogs and tramps. Local art and folk-lore are what we want.'

The morning came and with Mae gone from the house Jackson dressed and made his way to the stone. He had received the panicked messages from Peter and Samantha and told them to be there to meet him. They agreed even as they seemed reluctant. They met up at the stone as they always did, a new confusion, anxiety in them.

'What did we see?' Samantha spat at him immediately.

Jackson spoke 'A manifestation, a spirit. It can happen. Continue to pray here. You are safe I promise, it is safe to do so. I need you strong and loyal, He does.'

They knelt but Sally looked up. 'Why did it seem to come out of the stone?'

'It can be a gateway of sorts. I should not tell you too much. We must continue as we have, no questions. Faith must continue, strong like a rod of steel, strong and worthy.'

'A woman, she seemed ill, feral, and angry. Not a spirit, very human, flesh and bone' Pete added.

'Bow your head. End these questions. Touch the stone, heads down, focus' he instructed.

They did, Jackson levitated two feet from the ground, eyes closed.

After they left a local pub for a quick half Jen found her phone was buzzing and answered the call of Mae who sounded anxious.

'Everything okay with you?' Mae asked. Jen could hear the tremor in her voice.

'Mae listen- watch what you're doing, where you go. I've been somewhere today. I'm confused. Think I met an old friend but later think I had been somewhere else entirely. Things are not making total sense to me.'

'Wait, you've seen Katherine?'

'Briefly yes, not properly. Haven't really had a good talk yet with her.'

'Be careful Jen, I just don't think she is how she used to be.'

'You're right about that. And I know her parents are in town looking for her. I've had words with her father Ron.'

'Where is she now?'

'I don't exactly know.'

'Are you helping them look for her?'

'Again, I don't know. Not sure about doing that. She's our friend.'

Jen did not wish to upset Mae in the delicate state she would be in following the deaths of her colleagues but wanted to speak truthfully with her.

'Mae, come talk to us, help us get this thing finished. All three of us need to help each other, she is coming to all of us for some reason. We'll help keep you safe at the same time' Issy said on the phone.

'I hear you. I understand but right now I can't come.'

'Are you alone? You'll not be safe alone in your apartment.'

'I'll be fine. I'll be in touch.'

Mae told her and hung up. She had to prepare for what was to come. How do you defend yourself against an unstable person? Jackson had explained that Katherine may just have been involved in the deaths and even though she was a dear old friend her parents were possibly right in seeking her out to take back to where she could be watched and cared for properly. It did not explain how she had escape or seemed so lucid and helpful. The design work had come together beautifully and perfectly when she had appeared at the studio. It was all very confusing to her. No, none of that made sense she thought as she paced the lounge alone.

They returned to the open overgrown field lands around the outskirts of Witherbale to examine the stones in the ground before they intended to meet Tilda a second time. The sun was too bright, some singing could be heard and after arguing about the relevance of being in Witherbale and Tilda's songs Billy wandered out with Jen as Cassy looked out in another direction when she noticed a dog looking back at her. It seemed to read her face with such haunted, glassy familiar eyes.

'Look, you two go on up that street to the right I'll continue on ahead and message me if you see Tilda or something or someone work recording yeah?' Jen suggested.

She split from them and as Billy and Cassy ventured on off the right path Billy wandered alone absentmindedly soon enough. There was no sign of Tilda or sound of her singing in the main high street corner market area like previous days. Jen wandered out by herself, looked at the low roofs, the combination of very old architecture on the high street. There were parts which were fixed up but genuinely Victorian or older originally the oak and iron and metal structures, stone masonry stacked between up and above was a real pride of the town.

Jackson walked out along the riverside where he came to stand alongside Ron who stood and looked down into the river, his large scruffy dog at his side.

'Good day to you. Helps the mind doesn't it, walking the dog?' Jackson said.

'Or is the dog walking me? Yes, it does. Much to think about. See yourself in the waters?'

'A version of myself, as do you'

'Yes, of course. Maybe the version I might prefer to be. You need to clear your mind, get your thoughts in order?'

Jackson looked up and around them.

'My girlfriend, she is acting difficult. I try to reassure her, get her thoughts on other things but she can't focus. I don't have time for it, I'm a busy man. I can only do so much. I promise I will help but she panics and goes to her friends and is not telling me everything now.'

'I see' Ron replied and stroked his dog by his side 'Give it time. It may not be much to worry about. There is a bigger picture. I see you around young man' he said and walked his ugly scraggy dog away in the opposite direction along the riverbank. Jackson walked out and up by the Briggar stone form by the river edge out by the turn where the river stretched and crossed to the next town and out eventually to the sea. He knew the stone well, like many curious teens would come by and inspect or try to climb it. They never hung around long as either of the strange dogs came to watch or a peculiar sense of foreboding energy increased around it in the most unexplainable ways. This always pleased Jackson, it never made him fearful but that was never something he could ever talk about to others.

Being outside for a long while now he was beginning to become wounded to uncomfortable sensations of which he was ashamed, and it made him remember that he had to return within soon.

Chapter Twenty

The quite narrow back town street of Witherbale connected with the wider open route to the overgrown fields and forest off the to the left and as she looked out Cassy noticed an attractive slim lady with a dog at her side. The woman looked right at her with a pleased smile. Lily came to greet Cassy on the far town narrow trail, hand extended to her.

'Hello. I think you're with Jen, aren't you? She knows my daughter. I'm Lily. This is my dog, foolish old thing, just ignore it, harmless always need instructions anyway. Sleeps most of the time' she looked down to it with a tut and eyeroll before she smiled back at Cassy.

'Oh hello. Yes, we're making YouTube videos, vlogs about local history and also the new modern art and things and the connects between them, urban things going on. We're looking for things most reporters ignore or don't give enough attention to.'

'You're in luck, I know a fair bit about the land and places here. I've seen a lot, myself, and this dog here, some might say too much. Ask me anything, go on.'

'Okay...this whole area on the left, was it used for feudal things like slavery or things people try to forget and did any of that affect the community, the culture, like art, poems and that kind of thing?'

'Well, that's some deep and specific thoughtful questions. I could see you on television or these internet things discussing such things. You seem to have the mind, the taste for it, you do. Let's walk over the way, shall we?'

'I can't be long but that's great' Cassy agreed, and they walked together a while, the shabby dog snorted and huffed out alongside them as they walked.

Lily continued to offer what she knew, 'There are some folks in this further out part of town who have families affected by terrible events from such a very long time ago, generations ago but it did change the nature of the families and their fate distinctly. Wicked sorrows, tragedies befallen them which often seemed accidental but more often were due to arrogance or prying into things no other people dared. There may be forces on this world we should respect and avoid, other worldly forces we cannot easily comprehend. We are these days a largely godless secular land but even so it would not hurt to be wary of mysteries or the most unusual encounters or sightings. There are wonders unexplainable all over the world and even around us here.'

'You mean things like ghosts or supernatural or alien things?'

'Along those lines yes. Do you keep an open mind for the likes of those things?'

'I mean, I 've not decided if I'm a total disbeliever in anything strange. I do wonder about a lot of these things like Stonehenge, crop circles, witchcraft. But then some fake and are revealed later on after people have been duped. But then plenty still seem really mysterious and fascinating'

'Makes for good video reporting wouldn't they, some very unusual local mysteries, some hardly even known or discovered. I know of some. What do you think about that?'

'You know local mysteries people don't know about?'

'Let's keep walking. I may surprise you. I must say, I'm not simply taken in easily either but there are some things I think I can trust to tell someone as inquisitive as yourself. Let's take a look...'

They came to a wildly overgrown patch of land with two old, ruined structures behind.

'Old farm stables those. Before that...they used to find witches in out town or so they thought. Inside these the council people would torture and do depraved things to those suspected. Not all or many were actual witches. Many women and a few men died inside without trial of any kind in there. Also, some returned angry and violent.'

'Returned? As witches or ghosts?'

'Hard to say now. There are some local folk songs and poems which can be interpreted that way if broken down carefully.'

'A woman and a man, possibly brother and sister or crazed lovers, possibly both witch or something else escaped half dead and ran to the river. They took with them some locals drowned them and climbed into the Briggar's stone on the riverbank. They returned and caused chaos at times for more than three hundred years at least. They ruined some families, businesses but helped others, it depends on where the family lines rested, their deeds and business and links to witch trials. Believe that?'

'What is here to prove it or suggest any of their presence?'

Lily took her to the overgrown bushes, pushed them to one side and they looked through.

'Look down there. See the prints on the old stone path there?'

'Yes...but could be from anything at anytime. I do want to believe but I also want our viewers to believe you know.'

'Alright, I understand. Now turn but look over the path between the two old stables. Right ahead. What do you see?'

'The riverside. The broken stone path...it goes there so do the foo tprints...wait, hoof prints?'

They walked on with the scruffy dog at their side as it barked every few yards until they reached the riverside.

'Now look to the old Briggar's stone there. From here, look down where we stand and back up to it' Lily instructed.

The daylight came and hurt her eyes but split down over the stone toward them and back to the old farm stables.

'Look now in the river.'

The river ran red.

'Oh my god'

'The light does that, but it tells of the past events. The two wicked fallen ones and their killings. Now, would you dare return this spot at midnight to see much more?'

'Really? Such as what?'

'Can I ask-would you tell Jennifer about this? Who deserves it more? She always seemed a tad overbearing to me. My daughter would have really liked you I think if she had known you. So later tonight then, yes?'

'Alright, yes deal'

The scruffy dog barked and snuffled around near Lily as it peered up to observe Cassy.

Jen stumbled on as she studied the old stonework of the buildings around and along the narrow Witherbale streets. There were curious patterns, shapes etched in which looked almost like messages or an-cient hieroglyphics. What stories were there waiting to be interpreted?

The shadow came down around her, the breath over her neck and cheek and she turned, saw Katherine who still appeared drawn and ill as she stepped across the street where it cut into the road ahead and she stood half behind the wall there, one eye fixed on Jen, one crusted and rotten hand grasped the wall, the withered fingers tapped like scuttling insects.

'I see you, Katherine. I don't know why or how. I'm not the first, am I? Where have you been?' Jen asked with amazed nervousness. 'We've come to Witherbale, I listened to you. We've seen a young woman named Tilda, she sings folksongs about old local history, some of it sounds very real, some of it fantasy, some nasty, strange but kind of familiar...do you know her?'

She stepped forward, slowly not wishing to scare her friend away. There was some unusual colour to her pale face, bruises possibly or just the afternoon haze of dying daylight fading and shadows of early evening changing and playing with light.

'Won't you talk with me? You came back for a reason, right?'

She stepped forward, reached out to touch her arm. There was some spark or sentation like intense heat or fire on the skin contact. Katherine looked dazed and anxious as she looked back.

'Hide me...I returned but...hide me until...' she urged.

Jen nodded. 'I know Ron and Lily are out looking for you. I don't think they understand you. There is more it isn't there? Why did they take you away?'

Katherine stood and looked away through the trees and shadows around them.

'We did wonder, we never wanted to believe you had really left us, permanently. You just went after them didn't you.'

'My parents...' Katherine uttered 'Hide me.'

Jen took her by the arm gently 'Come stay at my place, I told you. Stay there for a while if you want that. That sounds okay doesn't it.'

Katherine gave a slow but grateful nod and a quite 'yes' before she disappeared away. Jen walked quick to the turn of the street and the road, but she was gone.

The moon was risen higher than it had been for many nights, clear and pearl pale white above the town. Ron took a quiet walk out behind the streets which he and Lily had led Jen and her vlog crew toward. He remembered the moonlight illuminating so many atrocious and depraved sights so long ago. He remembered Jackson being closely involved with the witch trials, the torching of innocent local subversive women who simply dared to speak their thoughts or be in the wrong place when there was a desire to witness such extended torture and slow churned death and pain which had seemed to satisfy and entertain so many. There he saw it- the giant wild lean bitch dog upon its hind legs and it danced where it stood as if crazed or trained to do so. This was no exploited, abused canine, there was a wicked joy in the fevered face of it as it danced over and across the bloody trail which led right the way from Briggars stone on the far riverside now in toward the town. This trail had not been there earlier, but he knew this evening he would observe things not viewed for the longest time. Now Katherine was out in town. There were games to play, there were old love to reimagined and respected as only he and Lily would dream of doing and knowing how.

Jackson placed his hand on the forehead of Ron, and it caused a shudder. It was a familiar and unwanted encounter. Ron knew what came next.

'I'm a myth, I'm a legend on two legs I will scar the minds and haunt the souls like you did, I won't hide or deny it. Respect what we can be, dead or alive or any other way' Ron called to Lily as she pulled up the body into the trees beside the river under the moonlight.

'They'll take tomorrow and forever more' Ron chuckled as he rushed toward town, his huge bastard bear beast man form creature, not seen for many decades.

Jackson walked out to look upon them with quiet judgement.

'There you are. You sound unhappy with your lot, confused. You must be tired with keeping track of our Katherine am I right?' he asked with a sly smile.

Ron turned to look at him, blood around his mouth, dog teeth showing, fur down his neck, over his hands.

'And have you been doing what's best for us all, you and your important town living?' Ron snarled.

He stepped right up to Jackson and sneered at him.

'So where is she?' Jackson asked.

'She's between her friends somewhere, keeps moving around' Lily said behind Ron as she twitched and crept low halfway toward transforming back to human form from dog. She cocked her hind leg, pissed against a tree without shame.

'Bad dog of mine' Jackson said. Ron fell to his knees. His head slumped, flesh began to melt, drip and flow like lava. His body began to take another form, less human, less canine, some patchwork of mammal species. The shoulders grew larger, hunched up and his torso extended, legs stuck out and jerked as pieces of skin and muscle fell to the grass with blood, bile, and sinew. The stench of shit, blood and semen drifted thick in the air around them.

'Well, hello again. Been a long time, hasn't it?' Jackson said with a smile as he viewed the silent large risen beast Ron had become. It appeared to be some mix of lion and goat though it did still hold his facial features and hands. Through large enough to do his serious harm it did not dare attack. It hung its head in shame, looked at him but turned away, swung into the trees down as it went. Jackson noticed the other dog with the face Lily across from him had it had been watching.

'Feel like a change yet?' he asked. She turned and rushed after the Ron beast deep away among the tall trees and brambles. Minutes later Lily watched Ron return to meet her in amongst the trees the light of day lit up his sour expression as he held back his thoughts.

'That Tilda, she knows of Briggar, really does know' she said with the hope he would do what mattered to their life in Briggar.

Ron nodded sagely 'Yes, it's her Pagan heritage. It is time for her.'

The sharp winds whipped his face when Jackson stepped up beside the crooked ancient local stone relic, the monolithic slab on the riverside. Once he had checked no others where around to see, he touched the reverse side which faced the river waters which flowed below. He noticed her face reflected up to him and with a scowl, looked away to the stone as it opened inward for him, and he stepped into a place no local alive knew existed. It closed to the outside world as he stepped into the hall chamber within, the high building ceiling far above hm as he approached the staircase and ascended, the chill around him familiar. He cursed as he marched up the steps to the main room. Under the flawed yet masterly carved walls stood the imitation Victorian era dining table with dresser cabinets to the left and lounge recliner positioned on the right. Tanks with thick liquid contained numerous unclear aquatic twisting and writhing forms as he walked past. Howls and groans rose up from below the rooms from the lower chambers. He tutted at the familiar sounds.

'Anyone here, hello?' he called out as he stepped around. He noticed a pile of plates and bones pushed down at the end of the long table and he frowned with plain dissatisfaction.

'Not again. This will not do. I will not take blame again. I will not cover up for your failures, damn you' he called, fist clenched and raised. He walked out to the far left to looked to a doorway into a room there. He pushed the door open and stepped in. He crossed the room and stepped to the window to look out and over the town. He saw cars in the distance which moved along the roads, people walking across the long path stretched beside the river around the side of town. There was a stench in the room, in the entire building he noticed, some new fetid aroma. The wall before him cracked silently, split just enough to let in some daylight down by his legs.

'See what happens, you know this, you've been warned' he spoke while still alone 'He'll not be pleased with this. You damn fools' he said and walked back out to the main wide room. As he touched the handle on the door by the upper right his smart phone buzzed in his pocket, and he clutched at it. A message from Mae. She was asking if he could pick her up from the studio in a short while. He messaged back and made his way back down the stairs and out across the grass to where his car was parked.

A short while Lily returned to the Briggar stone and found Jackson stood near it.

'Why do I see you here?' Jackson asked Lily as she stood with her scruffy dog some yards behind her watching them.

'We...the fresh air is good to remember, to see the horizon and the town from by the river. You know that. Shouldn't stay cooped up inside all the time.'

He gave her a dismissive look 'I am returning, you know that. I am doing good things there in town, you couldn't understand. Neither of you, even if you wanted to.'

'We could, we do try.'

'Take him back, he looks tired. You both do' he suggested. He turned and walked back to his parked car as Lily entered Briggar quietly and the dog followed her inside with a glance back to Jackson. It gave a vicious bark.

'Come now, we should cook our meal, keep our strength up' she called, and it rushed inside the stone which closed up silently behind them.

C hapter Twenty-One

They returned the following day to Witherbale centre, quite streets just as grey and the small, neglected council houses just as broken and ruined as the day before. Manda was not there yet in the pub, no crowd of locals, only a couple of people moving along silently. The bar staff were different. They each necked a quick beer for courage or celebration and walked out to the view the spectacle of Tilda once more. Down through the same streets and out to the small centre area they did not find her or a crowd waiting where she said she would be at that time.

'Where is she, we need her' Jen moaned as she looked about them. Billy also appeared disappointed. Cassy simply yawned and checked her sound equipment.

'Let's walk around for a while, maybe we'll find her in some other place, or we can find some other interesting stuff' Cassy suggested.

'The streets are quieter than yesterday' Jen stated.

They walked around for almost an hour but did not come across anyone of any use to help them.

'What do you we now?' Billy asked.

'Wait for the youth club stuff in a while.'

'That's still a couple of hours away.'

'We have a couple more beers, play cards or whatever.'

'I think we should look. There'll be more to see' Billy suggested in agreement.

As they came around a corner and approached the pub Manda stalked up to them, eyes blazing.

'Where is my daughter?' she yelled.

'We've been looking for her. Is she not around town today?' Jen asked.

'Every day she sings her songs in town. Every day, come rain or sunshine. They want to hear her; they need to hear her. So where is she today?'

'We don't know. We're as puzzled as you. We've been looking around for a while but not found her.'

'We'll all look around together. Look with me, together with me' Manda told them. Billy and Cassy glanced at each other but nodded in agreement. Until the youth centre was due to open, they walked around the quiet town for the few hours with Manda and checked all of the places where Tilda could usually be found. Manda seemed to appear disturbed, anxious, and increasingly desperate as they looked in doorways, pubs, markets, shops and through the cluttered small park and green land area near the condemned old mills and factories.

'This is no good. It won't make a difference. No good at all for this town' Manda muttered repeatedly as if she more concerned for the community than her own daughter.

'I'm sure they'll get by for a day without her songs, as lovely as they are' Jen assured her as they walked together.

'We've run out of time. The youth centre opens soon' Billy quietly remined her. Cassy shrugged with a nod.

'We'll have to go Manda. Call the police in a few hours, they don't usually do anything until a day has passed if someone is missing. I'll call you if we see her' Jen told her.

'Come back and help won't you. You can put it out on your social media film things, for help, can't you?' Manda pleaded.

'Right, yes, we'll do that. Bye Manda and thank you' Jen said as they walked away from her. Her eyes were wide with unblinking fear.

'There is some weird angle with her relationship to her daughter right, not just me thinking it is it?' Billy said a couple of streets away.

'Oh, there are some fucked issues there, totally. Not sure I want to know everything about it. Do you?' Cassy responded cringing.

'Look, Tilda will turn up. Come on, she's like in her thirties. Probably banged someone last night and stayed there or totally stoned like the hippy musician she is. So anyway...'

Samantha had joined Jackson at the stone to pray even though she continued to ask difficult questions and he wished she would remain as loyal and silent as Peter. Her head bowed low he looked up and gave a hand signal. The door inside the stone opened inward in silence, Ron stepped out, only half transformed into his canine self. He rushed out at Samantha, bit into her neck, clutched at her, snarled as he pulled her back into the stone, clawed hand over her whimpering mouth, blood down her neck. Behind him Lily watched from inside, waited and looked at Jackson out on the grass beside the river.

'Fill yourselves, continue the search' he commanded. The door in the stone closed and they were gone from sight as he walked back to his car.

A call came in from Issy as Jen walked with Cassy and Billy up a narrow street. She stopped and spoke to Issy who wanted to check in with her.

'I'm doing okay. I'm out filming with the guys, doing my vlogs. We've found some different place out on the other side of town. Hey footage from yesterday, some very weird spooky shit I'm telling you. Maybe anyway. The first part was that strange form behind me when I was interviewing locals but then Billy found the next part. There was a huge thing, a beast, a goddamn thing, big like some zoo animal but something else, something more dangerous. It had real eyes, human eyes but a body like some animal thing. It... he spoke, he said something about the stone, the Briggar's stone, a sacrifice for a curse...' Jen explained.

'Okay, I saw the video footage' Issy began 'Honestly, Jen- is it deep-fake or a trick? It's good, it's very convincing. You make new local myth or legend, use actors, hype it up, it goes viral, fame beckons even if it is found to be fake. Win either way.'

'That would have been great a fucking year ago. It's real Issy, I don't know what it is. I fucking wish I hadn't seen it almost. No idea how or what it is. It...he spoke, it's something real and it's said her name, it's said Katherine.'

'So, it really isn't some CG fakery?'

'No, and if it was, I'd tell you anyway.'

'Has she...has she been close with you? I mean spoken about things like she used to in college yet?'

'Not yet, not the same way. She's back but stays back, keeps a distance.'

'The animal man thing, what does he want with her?'

'No idea. He just spoke her name. Nothing more. You saw it. Mentioned Briggar's stone, her name and vanished. Don't exactly know where it was. It was on Billy's camera footage, but he says he didn't record it personally.'

She looked up and saw billy and Cassy gone from view.

'I'll call you back or message later. If you see Katherine, take her in, look after her.'

She entered a pub to her right which looked about to collapse and smelled of rotten things and bad cider. As they barman was eyeing them with suspicion she stepped up and spoke to him.

'Afternoon, have you seen my friends? Tall ginger young guy and dark-haired shorter woman. We're making a documentary here' she asked.

Blank glances as he chewed on something like gum or some hunk of fatty meat between his lips.

'You didn't listen to Tilda's songs' he stated.

'We did, we heard the songs, they were lovely. So?'

'Don't think I've seen your friends. Check the streets around here, don't waste time though.'

She ran out to the street, and they were gone from view. She cursed and looked left and right before she took out her phone and began to message them.

Three streets away Billy walked alone and continued, taking footage of scenes and the streets ahead with his small handheld digital camera. Half a dozen small children ran out from the opening on his left, waved effigies of stick women, pig faced men of clay and dirt.

'Hey, wait' he said but they rush around and past him too quickly.

'Wash them, in the river, heal them in there' they cried as they ran. He stumbled around and tried to follow them up the next narrow alley up on his right as they ran fast. He heard their small footsteps clatter away. When he turned and rushed up, they were gone. He looked around him and stood bemused.

Out on a different street Cassy stumbled on confused about her direction. The sounds she was hearing, voices, noises were too strange and curious to ignore. She followed their direction.

'There sounds should be heard...' she said as she came through rows of bushes to find a quiet wide grass area strewn with old fly-tipped furniture and junk.

'Where are the noises?' The sound of flowing, running waters came though louder, in their earphones over the recording equipment.

'The river. Okay' Cassy said.

Jackson stepped up on to narrow path between the old farm barn ruined structures foundations, he heard some muffled sounds. The sounds of bound and fearful people, he knew it. It used to be like fuel to him, a drug-like narcotic rush every time he took them in, pulled them down, judged them, offered them up inside or at the entrance to Briggar. He could do it this time. They were just ahead, through the bushes and behind the crumbled old barn ruins. There was blood down beside his shoes, stained the old stones and trampled grass.

'This is 1836 if I remember correctly' he said quietly.

'That is the intention. We're just playing, testing the land and the times, the locals. Entertaining ourselves sometimes. No problem there is there?' Ron said.

Jackson walked further in. He examined the torture devices, the well-used and familiar but reliable and sadistic instruments collected in a pile around the corner inside the barn structure and placed one of the larger ancient stone slabs. He picked one up, a long metal device which resembled shears or sharp tongs with extra-long jagged teeth and hand grips. He felt Ron watching with eager enthusiasm and curiosity.

'These are the ones, yes, I remember after so long. You've been testing for witches, have you?' Jackson asked without looking back at him.

'We have yet to really get into' Ron admitted.

'Found any?'

'Who knows. The good part is the testing, and the ritual am I right? The pleading and the screams, honest human emotion' Ron replied and let out a delighted low laughter. Jackson remembered he had Mae back at his apartment and work in the morning, a meeting or consultation of some nature. Human responsibilities. He placed the instrument back with the rest as the muffled moans and desperate sounds were rising only a few feet away from him. He caught sight of a pair of eyes which looked at him with genuine wide panic. He stepped away back out to the main wide path which pointed to town.

'Keep things tidy, not too much mess Ron. I know you get excited and careless' he commented.

'I'm getting better with that. That's what the practice is for as well. See you soon enough' Ron replied with a smiled as he looked down at the laid-out selection of instruments to use.

Along the riverbank under the moonlight Katherine floated with focus along inches above the grass below her as she carried ropes and barbed sharp utensils. Her eyelids only half open but some conscious anguish troubled her slight perception of her deeds as she reached the old barn structures. Lily set out the torture and death for Cassy by the barns and riverbank path. Ron walked on in the evening and met with Jackson.

'See anything familiar out here, take a close look' Ron said with a proud expression and stride across the overgrown grass. Jackson came out, reluctant to leave his journey at first.

'I haven't time Ron, I've work to prepare, a meal with my woman later' he told him.

'Come look, just a short while, we need your thoughts on the layout, the ways it should be. You remember this one?'

Jackson walked out with him, along the narrow path, through the field all the way to the barn ruins, the river beyond. Visible as ever behind that was Briggar stone.

'I know this location. There are markings through the field...a trail of blood spots...there...hair wrapped, tied to the nails, the posts...I know the one. Set up like back then, is it?' Jackson asked.

Ron gave a nod 'I believe it is. Lily has been taking the lead with this one. She was very keen to do so, has one or two young women involved.'

'Helping it or part of it?'

'She is undecided so far. Go on, Jackson do you hear?'

They stood a moment as the muffled cries and moaning was audible behind the ruined barn walls and below and through.

'Ron, I should not. Have your way. Don't let it distract from the priority of Katherine.'

Ron held up his hands 'Listen and remember.'

They did and he could easily see the fire light up in the eyes of Jackson as he swung his hands with discomfort. He walked on and around, through and in where he saw the bound and captive Cassy and another, tied and bleeding in the lower corner behind the barn wall structure. The smell of their blood and look of anxious fear in their faces woke his appetite. He looked back at Ron who smiled at him.

'Please, do take part. You know your own games.'

Jackson knelt down to look into the eyes of Cassy, and she moaned from behind the gag in her mouth.

His eyes flashed opulent shining white, and his face became translucent as he reached out a hand to touch her quivering face. He pulled it back quickly and moved back, aware of himself.

Ron scraped his own hands down the walls beside him as he spat, groaned, and looked back to Lily who moved out in the field in dog form.

'No I...I must go' Jackson told him 'Find Katherine after this. Hear me?'

Jackson walked away from the scene as Ron hunched low in dog form and rushed through the trees into the town streets.

Cassy came back to where Lily had taken her, the calm spot beside the old barn ruins on the riverside.

'Lily? Hello? I want to interview you' she called. She moved back in and around the broken-down walls and looked at the narrow path which cut through the grass direct to the river. That superstitious nonsense and interesting but just a made-up tale she thought. But she had always liked fairy tales when she was young. Always wanted some fairy godmother to grant her a wish to be as beautiful as the popular girls. That never happened in real life but Lily was so unusual and always seemed like a person who could do that kind of thing if anyone ever could. She was full of mystery and wise advice. Cassy walked up on the narrow path to the river edge. She looked into the water, saw the moon reflected. She looked up to the sky and saw no moon above her, only blue sky, and gentle clouds. The river water changed movement, began to church in such a strange way, swirled and churned in a manner which made no sense. She took out her vlog camera phone and began to record. She knelt and peered in close. After a moment of recording, she turned and walked back toward the ruined barn walls. As she moved in, she heard a gush of water. She spun around and gasped. From out of the river the most enormous writhing eel snapped and twisted up into the air. It was erect and the bulbous crazed eye on one side of its head stared straight at her. A tongue snapped and licked out from its amphibious mouth. Cassy fell to the ground in fear, her breath erratic and she pulled herself back toward the walls behind her.

'Wrong song, witch song is right...' a female voice said. Cassy had the camera in her hand still and pointed it in the direction of the voice to find Lily stood dressed in some long plain robe, garland of flowers and branches around her shoulders and neck.

Cassy dropped the vlog camera as hands clutched her and pulled her inside the barn ruins and up onto long wooden posts. Straps came over her arms and legs before the she felt the brutal smack which brought a deep darkness to her senses.

The wind seemed to scratch cold and harsh against her face as Cassy stood beside Lily and they came to stop a few yards from the winding river and the ancient stone which seemed to defy gravity and physics as it stood tall and half of it leaned over the water casting that long powerful shadow across the other side.

'There it is, Briggar's House' Lily said.

'Briggar's Stone. Why do you call it house?' Cassy asked.

'They lived inside and had done for the longest time. The Briggar clan. Brennar, Brinniar, Beniar, Benniah...language evolves over time. We can't see it now, but centuries ago there was an entire tall house here which cross the river, a small castle really. It was destroyed not long after the witch hunting and trials ended. It was stated as an accident, weather, storms, and wind but really it was knocked to pieces. They, the ones who resided inside are out, pissing about. Want to play with the mortals at human life and all the mundane daily trappings, the hopes, dreams, illnesses, deals and tricks, love, sex and living. Bastards'

'What are we here to see now, at this time in the dark?' Cassy asked as they stood with torches in the dark on the grass near the river as it rippled before them.

'Exactly that' Lily replied with a hidden smile.

The scruffy giant dog beast rushed out onto Cassy, knocked her to her knees. It had the face of Ron, his tongue wagging and gnashing, the back legs of a wild canine animal kicked and scraped the ground as his front arms pushed her down. Lily moved closer, unafraid and with a sickly delighted grin.

Lily stood silent behind the tall trees and watched Katherine arrive as she caught Cassy, tied her up and pulled her over to the old barn ruins beside the river. She watched while she transformed into her dog creature form and once satisfied rushed through the trees to distract Ron as he was approached from the opposite side of the old, ruined barn structures. They let Katherine do the work they knew she had been instructed to carry out by Jackson once the spell had been cast years before.

As Katherine tied and tortured Cassy up on the side of the barn ruins, moonlight overhead she came aware of the terrified face which looked at her. She looked at the face of Cassy, around at the ruins of the old barn. She let go, stepped away and moved away, outside and through the trees, a feeling of shame or guilt and a need to find Jen, Issy or Mae, to get to them, use them get to Briggar.

Chapter Twenty-Two

Jen saw Katherine return from somewhere, noticed the tired exhaustion in her features halfway across the road on the lower side near the woods.

'Hey Katherine, you're back. They want to see you, your parents, Ron, and Lily' she told her as she moved to her. Katherine stepped back returned to safety of the shadows of the over arched roof of the carpark beside them.

'Where did they go?' Jen asked, 'My friends have gone somewhere; I can't reach them on their phones, and we're supposed to do this presentation at the community centre.'

'Witherbale...had witches' Katherine murmured.

'I know, we've been told by this Tilda woman, she does songs and poetry about it. You know any more?'

'Hold me' Katherine said. Jen could not ignore the fatigued and dishevelled state of her old friend.

'Katherine, do you really feel alright?'

Katherine stretched out her arms from the shadows. Jen stood and looked at her old friend, what she could see. There was damage there she knew it. She did think Katherine might be a violent person, unpredictable. There was some fermenting anger there, quiet but it was there, it was going to burst out she could see it.

She moved in, gave the hug. The pain came in quick to her neck, a jolt, her ribs and back. She thought it was because Katherine was crying, her chest and torso must have been racked with pain and fear, all kinds of unexpressed emotions rattling through her, in need of release. She let it rattle over into her. She shifted, could not step away and so let it continue. Katherine held her tight as the opened wide wings stretched around them, held them together until it was enough. They shuddered, shared a thought or memory, a vision of some event which was horrible but so real. Jen pulled back, looked to see a street, a way familiar from a long time ago.

'Your home. We should go there?' she asked quietly.

Jen was exhausted, drained. She slept instantly. Hours later her eyes opened, and Katherine was gone. She took up her phone and messaged Issy. A positive message came back, and Jen replied to not tell Mae just yet. Katherine knew the Witherbale 1836 lore, it was filtering back into her conscious memory over the next day since she had observed Ron and Lily stalk out along the riverside. She had moved out there with quiet care, to the old farm barns, curious to remember the place and events. She moved around in the night alone, spectral, floated through the hall and returned to observe Jen while she slept. She contemplated when to feed. She did not wish to harm her old friends, but she did need to open and unfold parts of the town while Ron and Lily were out and playing their games in the hope that it would unlock or release more memories. She could see the Briggar stone from the window of Jen's flat which should have been impossible, but she understood it was the effect of what they were doing. It seemed to move and watch over them. Eventually she took hold of Jen and wrapped her unfolded wings, whings made of cosmic energy membranes which came together around both. The teeth of the wings pierced into Jen while she slept, into her ribs, neck, arms, sucked energy, and blood out and into Katherine. In the morning Jen woke, felt weak, dazed, and found Katherine gone from the flat. She showered and noticed the numerous small marks over her body.

Jen arrived at the lower side Witherbale community arts centre. It would take some serious coordination, but they had managed to come to an agreement with the manager Gareth Shawleigh to hold a short art event to highlights a variety of local talents, all connected through clips of their vlog diaries on a backdrop display. They had sent up social media posts all afternoon and spoken to a few dozen people out on the streets around in the last few hours. It seemed like it would be a great evening, all until the team split apart. She walked out before the main entrance doors to address the gathering crowd of interested local towns people.

'Hello everyone, my name is Jen. I'm a vlogger and reporter and we'll be celebrating local talents in art, poetry and more here tonight. Come inside please and have some refreshments until the entertainments begin' she told the gathered crowd and onlookers outside the community centre.

They made their way inside while she walked into another room with Gareth the caretaker and community arts coordinator.

'Wasn't it more than just you doing your thing?' he said.

'Yes, it is. They're around, the others. I mean, have you seen Billy and Cassy recently?'

She asked.

'Earlier on, a while ago. With the other one, what's her name, she looked a bit of a state' he commented.

'Oh that...that's Katherine, my friend. Where did she go?'

'No idea. Went off with them, probably getting all this stuff ready. How organised is all this?'

'It's all in place, don't sweat it.

'Go check with the performance artist or Tilda, out around the carpark at the side, they were there with props and equipment weren't they earlier?'

'Yes, that's right. I'll go have a look. You keep the locals here in good spirits,'

As she stood and tapped messages on her phone Billy came up beside her casually.

'People are coming around aren't they, showing some interest in our arts event. Good idea'

'Where've you been?'

'I went looking around other streets. Saw some weird little kids with hand-man things, effigies, or something, think they knew the poems of Tilda, so I tried to follow them. They disappeared'

'Where the hell is Cassy? This is humiliating, this whole thing is falling to pieces.'

Billy 'I'll go look around for her nearby, you keep this event happening, you can do it.'

Billy walked out down the street near the community centre. Ron came out before him at the end where the road split.

'Oh, hey mate, have you seen my friend Cassy, she's missing.'

'Is she? No, I don't believe I have. You and your friends been looking for my daughter still?'

'Yes, well we were and we're doing this community thing tonight. We haven't found her around anywhere near sorry.'

'Right. Billy my friend come out for a short walk. I know the town so well, have watched it for what feels like centuries you know. I've seen shadows move, things out by the river you should witness.'

'Well does that have anything to do with Cassy?'

'You are interested in truth and hidden histories, yes?'

'You know I am. I need that stuff.'

'Cassy was down by the river; I believe my wife saw her a short while ago. Follow me now, let us not waste a moment.'

With that Ron led him away along narrow alleys and quiet streets out to the open fields which led to the riverside. A pallid grey sky hung over them. Billy heard some low drawn sounds, a slow moan from something not too far away. Was it a person or animal? Hard to decided.

'Ron, listen. My friend Jen had this bad news, and I don't exactly want to screw her over...'

'It's about getting what you should rightfully have in life. You're good at this vlogging reporting thing, you'll get what you deserve.'

'If you think so.'

'I do, I told you that much. So, it's up around this side area and right toward the river my wife Lily saw Cassy, I think. I think she'll have been investigating the old barns. If she's lucky she might even glimpse a witch or something else'

Billy stepped out ahead of Ron to the edge of the riverside and turned around. He saw the tall but crumbled ancient barn structures.

'You'd think they would have been knocked down long ago' he said as he walked over in and looked in alone. 'Hey Cassy? You in here?'

There was some faint sound, a quiet murmur he heard. Was it behind the wall, in the next section of the ruin? He stepped in around the broken stone wall, vlog camera switched on and in his right hand, held up with the slightest shake of nerves.

He turned and saw Ron was not behind him.

'Ron? You with me?' he called. He shook his head and stepped forward into the next section. Where he found tall wooden posts which had been erected in some specific manner. These posts looked new, the wood not yet aged, some strong nails held them together, bright and glinting under the brief glare of late daylight.

'She sings the wrong song...' a female voice whispered. He spun and caught half of Lily hidden in shadow stood on the other side of the barn walls. She watched him as hands clutched him, tugged him down and a violent knock sent him unconscious.

Jen passed on through the bustling crowd of people near the refreshment's tables, down the side corridor to the back of the building alone. She did not think Katherine would go and meet Billy or Cassy. It had seemed like she wanted to be hidden but she must have changed her mind. She reached the doors at the end and pushed them open to look though.

'Billy, Cassy-hello, it's me?' she called as she peered down the hall, a quiet echoed of her own nervous voice was all she received. She walked up and out to the main entrance to stand on the street and wait.

Ron came up as he noticed Jen stood in the street alone and confused.

'Been a long couple of days. We need her back. So, you haven't seen Katherine in town yet?' he asked as he looked at the community centre building behind Jen.

'If I had I'd ask her what she found when she left us. Why she did ask us for help one last time. No, I haven't seen her. If you go back, I'll give you a call or message if she comes around like I said.'

'You did say that, yes. So, what's this place here now?' he asked.

'It's a community arts hub. Locals can express themselves here through art, music, poetry, that kind of thing. It's therapeutic and good for people. I'm doing a thing here later for my vlog channel, internet stuff.'

'Creative things, art things, that's important, is it?'

'I like to think so and a few others too. Katherine did, she was very creative and imaginative.'

'Did she come here, to be creative?'

'I don't know. We didn't know much about it back then; it's only been like this for a short while.'

He stepped away 'I'll go walk for a while longer. I'll be around if she turns up, remember that.'

'I will, yes'

'Ron wait, you haven't seen my friends Billy and Cassy have you in the last few minutes?'

'...no, I am sorry to say I don't think I can help you there. They'll turn up won't they. Like my daughter?' he said with a brief sneer as he walked away from her.

Gareth had a frustrated expression over his drooped middle-aged face as he approached Jen by the main doors.

'I can call this evening's events off. It was a nice idea, but I really think you should have planned it well in advance, personally.'

'No, these days people do very spontaneous events using social media' she retorted.

'You mean like walking off and leaving you in the lurch to look a fool in front of locals?'

'No...I'll go back in and look around.'

Jen spun away from him and headed back inside past a couple of the local creative people they had called in with promise of a great evening. She avoided them stares as she stormed on further down the corridor to where Billy had been talking to some musician guy earlier. The smell came pungent and vivid. A voice could be heard, female and soft. It sounded familiar. She could hear two female voices talking, laughing casually. One of two sounded like people Jen thought she knew but could not clearly remember. She stepped on alone, turned the corridor through some doors. A door slammed shut in the next wide room. She turned around, a moment of hesitation before continued. She reached the main hall and with the voices louder she opened the doors with an optimistic smile.

'Hello?' she called and looked at the wide empty hall. No people could be seen anywhere. She walked around, the few tables set out and materials and kids' toys on the floor in the far corner. Something fell and notes tumbled from a junior xylophone.

'Hey Billy? Cassy, you two down here?' she called as she looked around her. A voice was muttering something in response somewhere over to her left. She moved across feeling a chill breeze move over her.

She could hear the song words from Tilda. The words were of things she knew from her own life, things of this small town but her own experiences in her teen years.

'Tilda, is that you?' she called. Entered the room to her left and fell to the wall beside her. The sight of the walls around smeared around her made her cry out and shudder. The words were ones she had heard sung only a day before, only minutes before.

'Shit, what....the shit...' she uttered. Someone moved under shadow, glided out at the side of her vision. She spun her head, the person quickly gone. She had seen a woman she was damn sure of it. Had it been Tilda?

The words on the walls were the song lyrics but why. The song of some ancient time, some local tragic death and destiny. Outside of the room footprints were marked across the hall. Prints of dark red smeared by hand. The trail of footprints she followed as the voices came back to her, whispered arguments, and screams. Her own name came next.

'Tilda is that you?' she called.

The wet red footprints led out back to a yard area. The door behind slammed as she walked out. The sight of it up into the trees sickened her and she turned back but the door was closed, jammed shut as she pulled and twisted the handle.

'Billy, come out here. Come now, help....me' she said into her smart phone. The body in the trees swayed as it stared down at her. The eyes gleamed wet and sad as blood flowed down the pale and broken face of Tilda. She heard the songs still around her, sung by some other unknown voice. She saw the back of a figure carrying another as it shifted and disappeared up a side alley. She rushed to catch it, but it moved too fast. A trail of blood led out to the alley but stopped abruptly so far in. Down at her shoes she noticed two small, bloodied objects. She knelt and saw all too clearly, they were freshly ripped away lips. She fell to the wall at her side and threw up onto the cobblestones.

'Oh, fuck me, that's horrible' she blurted. She ran back through the arts centre, the walls a blur, her senses swarmed, a fuzz of manic fear and panic around her. She made it to the front entrance where the crowd was gathered. Her stomach flipped and she threw up a mix of painful colours before her boots, wiped her chin and looked up. Gareth stood and looked at her in shock.

'Don't....don't let anyone in there. Call police. Get police, call it off now. Call police' she managed to split out. 'You haven't seen Billy or Cassy, no?'

'Sorry they still haven't turned up. I'll give it half an hour and then I'm going to call the even off. Sorry'

'Fine, whatever...'

She stepped away while some of the people noticed her and started to murmur and whisper. She ignored them and looked around her for any sign of Billy or Cassy.

Jen looked around her as she stood outside the arts centre. She glanced up and down the street as cars drove past, random people laughed and argued among themselves ignorant of her dilemma. There was a familiar figure out on the edge of the top corner of the street. Was it Katherine?

'Hey Katherine, is that you?' she called and began to walk in the direction. Too many people were walking right in her path as if she did not matter, like she was street garbage or a nameless, homeless vagrant. She managed to make her way up to the street corner and look around her. The next narrow road had some familiar element and so she made her way along.

'The streets...aren't right' she said. She backtracked a couple of streets. Clouds seemed to change, move in the most noticeable and eerie manner while buildings seemed to come up and block her path before she expected them, roads cut off or changed direction before she had chance to notice, or head down them. This was a less familiar part of the greater town area, but she was not anywhere near as forgetful or absent-minded as this was making her feel somehow. What was going on? She was experiencing the sensations and feelings Tilda had been singing about and what had been written in the poetry on the walls along the old factory side and half demolished housing.

Billy and Cassy were missing, gone, blood down the corridor. There was Katherine stumbling alone on the side alley outside the community building. She looked dazed, distracted.

'Hey! Katherine, wait! Wait for me!' she yelled and rushed up.

'Oh fuck, shit oh shit' she murmured.

She fell back and turned to see Katherine walking out down the far side road to the edge of town. Loud barking was echoed from the end of the road. Jen followed Katherine out as the paths and road bent and warped, twisted to confuse and the large dogs in the streets near to them. Katherine came to stop as Jen approached. She spun around and hugged her tight. As Jen lost consciousness, her eyes closed instantly, the tendrils slid out from the sides of Katherine and fed from Jen as the patches of energy emerged and folded around them as wings. Katherine took what she needed. She placed Jen further out and continued with her task given, her mind still not entirely her own.

Ron watched Katherine stalked in through the rows of the sheltering trees in among the ruined old barns beside the river to them.

'Will that do? We have this one. Her songs will stop now. They'll find her new poems; we've laid a new lore down. Pleased with that?' Lily asked as she motioned to the bound Tilda.

'I'll get that footage out the way the young ones do. Here's the folksong lady troublemaker. That's no problem now my dear' he replied as he brushed her shining hair.

Katherine placed Billy down beside the bodies Cassy and Tilda which had already been butchered and tied and bound in place. He nodded in approval as he and Lily changed her form more than once, the Witherbale back area street shimmered, quaked in time folds.

'She is there to bring back to Briggar' Lily stated her lower half that of some kind of deer or goat.

'We have more to do. We've waited too long. You are feeling better aren't you, like I promised you would?'

'I didn't think we could feel like them.'

'Yes, and they will understand our anguish of so long.'

'Ron, I think I saw Katherine fly again, tonight. She hasn't done that for so long. Is that a problem?'

'Katherine, you must be careful!' Ron called out 'Looking ill again, and you were doing well after seeing Mae. It's not good for you. We could take you back, but we want our time too. Think of Jackson. Remember we are all back in town now.'

Lily shook her head and walked away from him.

'You saw that? Jackson's problem, not ours' he said with a filthy laugh as he turned to face Katherine 'Go now, go back to your friends. Go play in the town while you can.'

They watched her glide away between the trees out of view. As they arranged the runes and checked the straps and ties over Billy, Tilda, and Cassy they soon enough heard footsteps over the branches and soil near to them.

Jackson stood with with Ron and Lily to the side of them. Saw signs of their recreating of another old lore monster and myth. They stood before Billy and Cassy in the stocks as the moon shifted in silence.

'I see the old lore of 1836, the witch trials and deaths and river beast times' Jackson observed with a slow nod of his head before he glanced to his wrist watched. 'Are deaths taking place? More lives leaving us as old lore is resurrected?' Jackson asked as he viewed some of what Ron and Lily were constructing out in the fields by the old farm barns and riverside.

'It makes us feel proud. The town needs the fear, unexplainable, drives them to the other, keep balance' Ron said, his body an uneven contortion of spider limbs and canine features which spoke. They all stood among the trees and Jackson waited for answers as a chill breeze cut threw the trees and touched each of them.

'See how Lily made sure the trail of witch footsteps led through the barns to the river where the hungry worm would come up to devour them or so they thought?' Ron stated with no small pride.

'I've seen some kind of river worm thing. Where did that come from?' Jackson asked.

'I've waited so long for such a transformation. I took a head clean away, swallowed whole. Teeth marks on the riverbank, the trail of slime and hex spell markings?'

Jackson nodded as he took in the evidence around them 'The detail is a credit to you. Ron, keep from my apartment. I see you are loyal and capable, your memory strong and reliable. My woman doesn't need the night terrors she had experienced of your shadow, shape of the back rooms and garden, understand?'

'I apologise for the visits' Ron told him 'I found it difficult to hold back my will to show what I remembered and was eager to do once more.'

'I see, but simply collect Katherine. I will be back to Briggar soon when you have her to make sure she is secure. Any signs of Katherine so far?' Jackson asked.

'Maybe a few clues, trails we'll look at next' Ron said as he patted Lily who had become the large dog at his side.

'Your dog gets enough exercise, I think. More than usual now?'

'The way things are, I suppose so. A loyal dog does help. Good times and bad. Good company. I love her dearly.'

'I know that' Jackson said and looked down at the dog as it sniffed at his shoes. 'Do anything for her would you?'

'It's about finding our daughter right now. You could come help if you're not far too busy with your job in town. I know you are well suited; you know parts around town many folks have never seen, or not for the longest time anyway. You look like you want to be out looking around. You've got curiosity in your eyes. Your job getting boring, is it?'

Jackson stepped out under the clouds and trees, peered in deep at the wild brambles and bushes around the part of Witherbale which led on toward the winding river behind.

'You've got those old farm barn ruins right over that way. You been looking over that way yet?'

'We're started yes. But please go look around for yourself, you might notice something useful or significant.'

Jackson glanced at him. The smirk upon the face of Ron irritated him, he knew it too well, but he controlled his anger, the urge to smack him down where he stood.

'They should all know you, you and her' as he waved his arm out and pointed to the town behind them.

'No, they should know Briggar stone and a sense of wonder. Any fear and bloodshed should be unexplained as it happens.'

'Just because you're confused doesn't mean you and her are not what we've been telling you are for the longest time, doesn't make it less true.'

'Stop. Don't say anymore.'

Jackson looked with silence fascination. He was impressed, even slightly envious.

'You could come out and join us, take part?' Lily suggested down in her canine form.

She watched him lick his lips, his hands brushed his suit, straightened his tie.

'No, you both enjoy and see the results. Best of luck. Lily, you are close on her, aren't you?'

'Katherine? We have seen her. We know she is in the area. She is trying to be with the friends she had, trying to help them.'

'So, stop that. For me, and all of us' he said and kissed her cold pale forehead. He touched his lower chest; she understood the notion.

'We will. We want her back in Briggar, the family way.'

'That's it, exactly it' he agreed with a smile. He had the urge to stay and watch the blood pour, the screams cut the night air with them, but he was a man of refined ways and attitudes these days.

'It's more than five centuries of helping you out here, in this town, making them scared, making them think of more than cars and money, lifestyles and insecurities. The wonder of the mysterious, the fear of the unexplainable but we need our time too' Ron suggested to Jackson.

Jackson shook his head as he clamped a strong hand onto the shoulder of Ron 'No, no- they're local folktales, legends they know, familiar and part of the identity of the town. They should not be broken down or changed at this point.'

'If not now, when? We should be the things they know, fear, wonder about, even respect or worship,' Ron blurted and spat between them 'The things they sell to tourists, put on t-shirts, keyrings and shitty web blogs or podcasts. Us, us, and Katherine. It's a disgrace. I and we want and deserve better!'

'In time, Ron'

'Centuries have passed. Times' been and gone. You have what you want, let us have this, give us a century of admiration, a few decades. We are having it, we are.'

'Ron, don't fuck about with Briggar and her. I can go there and do things.'

'You won't. Not now, will you?'

Ron and Lily then tortured each other as examples of the successful forgotten lore and activities for Jackson, as he turned and walked out of the woods back to town. They knew they had him thinking and considering his past, his real self, even his mistakes over the centuries.

Chapter Twenty-Three

'Another witch to hang, the worm awaits' Ron declared as he stepped around in a circle under the shadow of the tall trees 'No honey, no cakes, no good. Weak witches. Her lying words have ended now.'

Behind the old barns, Ron walked forward dressed in some old-fashioned official ceremonial robes, stepped up upon a platform between the ancient low barn structures. He looked out to view Cassy and Billy who were held down between the stocks and bound in place to hear his words. Billy was scared but angry too.

'Aren't you...are you looking for her, your daughter?' he asked.

Ron tilted his head as she stepped around the barn grounds 'She's around town, we'll find her. She knows we're looking, anyway that's beside the point. Right now, we must decide upon your outcome. Where was the berry cake, where was the honey?' he chided. Cassy writhed, struggled in her bindings across from Billy.

'What have we done? We're just making films. Our friend Jen wants to help the town, that's what we want' she offered.

'Misguided. Her and both of you' Lilly announced. Both felt the bindings pull and twist around their wrists and ankle, around their backs and legs. The wooden stocks opened over them. They were grateful but hesitant to move.

'This is our chance' Billy whispered to Cassy.

'I don't think so. I think we've pissed them off. It's a trick' she replied, tears in her eyes.

He struggled with the ropes over his back and legs, pulled and tugged without unleashing himself. Some slack came.

'Wait, they're loose. They are. They're moving us, that's why. It's our chance, see' he repeated 'Pull your ropes, free yourself.'

Only the moonlight shone down over some of the path near the and parts of their bindings as Ron and Lily were further out beside the river checking the position of the moon and instruments, they would use to inflict punishment and pain. Ron perched the digital camera taken from Jen and recorded the footage with immediate upload to the YouTube channel and socials. Locals were seeing distorted clips minutes later, knew what they saw was somewhere local, something to fear and respect, new folklore to believe in. The flow of the water rippled and changed down behind them. The ripples stirred, sudden whip and splash of water came up. The sharp fins broke through and dipped down once, twice and Ron rubbed his hands and turned to Lily.

'Wonderful, this what we need. Not the old shit from the Jackson' he said and turned back to see the progress.

The water poured over the sides of the riverbank with loud splashes, the beast leapt out. A vulgar wide mouth gaped open to the air above, dozens of jagged teeth shone bright. The river worm beast rose and snatched away the head of Billy in one eager bite, his immediate scream snuffed out, his gore and blood sprayed across the barn wall ruins behind as Cassy yelled hysterically and struggled in pain. She pulled and struggled as Lily came from behind the wall to her side and snapped her neck with gleeful ease, cut her throat with a long-jagged fingernail and sucked her blood with delight. In her walking sleep she was satisfied after a long moment and walked to the riverside to inspect the huge river worm beast as it splashed and writhed in the water. It stared at her, fresh blood dripping down its body and she slowly shook her head.

'Weak witches. We...are...powerful. Like...them...' the river beast spoke as it lower into the bloodied water around it, bulbous eyes wide and sickening.

Lily looked down and around at the lifeless broken bodies of Cassy and Billy.

'Would he have done such things, in this manner?' she asked.

'Oh...yes...' the worm beast spoke, and it descended into the water. She wiped a tear from her cheek as she moved back beside Ron. From behind her Ron looked with a triumphant expression with adorned his face, blood over his chin. He came and put an arm around her as they looked at the bodies.

'The worm has fed for now. He can have the rest later. As it should be. To be what they never let us be. Our time, our lore' he told her 'All fours now, come.'

They put on their robes from within duffle bags behind one wall and walked away into town.

Jen stood on a street, minutes out from the community centre, and heard the buzz of her smartphone. She withdrew it and saw the new clips line up to be seen had been posted and linked to her vlog page channel. She clicked them, curious to know what someone was sending on her own channel feed, and she stumbled back with a pained gasp as she saw somewhere among shadows of trees and broken brick walls the faces of Billy and Cassy as they were held stuck in some kind of traps as they bled and moaned. Behind the light shone down on the river as it rippled silently, and some large form moved through it. A huge tail snapped and splashed out and an eye the size of rugby ball blinked out toward the camera.

'What the fuck...' she uttered and dropped her phone.

'The river...somewhere on the riverside...' she muttered to herself. Some form moved around her. The familiar silhouette, the long hair and tattered dress and jacket. Was it Katherine? She thought so.

'Wait! Do you know where they are? Katherine, wait!' she called and ran to try to follow the figure as it darted through an alley and down toward the park and trees further out.

Jen followed what she thought was Katherine or someone like her. She was led out to the edge of Witherbale beside the old, ruined barn structure. She walked on and the screamed released from her mouth woke all sleeping wild animals under bush or trees. The bodies of Billy and Cassy lay motionless and horrific when her eyes looked upon them. She fainted instantly, fell to the mud and grass. When she woke, she saw them still, knew it was no nightmare and with trembling hand dialled for police and ambulance. She stumbled a couple of streets near to town, her mind a nauseous fog of torment and sorrow.

Ron stood by the taxicab building and noticed her as she walked alone, her eyes glazed.

'Dead...both of them...Ron. My friends...dead...called...called for ...' she muttered as she cried and rubbed her head with her palms and fell against him. He held her and patted her on the back, rubbed her shoulders.

'My word. Terrible, horrible news. My dear girl, terrible' he said.

'Followed...Katherine...' she muttered.

'Jennifer, if this really was done by our Katherine, you must tell us where you think she is. She needs to be inside our home, treated with her medication.'

'Maybe...maybe not her. So violent, so sick...might not have been ...police should know, they'll know what...'

Jen saw the scene in her mind, the remains, the torn flesh and bodies, the blood on the ruin ed walls. It sickened her and she threw up onto the grass by the narrow path beside him.

'She is near. You think your own daughter is a killer? Why think she did this to my friends? Why?'

He looked at her, his face calm but displeased.

'Katherine is dangerous and unstable. I don't want to believe it but...it is possible.'

'Anyone might have done this. And the people Mae knows who died. It's serial killing, some sick sonofabitch psycho or some drugged up bastard scum maybe.'

'Maybe. To be sure, to really know for certain, Katherine must be taken home. Can you get to where you live easily?' he asked.

'I'll order an uber now. Police will probably come around anyway.'

He waited with her until the car arrived and took her away.

Jackson heard the scratch by the window after midnight. He sat up curious and looked over the curtain was drawn. Must be cats or dogs near the garden below the window being a nuisance he thought. Ron was an inch from the window. He had peeled back the skin from his face, taken off his lower jaw and pushed his left hand through his cheeks over his tongue which dangled down by his stomach and licked up against the window slowly as he grinned at Jackson through the window.

'Too much, too soon. You've seen the way it works. Too much' Jackson said with a disappointed expression and a slow headshake.

Ron swapped back his dangling long tongue into his mouth, pulled back his hand from his face and reconnected his lower jaw. He gave a frown.

'Trying things out. I Like to practice' he said.

'Not here, you fool. Go back, go elsewhere' Jackson told him. Ron shrunk away into the night. Ron formed the folklore beast of 1589, a wide and gargantuan horse hound man, hooved legs clacked on the ground below him.

'Good likeness, yes. No reason for it...' Jackson muttered as he looked at his phone screen absentmindedly.

'I like to remember; think I could have been the one' Ron croaked through his animal lips.

'You play your part, both of you. You have always been needed, necessary and valued.'

Ron twisted, shook, and hunched while he grunted and coughed out a thick pile of hot viscous bile. He reappeared as the monster form of eighteen sixty-three. The head of a muscular bull, body a cross of scales lizard arms with and furred goat legs.

'No Ron. No more, you'll tire yourself and I can't have that. You understand. Not now'

'I can be this, bring it back to the town, like last time. Someone should'

'Not you, no, not right now. Just get Katherine back inside. That is all we need to focus on.'

Jackson stood and stared in silence. He looked at the creature he had portrayed centuries earlier, a forgotten mistake, a curious sketch of wild monstrous anger for the people. He admired the devotion and adoration, but the misunderstanding was infuriating. Ron fell, collapsed to the ground. Jackson simply let out a tut. He knew the form could not be held for any amount of time, such quick transformations drained energy so rapidly.

'Where is Lily?' he asked.

'At Briggar...cooking as usual' Ron managed to gasp.

'Go eat, don't be late. Keep strong, back out tomorrow to keep searching. No more of this' Jackson said and pointed his finger up and down at the thing Ron had presented to him.

'You were this once.'

'Yes, I was' Jackson agreed. 'That was the past, Ron. Time for new reform, new games, and lore for the people. It's been and gone. Now go'

A short while later, through trees and under brambles Ron came and found Lily as she wept alone. She looked up at him and cried out 'We're doing bad things; we shouldn't be out. We should just get Katherine, only that.'

Ron sneered, shook his head, and fell to his knees. His form changed, his claws and limbs grew out. The fur bristled, he howled and scraped the ground. Lily watched as he bounded away through the trees and walked after him slowly with a look back at the one, they had killed who walked and spoke like before.

They rushed to their den to clothe and whisper what they had encountered among the trees of the woods.

'Who was that? Tell me now' Lily urged.

She was breathless, nervous, and excited all at once. She was thinking of all the possibilities, he could see it in her eyes. He knew she might get carried away and make mistakes, he had no time for that.

'It is something released by Katherine. And that means she is healthy, is well, nearby.'

'She has released something from before or from the other places. She said she could do that; didn't I tell you?'

'You both were interested in possible evocation and creation yes. Just remember now, we are out to do what we want to do, and we may not have too long to do that. Jackson could come down on us in a matter of days. Keep that in mind. Anything she is doing is her own game, not ours. Let us rest. We have more to do with the next one' he told her. Arm in arm, they returned within the Briggar stone.

Mae had spent a whole day in bed, hardly ate any food or drank much at all. The knowledge of her dead work colleagues had hit her hard and seeing Katherine at the same time, her head was a fog of confused anxiety and nerves. Jackson had told her to stay away from the studio, rest for as long as she needed to and find some calm while he would talk with police and check around the studio road by day. She was pleased to be with him, glad of his sensitive and caring ways but she had some troubles questions in her mind of some of his secretive habits and journeys alone. In the late afternoon she dressed casually and when he left the house she followed at a distance. It felt wrong and foolish, and she would be extremely embarrassed and scared if he noticed her, but she wanted to know why he seemed to walk out to the old stone on the riverside alone regularly. After twenty minutes she saw him arrive there and there were two other people there. He spoke and seemed to know them, and she watched them pray or chant under his command. It was incredibly strange and made her wonder why he kept this behaviour a secret from her. It was sinister and creepy, and he must had known she would think that. Was he a pagan or was it even some kind of cult worship? Was offering or sacrifice involved? She began to think all kinds of terrible things before she quickly rushed back to the house and consider if she should really be with him at all.

Jen was lost between streets in further Witherbale east side, a panic attack disturbed her focus and inner self. She collapsed, blacked out where she stood. Katherine came and laid hands upon her, whispered and chant and walked away. When her eyes opened, Jen moved along on the ground up a quiet side street. She was close to the river, she could smell it, could feel the breeze from the moving cool waters and open land near the sea. Her senses felt much more focused or rearranged in some way, but not her eyesight. She held out her arms and fell back as she saw long fur coated talons, claws and below, similar fur coated legs, large and muscular. To the right of her a long tail flicked and snapped out, hit the wall to her side, the window to her right, where she caught a reflection which made no sense but from where she stood and how she moved...it must have been...no, could not be...she was no longer human? She saw as her own body some kind of large hybrid feline cat form, fangs in her mouth, yellow eyes, sleek fur over her lithe body. She slowly shook her head as she watched herself move.

'What...am I...I know this...' she stated quietly. She bounded out and around behind the derelict ancient farm barn ruins on the riverside further ahead. She could smell the dogs. Those strange huge dogs unlike any others. She sniffed the air around her, licked her lips, purred, and slunk down low to wait. She was could not think of any question of why or how only follow what felt like a natural animal urge or instinct.

Jen as the feline hybrid creature moved down between the large dogs which jumped back further apart startled. They appeared bewildered and scared. They had only known each other to be the most fearsome and unexplainable creatures around the town for many decades or more. They barked and growled briefly at the unexpected hybrid creature before them. It fascinated them but until they knew what or who it was, they knew it best to retreat to a safer place. It stalked after them easily, grasped a hold of the slower dog, held it up and stared into the eyes of it.

'Where have you come from?' the dog asked, front paws up and desperate to touch.

The creature held the dog high up as if unsure of its own strength.

'New, are you?' the other dog asked from the side of them before it barked loudly, came closer and snapped at the feet of the creature. It stepped back, hurt angered and dropped the dog. Both dogs stood and looked at the thing with its stretched out wide wings which blocked out the daylight behind.

'I am dream' the feline creature uttered.

It rushed at them, flew up into the sky above and was gone a moment later. The dogs looked at each other, looked around them and rushed away within the wide overlap of an untamed stretch of trees.

Chapter Twenty-Six

Jen opened her front door to see Issy there, coat pulled tight around her against the cool autumn breeze of the day.

'Is she with you, is she here?' Issy asked looking over her shoulder.

'She was. Gone again but I feel like I have more of a feeling of where to find her home. Not exact but I think now she's been with me, close to me, I've connected with her. Sounds stupid right but that's how it feels.'

'You were safe with her near you last night?'

'Of course.'

'Jen, honestly-you weren't worried?'

'Let's get out to town and get there. We can't waste time especially with Ron and Lily trying to find her as we speak.'

'You don't think she did what you saw?'

'No. I think we don't trust Ron and Lily, not entirely anyway. There's more to them all disappearing three years ago. They're not telling us everything.'

Issy shrugged 'Okay then. Well, we don't have Mae with us but let's find the place and see how that's helps us. Will Katherine be there?'

'I don't know. Come on'

Jen and Issy surfed the net for a couple of hours on their phones, checking back and forth to find eventually a collection of papers and articles over websites which told the details and supposed events and characters of the witch trials and deaths in their area centuries ago.

'This is what you've found in connection to Katherine's family and the home. We're not getting very far. Are you just trying to make things fit?' Jen asked.

'No, look her father Ron, he was fascinated with local superstitions. I remembered some of this, it came to me suddenly. The paintings in their home, the poems Katherine wrote and told us. Some of it had family connections to local history' Issy countered.

The walls rumbled, some strong vibrations came under them and moved along the building. They looked at each other.

Jen turned where they sat 'What...?'

'Witches in this city, this town. Murdered, hung a bunch of times, maybe for entertainment or genuine fear. But witches are bullshit right, the kind you see in movies and Halloween masks?'

'It was probably men or a fucked-up mob killing lesbians or women who had opinions for sure but then, witchcraft...I don't know.'

The lights flickered above them.

'What is this?'

'Ignore it. Listen, when your colleague was attacked did you mention seeing wet footprints and the sounds and they were hung up in the tree?'

'The witches were hung, the sounds like bells and crying.'

'Exactly. Same thing with me and my friend on my work project. Exactly the same. It's here in these articles on the websites, the tongue taken out of their mouths, the skin taken after they were hung up and drowned in the river after.'

'So, I can't deal with it. Why all of it and around us?'

'That bit I don't understand.'

'What is the solution, or do we hide or what, if it is otherworldly unnatural things what are we supposed to do?'

'Fuck, this is so much to handle.'

'It really is'

Jen collected her jacket and phone, and both began their walked together toward the main streets of town following whatever instinct or unknown feeling might guide them to the hidden home of their old friend. They hoped they would not hear the barks of the dogs of seeing Ron and Lily before they reach the place.

As they walked, they talked.

Jen looked up at the arching tall trees which reached to the autumnal sky above as they moved on 'It does sound wrong, but she might be here. I'm pretty sure it was still up for sale last time I came past it. Word got around about her, and her parent's possible deaths or family trouble didn't.'

'I just think I sort of offended her. The ways she made off so quick and didn't turn up later. She used to flit really quick from one emotional state to another.'

'Because her parents are looking for her. She's what, she as us, around twenty-three now?'

'You can't understand their being concerned, it's their family way. I think they were a very close family just unusual, not like most.'

'They smothered her. She couldn't have a boyfriend or girlfriend easily because of them. They made her so introverted. Could have been religious or just way paranoid. It was mental abuse; they knew what they were doing I think.'

They walked on past the town library, the junior school and park on the other side of the high street where Jen began to look confused.

'I'm sure it didn't use to take this long to reach it from college back before she went missing. High street over there, we're here, the park there...' Jen said as she looked around them to focus her surroundings.

Issy stopped and wondered with a puzzled expression 'Are we a few streets out?'

'No, we should be able to see her street from about here I'm almost certain' she said as she walked to the end of the street, crossed the road, and found a disused condemned small block of flats and the old doctor's practice.

'Where the hell is it?'

'You're lost. It's just not around here. Good work. Let's go back and try again.'

'No, this is ....it isn't right. It's this area, this part of town. Something is wrong here. You knew her street, don't you?'

'I... I'm not totally sure I do, I can't seem to remember the name and if it was in this part of town, sorry.'

'It should be here, ahead of us, her house should be here. Right here'

The wind pushed along beside them up the narrow side street and it carried the barking of a dog so guttural and raw like a voice which called out.

'Hear it? Doesn't sound like the usual dogs around here. It soun ds...' Issy began.

'I know, I know. Keep moving, ignore it. Straight on and... left I think' Jen replied. Issy did not look the look on her face, a nervous anxiety in her eyes but she followed anyway. There were a few people who passed them every so often, some focused solely on the addictive screens of their smartphones held out before them, others with eyes down or straight ahead, no interest in acknowledging the world around them. Some familiar shape, a human form moved from one side of the street to the next up ahead of them, too fast to be clear but Issy thought she caught eyes flash down to her for the briefest seconds.

'You know, I swear I saw a glimpse of Katherine further up there' she said.

'Good, maybe you did. Come on, we shouldn't stop yet' Jen reminded her.

'I feel like we've come around in a full circle. Do you feel that?'

'Oh, don't even think that. How could we? No, we've only been moving forward with a few careful turns. Look, we'll keep going another twenty minutes then hit a pub or coffeeshop. Sound good?'

The sudden barking cracked out from a street behind or ahead of them. Which was it? It was so hard to be sure.

'Did Mae say the dogs were really big, unbelievably large? And that sounds like...does that sound like words, those barks?' Issy asked 'Did it sound like her name?'

'Oh, come on. No, no way. Another street, keep walking, don't think about it.'

'Sounded like...like her name...'

They turned a corner and daylight seemed to twist and flicker above and around them. Shards of light shifted, clouds above moved with a dense but firm purpose and shadows shifted as they took a few more steps ahead blinded by the light until the view came clear and somehow familiar.

'The barking has stopped. Hey look, there it is' Jen declared. There before them stood the house they had visited numerous times when they had all attended college, those blue curtains in the upper windows still there, the weird garden ornaments which resembled angels and lions sat as they always had in the front garden beside the rows of bright flowers.

Issy turned and looked back behind them. 'What street is this?'

Jen peered down to where they saw the street name beside the house opposite. 'Barley street, isn't it? Sounds familiar?'

'Yes but...up there is Dickson Road and didn't that used to connect with Waddly Close before meeting the main road into town again?'

'Maybe, I'm not entirely sure. Look we're here, we best just get inside if we can.'

Jen and Issy outside where they looked ahead to the house Katherine used to live in. The air around them had an unusual throb of vibration around them, the buildings to their left and right appeared to move where they stood, shifted just so slightly on the hard concrete somehow. The door was open, they moved in with quiet hesitation, some sound inside, a quiet shuffling, clanking noise repeating. Was it calling, a voice inside? Jen walked on to the door hand on the frame.

'Katherine, it's me and Issy. Hello, you here? Ron, Lily?' she called as they entered.

Issy came around behind her, breath touched Jen over her neck.

'Fuck my heart' Jen spluttered as she turned to see her.

'It's me, just me' Issy said.

'You bloody scary bitch. Okay, come on, come in with me. You hear that...a voice or something else?'

They were walking together on edge. They clearly heard the noises, the footsteps not far from them, the breathing close behind them but distant somehow. The flashes of weird shapes among the trees and buildings had continued as they moved on. Some of the images were so ferocious and sickening, somehow familiar and regretful. She would not leave them but would not clearly help them in their search for safety either. They knew Katherine was somewhere also watching.

Was she guiding them? Haunting them with relish? These two beastly entities were around them at the same time, but each with different intentions as they made their way to unpick their past mistakes and glories, deaths and disasters included.

'They're on us.'

'Katherine is there. You think she is aware?'

'Yes'

'But like, if we have souls, is she still there conscious. She experienced her death, but does she know how or why?'

'She is trying to help us.'

'Can she...can she want to?'

'That's not the question. Do we want to?'

They approached the family house surrounded by fog and cold chill.

'Now we see it' Issy said as they stood before the old detached large house.

'It was always here. So strange. Come on' Jen said.

'What's the point of being here?' Issy asked.

'We'll find out. Let's walk around the house quietly.'

They cautiously stepped around the narrow path. The house had a 'for sale' sign pitched in the lawn but seemed to still be unoccupied.

'I can see through the back windows. This house, her family, they were nice, friendly.'

'No, we thought they were. Turns out, they were lying, manipulative bastards.'

'It goes deeper than that. She told us things we didn't believe.'

The chill seemed to breeze past them up toward the side of the house. It turned her attention to the top right window.

'Her room' Issy said.

'We can't get in.'

Lily appeared in the garden in the corner under the shadow of trees and bushes surrounding them. She stared at them with a fractured psychotic grin. She moved to them in a split second, grabbed Issy, pulled her down. Pushed her into the back garden away from Jen.

'Help me' Issy moaned.

Her face was pushed next to a pile of rocks at the side. Lily pointed with a face; a smile familiar to them. She let her go, moved back, and pointed to the rocks. Issy came to her knees and picked up the largest rock, threw it up at the back door. They turned the handle and stepped inside.

'Katherine wants us inside' Issy said. Jen had seen it silently before it disappeared.

'So, we're in' she said. They climbed inside up the stairs quietly, flicked on a lighter to illuminate their path. They climbed the stairs, stumbled around. A squirrel chirruped and shook them up as it bounded away.

'Little fucker' Jen commented.

'In the room'

The walls rumbled. Thumping, thumps over and over in time with their own footsteps into the room Katherine had grown up in. A disembodied low laughter echoed around the house.

'I don't like that we're in here. It feels wrong, feels like a trap' Jen said.

'There's nothing in here, its empty. Okay so we'll get going I suppose.'

'Wait, just let me walk around...'

'You hear that, feel that?'

Once they stepped inside the light from outside changed, a deep heavy cloud moved over the house, darkened the already shadow filled rooms, thickened the black around them as they walked further in together. The house was a plain detached old home, the décor simple but outdated, wallpaper and furniture remained from the eighties or before. They had not been a wealthy family and had furnished and decorated and renovated the rooms themselves or that was what Jen remembered Katherine telling them.

'This house is a really strange shape. Was that staircase there before, do you remember?' she asked Issy as they looked at the winding staircase which twisted up in the hall before them to the first floor and down to some basement possibly.

'I don't remember it being there but…I feel like I do know it. Like I've seen it before. Weird' Issy replied.

They walked on ahead to where Jen though the sounds were to the kitchen further back. They found nobody there, but a dank smell started to rise which was sour and unwelcome.

'Is something dead in here? Oh, that smell…' Issy said.

'That is really bad, oh god' Jen responded.

'Let's try another room.'

'Yeah, could be a dead cat or rat or something. Hopefully, nothing bigger'

Neither wished to find anything like that. They moved on back out to the staircase.

'Up or down?'

'Let's do up. See her bedroom, I think that's a good idea.'

'Right, yeah'

They walked the stairs together as Issy heard some faint sound below like whispers or footsteps, possibly outside the house as they passed a small window. She peered out as they passed it but saw no one out there.

'So, where's Mae?'

'Her bloke had plans for her. Plus, she's not totally feeling the same about this as us, is she?'

'Isn't she, how do you mean?'

'About Katherine. They didn't connect as well as we did, I don't think, not really. I think they had an argument when Katherine turned up to see her. Probably best Mae's not here. I don't think she'd be helping much anyway.'

They came to the bedroom and the door was open. As they stepped inside the house shook, some severe rumble from down below.

'What is that, earthquake or what?' Issy asked, eyes wide.

'I...I don't know' Jen replied and stepped to the window on the right and pulled the musty moulded curtain aside. The view did not feel right, it did not make sense she thought.

'How cand I see that part of town outside but from a different angle?' she said.

'What do you mean?'

'Have a look. It doesn't seem right. I see this direction but...below us the river, like right below us. Hey, look-Mae's design studio just along on the left too...'

'Oh, hey...that's right. That...how are we seeing that? No...is that right?'

Issy rushed from room to room upstairs and the laughter grew into a hollow guttural howl. The thumping and banging increased. As Jen stood by a doorway she was touched. Black cold hands held her, pulled her back toward the staircase.

'Issy...' she muttered 'Issy.'

'Wait a minute' Issy replied distractedly.

She looked around and recognized so much.

'This...this was my room. My bedroom'

Jen looked at her confused but as both looked around the room at the walls, the furniture, Jen saw other things, her own teenage belongings, the wallpaper of her own teenage bedroom.

'What is this? I see my room…you see your family room?'

'Yes, I do. I really do. How are we seeing this?'

'This is our home. Was…it was our home too' Jen told her.

'That doesn't make sense.'

From up on the stairs behind her, Issy was held with force, the low laughter burned her ears inches away from her. Was held, shaken over the staircase, arms bound only able to look down at the fall below her if it let go of her of her arms as she balanced on the top stair.

'The river' it said from behind her.

On the walls of the abandoned old family home Jen and Issy noticed large paintings of animals in the style of which Katherine used to paint in college and they did still look surreal and more mysterious, more fascinating with their bizarre animals and creatures. Just like the ones she had told them about in the sleepovers, while smoking weed and, in her poems, and short stories. Now these images and stories seemed so much more important.

Issy rummaged under old magazines and some dusty boxes in one empty room. She cut her fingers on pieces of glass and paper, but something emerged which caught her attention. She pulled it out, held it up to the light from the small gaps in the paper-covered windows. Handwritten letters. She read them. Issy came out the room and held them now the haggard figure let go of Jen, who toppled instantly from the top of the staircase. Issy leapt forward desperately, their hands grasped each other, eyes wide.

'Got you' the voice croaked out.

Jen held on tight with no words and tears in her eyes. They both fell and Ron with his face rearranged into the form of some four eyed wild boar with gleaming drooling fangs knocked them, kicked them all the way down. When they hit the last stair, they stopped moving, fallen into the heap over each other. After a few minutes Issy raised her head and slowly looked around them. Lily was stood in the doorway of the kitchen room behind them, waiting to see if they still had life in them.

'Jen, move, get up' Issy whispered as she gave a gentle quick nudge to her friend beside her. Jen let out a quite pained sound as she opened her eyes a fraction to see her.

'Can you stand?'

'Maybe'

'We're leaving. They're watching but not moving toward us,'

They saw the front door open slowly of its own volition. As they help each other to their feet they made their way across to the doorway Ron stepped out toward them but slowly with some difficulty. They could see Ron and Lily seemed to be struggling with muscular twitch, some spasms over their bodies. Their eyes winced, arms shook, and Ron growled as they moved outside.

'Look at them, what's happening?' Issy asked as she and Jen stepped outside and rushed up the street together.

'Fucked if I know.'

Issy turned and stepped back to look at the room they occupied. Jen was right. The view was from the other side of town, it must be. There was no way they should have been able to see what was out there from inside that house in that part of town, miles from what was visible out there. The rumble occurred another time, more prominent below and it seemed to swirl up and around through the house. They both stumbled where they stood, leaned against each other for support.

'I don't like this, it's fucking weird. Are we high, I mean like on the mould or dirt in this old crappy house?' Issy asked.

'I don't think so. Look at the wall' Jen said. The paint and wallpaper peeled, wet lurid substance behind, the sky shone through. The barking came back, it seemed to be inside the house, below them but rising.

'Let's leave, please. This is freaking me out' Issy uttered.

With another sudden shake and rumble below them Jen turned and saw a thick book over on the bedside table slide to the edge. She moved over and took hold of it.

'Yes...' a voice was heard somewhere in the house.

'Katherine?' Jen said and saw the face in the mirror and Issy was stood with Katherine at her side in the shadows behind Jen.

'I'm feeding them. Look out, read...the book, see my paintings' Katherine told them.

'We let her take us, use us and she can do what she needs to do. Get the dogs away and sort the other place.'

'Take us like...how?'

'Don't ask. But just...it'll stop the deaths; it'll heal her and more.'

The walls around them continued to rattle and creak as they stood and stared at the house around them, walls of plaster and stone that somehow seemed to pulse and warp in time to their own rattling heartbeats inside their nervous chests.

Chapter Twenty-Seven

They sat together and looked through the pages of the tattered old book. It was some old journal, the writer terrible and hard to decipher but they believed it was that of Katherine. Issy took out a large folder from a drawer beside the bed. She opened it and found a collection of paintings which both instantly knew and remembered.

'I know these' Jen said.

'Yes, we do, we know them. She painted them back when we were in college. Look, this here, the river worm creature. And this one...the werewolves...'

'No, they were not werewolves but something different...shapesh ifters...'

'Oh, look at this one...these women, together, inside each other but apart and in the air...one has the head of a cat, the other...'

'...the other has huge wings from her back, and a bird head...'

Jen continued to flick through and stopped with the pages open on a spread two-page illustration, great in detail. Town streets with the buildings transformed, distorted and staircases twisted up into the sky. Between them stood some large contraptions of torture, people inside and out, strapped, and buckled in. At the base of these two figures with wings, their heads bowed.

Jen looked down, heard the bark and howl from outside below. 'She did make these up, she...remembered them. Like we should'

'What?'

'Do you remember them?'

'Yes, she painted them. We saw her sometimes when she was doing it.'

'No, listen...'

Issy- 'The letters mention us. The three of us'

Jen 'Oh, is it okay? Sound good?'

'Overall, I suppose but...not all the way through. I mean she mentions our shitty behaviour and dumping on her more than once...we know it's true.'

Jen nodded, head down 'Yeah, it is.'

'I'm not done reading. More of it reads like so much of the stories she would make up, we're in stories, they sounded so strange, like fantasy tales. So that was Mae...where is she?'

'Passed the college. We'll see her at the pub if she turns up.'

'You sound pessimistic. Wait, her boyfriend...'

'What?'

'Here in this letter, Katherine mentions him, him and her togeth-er...'

Jen looked at her 'Like they were a thing?'

'Let me finish reading...'

They read over the note pages and learned of Jackson as someone called 'Beniah' and how he had been abusing and torturing Katherine as 'kah-Tahreen' for centuries where Briggar stone had once been a house which belonged to a man whom Jackson tricked and murdered. The stone took the name of the man. House had existed in their world and out of it at the same time, until it was under attack somehow.

'Mae must know about it. He's not who he said he was, he's even some other thing or...' Jen reasoned as she looked over the pages.

Issy tilted her head 'Maybe, we can't be sure.'

'Oh, come on, the way she's been acting.'

'That's just her. Maybe he didn't tell her. Blokes often don't tell you if they've shagged your friend, you know that.'

'Yes, but we weren't exactly her good friends all the time, were we? It depends when and how he was with Katherine but in these pages it doesn't sound good. She really wanted him...he seemed a good guy with her but...'

'What?'

'The pages don't go up to when she died. Or I don't think so...hard to tell.'

'Oh god, Mae is going to meet us. Do we challenge her, if this is because he fucked her over-Katherine, and she knew...?'

'Her workmates have died this week too.'

'Yes, but that doesn't mean she doesn't know or did have some involvement with what happened.'

Sudden sounds of crunching twigs, rustling bushes yards away. The rumbling groan into low slow laughter.

'Katherine is around us. She's near. Do we meet Mae, yes or no?'

'It could be Mae she wants.'

'Exactly'

'She might think all three of us are to blame but it just has been her and Jackson. What do we know besides what's on those pages-do we hand her over?'

They looked at each other as they rustling sounds increased, the low guttural laughter from somewhere around them. There were loud howls and screams outside. The view from the window was different. It was that of the other side of the high street and library up ahead, how it should have been the first time they looked out. The walls throbbed and the rumble returned. The shadows moved and Katherine was no longer in the room with them. The smell was so overwhelming and fetid they struggled to breath.

'Come on, we must leave' Jen advised 'I think this will help us.'

'Agreed, totally'

They rushed down the stairs and in the hall some sound echoed up from the basement.

'Hear that from down below?'

'It's not her so let's just get out now.'

The door was jammed as she gripped the handle. She struggled and pulled on the knob, Issy moved to add some force, her hands over Jen's own.

'Fuck it, come on. Shit...' Jen moaned.

'Turn, push it, we can do it, push down.'

'I'm trying, fuck...'

Jen kicked the door and twisted her hands over the lock with Issy together. It turned finally. Dogs barked from somewhere. Some voices argued from another direction, but they tried to be ignored it all and simply leave the house. Silence came. Footsteps. The lock turned; the door opened to them. Jen and Issy looked at each other before they moved quickly back out and about them.

'See any dogs, you heard them, right?'

'Don't see them. Let's get further away to my place or yours'

They looked up and down the street, sound of cars passing, some random laughter burst out. Their hearts were ready to burst and each of them felt nauseous. Katherine appeared looking drained, deathly pale as if washed up from the river, veined, bruised and so Jen hides her at her flat. At the same time Lily and Ron walked the streets of town call out for her. Katherine stood in the back alley to the apartments and spoke out.

'I'm sorry. You have success now, you are the vlogger, the revelator of local times and truths, connecting the people in a good way.'

'But...that's it?'

'It's time. Not what I wanted but the deal was made. The deal is broken so...'

'The deal with who? Your parents? Make a new deal then!' Jen urged.

'We'll see. It must end before it starts again. I need you. Let us be together,' she said. She looked to have more vibrant life and colour in her features but still not entirely healthy as they were before her.

'Your parents, where are they? Are they still looking for you?' Jen asked.

'They wait. They understand,'

She took them closer to her. Her chest opened out like a flower of flesh petals blossoming and they were drained wilfully. They sat together briefly until Katherine sat up and opened her eyes wide.

'We must go to the stone together. I need you with me. You will come?'

Jen and Issy sat up dazed, smiles over their faces.

'Of course. We know we should,' Jen replied.

'We feel it,' Issy agreed.

'What about Mae?' Jen asked. Katherine led them out across town in the dark of night.

They walked back through into town together; both experienced a lightheaded elation. Colours, shapes, and movements around them all seemed much more vivid and real in new but familiar way. Out on the edge of the Edgeton Road stood Ron and he watched them walked toward them. He gave a casual wave.

'Oh shit, let's try to avoid him' Issy said quietly under her breath to Jen.

'Hello there' Ron said 'She came back, we found her. She is better, we fed her. You may not see her again. Thank you'

'What for?'

'Being with her, when she needed it.'

'She came out to be with us again and see the town...' Issy said.

'She's been cooped up for too long. It might have seemed the right thing, but it wasn't' Jen added.

'Well, you've seen her, and you've seen what kind of state she is in. We all care greatly about her and so we thank you. You're welcome.

'So, you're taking her back to the other place you live at? Just like that?' Jen asked.

'It is the best place for her.'

'Do you like it there?' Issy asked with some bravery.

Ron changed his expression to one of curiosity. 'And what do you mean by that?'

'That's where you've all been but did you all really want to be there?'

'We were only ever going to live right in town for a short time. Our other home is where we should be.'

'Says who?' Issy pushed.

'Leave it, Issy' Jen urged hand on her arm with a gently tug to lead them away. 'See you around' Jen said as she nudged her in the side, and they watched Ron and Lilly depart. Lily seemed to offer a sympathetic look as they quickly walked away up the other road.

'Where is Buckley Road?' Issy asked as they walked together in a rush.

'I...good point. And we should have passed Mason Street by now I think...look there' Jen said and pointed up ahead. They were amazed at what they saw. The old bakery and the cinema stood together as usual, but the street had a new name, Chalkley Street.

'When did they rename this street?' Issy asked.

'Some very strange things are taking place. Let's get to the flat right now.'

They made it back to Jen's flat and Issy stayed the night, slept on the sofa after they remained up for a few more hours discussing what they thought they had experienced in the hidden old house and what the paintings and journals of Katherine meant to them and what might happen next. Jen was woken as her name was whispered from outside the bedroom. She got to her feet and stumbled through the hall.

'Who is there? Hello?' she called. She moved close to the coat stand and quietly picked up the umbrella as some tragic form of self-defence. Katherine stepped forward from within shadows.

'Hello Jen. You made it' she said.

'Yes. We found things, some answer questions and other things create more. You were always telling us, showing us things.'

'I was. I remember, I have looked at them. We are special all four of us.'

'Right, I get that. We get that but I've become something. It was a thing, a dream of being, I told you years ago. I woke as it, flew in the sky over our town. How did I do that? How did you let that happen?' Jen demanded.

Katherine stood calm and composed 'Listen to me. You let it happen. It is in you, a part of you, to be that creature. That thing comes from you, and you come from somewhere else. You know that thing, deep inside. That is okay, it's alright.'

'What was I?'

'A species known in dreams, in other worlds, from places elsewhere, places of joy and freedom, of unlimited possibilities and hope and peace.'

'Have you been there? How do you know of a place like that?'

'I'm not totally sure, I only know of it. I believe in it. The more I believe, the more it reveals itself and that is how it used to be.'

'It did, didn't it, back when we were younger. It was what you drew and wrote about and told us about from your dreams and ideas.'

Katherine nodded 'Trust in me and soon you can be that thing again, you can know the other places, endless peace and things which can only begin to be known in human expressions of art and speech.'

'Have you flown?'

'I have been what I am. I have flown, yes. I am a different being when transformed, we are similar and connected. You know that yes?'

'I always have, yes.'

She looked at Katherine 'It hurt you didn't it, to let me be that creature?'

Katherine gave a nod.

'I wanted you to be what you had dreamed, to know it. Some dreams are memories or offers laid out to us, visions, and prophecies,'

'You need to rest more. I can see you look exhausted again. Are there others who change or fly in town or elsewhere?'

'The Great Cull happened. There are I believe, dedicated ones like me who live hidden, they who know those who change, roam as beast, bird, swim in the waters and more. They bless and protect. I don't know exactly where...'

'But you've dreamed of them?'

'Yes'

'So, you are sure and believe?'

'Yes. They exist. They care and look after those gifted, blessed dream beings. Like you, like Mae and Issy too. Go rest now. You are safe.'

'Will be that thing again?'

'Possibly. You think you can all help me?'

'Of course. We see it is very important. We don't want others to die. We will help.'

'Sleep now, like Mae and Issy.'

Katherine returned to the shadows. When Jen moved ahead, she touched the walls and found her gone entirely. She returned to the bedroom and lay back beside Issy to sleep and rest for whatever they had to confront next.

Outside on the street Jackson wandered slow and careful and eventually faced to see the front door of the home. He stepped toward it slowly.

'This ...is...it...?' he said low and unsure. The Briggar stone edged in behind it up on the left. There was a haze and fog as the perception of his surroundings contracted and warped.

'I see...yes...' he said.

The giant dog came and rushed out to his right. The mouth split open unnaturally wide, a tongue like that of a lizard snapped out at him as the dog stood on its back legs. As it barked another bark echoed out from around him. Jackson returned to gaze to the old home, but it had shifted. He was staring at some other house among many. He spun where he stood, confused, and angered. The dog stepped toward him, the large, opened trap-like mouth snapped as it barked right next to him. He stepped back with a slow nod, turned and walked away. Down the street a figure walked along. It was Katherine, he knew it instantly and saw she looked like a corpse. She glanced right at him before she floated out behind trees and was gone.

'Bitch' he spat.

Chapter Twenty-Four

The following day Jen could only sit before her television wondering what the hell her life was supposed to be without Billy, Cassy and the vlog posting. Their families called her, and she replied quietly telling them only that they had been found out by the riverside before the arts event could take place, she had called the police, the families took over and she communicated with both. Issy sat with her in the flat and occasionally made a few calls to her own workplace with the council youth services mentors to check in and explain she would not be in that day. Late afternoon once they had eaten some basic noodles and beef Issy suggested the pub and meeting Mae.

'Okay, that would help me and I'm sure she probably needs it too. Thanks for the support Issy, we'd be lost without you' Jen told her.

'We've all been lost without Katherine. We need to figure it out. People we know are dying but she's shown us our significance in stopping it.'

'If she herself was not the one...'

'You've been telling us it wasn't her.'

'I know...Katherine is different. She is not who we knew back then, but somehow is that and more. A lot more. let's get to the damn pub.'

She shook her head with a sigh as they pulled on their jackets and left the flat together.

Mae wandered out away from the bus stop alone aware of the noise of the cars driving past, people chatting, calling across the street, a dog bark somewhere. Not sounds she was afraid of but each one alerting her to sudden audio nervousness. The sounds she had come to experience over the last week of death, dying, haunting was in her head and would not be gone yet. She expected to hear them for real at any moment as she walked out to join her two loyal friends. She hoped there was a useful reason for going around to places they had left behind with no intention of visiting again. They each wanted to move on, away to be better people with their skills she thought. They were doing it so why all this now? Her phone buzzed, a call from Jackson. She messaged him a response which suggested she would return to him soon. She would because this whole adventure was a fucking childish joke, she told herself. Issy and Jen might be entertaining themselves, but it was very sick and inappropriate. Was it how they were dealing with the deaths of their work colleagues or remembering Katherine?

Mae turned and saw Katherine yards away among trees and beyond two full junk skips. They stared at each other for a long silent moment. It looked real, physical, flesh and bone covered in tattered soiled ragged robes this damaged worn and decayed woman but stood there among the things of the world. She blinked and Katherine was gone. Her phone buzzed and she stumbled back before answering.

'Jackson wait, I've just gone out but not for long. I'll be okay. I won't be too long. I do think my friends are in some way right about something but confused and I need to meet them briefly about something connected to our college friend Katherine who died before we graduated.'

'Katherine from your college days?'

'Yes. What Jen said earlier, I need to speak to them. I need it cleared up. Listen, I'll be back. I don't want to be out, but I'll only be a short while. Let me be. I will call you soon.'

'I'll come meet you, I can't have you out there alone.'

'I won't be.'

'Do you know where they are?'

'Not exactly, sort of?'

'So, I should be with you until then. There is something really fucking dangerous out and around don't play it down.'

'I'll call you soon.'

'Mae no...'

'Yes, I'll get them home and get it cleared up. Speak soon' she told him.

The low grunting sound drifted around her, under and somehow through her. She looked all around but could not see anyone. She walked on quickly as she called up Jen on her phone.

'Hey, I'm not from where you two are. At her old home, right?'

'Oh Mae. We've been there. Somehow, we remember or...we were led.'

'You're there now?'

'No, we were inside but there's something in some letters, like diary letters she wrote I've taken. We'll look you're okay. Where are you?'

'Just off the bus next to the college. Just passed it. Do I go to her house to meet you?'

'Issy says at the Ox and Deer pub. We'll meet you there and go to the river together, okay?'

'Right, I'll be maybe twenty minutes, see you there.'

A half hour later they sat heads bowed and quiet as they saw Mae enter the pub and come to join them at the table in the back corner as they gave pained sombre smiles and a wave.

'Really, sorry to hear about events Jen' Issy said with arm around her. Mae poured more wine for each of their glasses.

'It's really terrible. What reason? Police spoken to you about it? Don't think there'll be more. Like it seemed accidental really, I think' she said, offering reassurance.

'They seem to think that too. They'll investigate but I saw enough to make it probably seem that way. Just accidentally tragic'

'But you're not entirely sure?'

'There are some things about what we were doing where we were that make it seem like there was other things around us that were dangerous, less familiar or rational things.'

'That small town area is kind of desperate, backwards and has that atmosphere. Just how it feels.'

'You think it is Mae?' Issy countered.

'I'm just saying it's not the most up market and safest place but let's keep optimistic and careful.'

Issy and Jen stopped together.

'Wait, let me say something' Jen said.

Jen walked out before Mae.

'These letters, they're from Katherine. Honestly, you recognise the handwriting, don't you? I can't believe it but look at them. She guided us to the house and out here' Issy exclaimed. Mae did not feel comfortable with the news but was intrigued.

'Okay so...anything there that might be helpful to us while she is back there somewhere?' she said.

Issy continued to quickly read over the pages she held before them. 'Hard to tell...shit, you know, I can see she wasn't happy from this.

There were things knocking her down, she seems to have had some bad ideas of things she might have done to others or herself. God, we didn't help you, did we? We really didn't help her...'

'Alright but what's there that helps us how what to do for her. I mean, if we can't it's just the river witch killer doing whatever she wants with no end to any of it. Keep reading'

'That's all a lie, that's Ron and Lily and... it's a not the real truth' Jen argued.

'How are you sure of that?'

'We've been in her family house. We know the place; we saw our own rooms. You would too. The three of us are linked to it and her' Issy added.

Mae looked back with disbelief. She looked to Issy 'You're going to work tomorrow considering what we're experiencing?'

'I know it sounds a bad idea, but I can't...I'd rather be with the people I work with, finish my work, and possibly protect them too. We've got a project to finish with the young people. Plus, hasn't Katherine changed? Now we've been to her home, there's a difference isn't there?'

Jen added 'We can hope so. She seems more awake.'

'You've both seen her now?' Mae asked as she looked at each of them.

'I haven't. Not properly yet. Or I don't think so. I haven't spoken to her' Issy told her.

'We've been in her old family home in town. We finally remembered how to get there.'

'Yeah, I could not think of the exact street name, I was thinking about that.'

'She let us go, led us there you see.'

'And you went there with her?'

'No, she wasn't there. She was.... somewhere else' Issy said.

'So, what did you see in there? You weren't being too clear on the phone before.'

Mae said.

'Remember Katherine used to talk of big monsters, fantasy beast creatures, folklore like giant dog like horses, birds like planes and more.'

''Coz she was an artist. Was always dreaming. Wish I could think of crazy wild things like that, escape to some land of fantasy things even for a short while when the world is too much...'

'Dogs like huge horses, yeah. Wild'

Jen and Issy looked at each other before Jen spoke 'Her paintings of the fantasy creatures and people, journals with stories about them. It just, now it means more.'

'What do they mean?'

'It's hard to say.'

'We experienced something in there. We understood something about us and her and other things...'

'You mean about her mental health, her illness?'

'Mae, it's just not like that.'

'People we know have died since she returned. She either was involved or let it happen and knew it would happen. You want to protect her?'

'She's gone with Ron and Lily now so...'

Issy look at both with an urgency in her eyes 'When do we go, follow her to the other place? She could be there already.'

Jen 'No, she's gone but she'll tell us when.'

'So, we just continue on as normal?'

'And we can't go get her?'

'Knowing what we know about Jackson now-Ron and Lily out and around in town…no we wait. She can use us; she will collect us.'

'Be very careful. I do think she's sick. Don't get her more worried about weird shit. We're supporting each other know she'll get past this. We all will. Sorry, I have to go' Mae said.

'You're not going to come with us to this place where's she's been?'

'I think she doesn't know herself, doesn't know right from wrong. She is special and I love her but…'

Issy shook her head 'I think we should pay attention to what Jen's saying. She's no idiot, she doesn't say things for attention. Yes, bad things have happened but there's more to it than just her being ill. The house, the old poems and paintings suggest deeper things beyond her.'

'She's been on you as well. Look, we pissed her off.' Mae countered 'We let her down and she has remembered that. They can probably help her more than us. She's been watching and taken people around all three of us. It's about our college time and us. We must have done something stupid there. Look, I'll see you at the weekend or call.'

'You should. Okay, the weekend'

'I don't feel good being there. I will, I'll meet you. It's just troubling me. I'm with Jackson. So, don't worry about me.'

Mae stood and left them, a kiss to each on the cheek and a brief hug as she went.

'She won't listen.'

'I can understand, I mean me and her have had some fucking tra uma…'

'But she needs to be with us, go help Katherine. Why won't she listen to us?'

'I suppose it hit her hard. She's more fragile, the way she is.'

Issy looked up at all the people sat and stood around the pub who talked and laughed among themselves unaware of their troubles.

'So...is Katherine a witch?'

'What?'

'Katherine is some kind of witch, isn't she?'

'I don't know. Maybe or something else like...some angelic creatu re...I don't know.'

'Not that witches should be scary, I mean an empowered, liberated, independent woman utilising the energy of the earth around us and magic or whatever. That part is quite cool though' Issy said.

'We want to leave this city, this place we thought we knew.'

'We can. We probably should now. It might be confined to here; we might be able to escape it.'

'We've seen we can affect -her-but I don't think we'll outrun it. We have to do what she wants from us. She's only been showing us what she can do. We could have been up in those trees, but we were left.'

'Right and not if we do what is required. It's one of those old things, 'spirits can't rest' thing.'

Jen looked around and stood, pulled on her jacket.

'Shall we go walk out to the riverside then?'

They walked out down the narrow side streets, pulled their jackets tight against the cold breeze as the sounds of the river grew clearer. The long view of the tall tangled old trees filled their sights as they approached. Out way down on the left they saw the Briggar stone as it appeared to gravitate toward them.

'There it is. That rugged old stone. She wrote about it, spoke about it' Issy said as they walked out.

'She did, yes' Jen replied.

Some time passed as they moved right up beside it, stepped around it with the river in motion behind them.

'What is special about it? What is the real significance to this old thing?' Jen wondered.

'Could be Pagan worship, fertility thing, a sacrifice point to other gods or...just a blood great stone.'

They waited for over twenty minutes, but Katherine made no appearance. Something like barking snapped out from around them not too far away.

Jen breathed out and sighed 'Let's get going. I think we'll probably see her in town. Or maybe we can distract her parents.'

'Right, yeah that's an idea' Issy agreed, and they started back toward the closed in streets of town.

'Wait, Issy...wait' the faint voice whispered as they walked. Issy turned back but saw no one near out on the field around them.

C hapter Twenty-Five

In the woods Ron stood with the shredded and mutilated body of Billy at his feet as he looked up at the hole into another place between the reality around him. It pulsed and wavered and through it he could hear Lily in the kitchen within Briggar. He took up the dead body and pulled it into the hole with both hands, gruff grunting and groans as he did so. Lily turned and looked out to the lower hallway inside Briggar where Ron appeared as the dimension hole shrank up and closed to nothing silently.

'Hey, I needed you to keep the hole open for me. Could have been stood in the woods with this one for hours by myself' he called over.

'Oh, I'm sorry Ron. Wanted to keep going with cooking up the stew and dishes in here. I know your appetite' she replied with a sweet smile.

'Fine. I'll take it through to the others, skin it down and prepare it. Listen out for those two anytime' he told her.

A short while later Katherine stepped out of her room and met with Lily in the kitchen as the stew steamed and boiled quietly on the hob and Lily sat with a cup of herbal tea as she looked through an old book of creation myths and faith scriptures.

Lily stirred the soup on the hobs she had been cooking for over an hour 'They must do it over again, Ron wants to be him, to do what Jackson did only better.'

Katherine heard her and scoffed 'Do you want that?'

'I don't think I do.'

'Let them continue. Let them go right ahead. My sisters know me now like they did. They are coming home to us.'

Lily tested the soup. Not quite right. She quickly tapped in a heap of turmeric and thyme.

'So, a meal is cooking away there?' Katherine said.

Lily offered a delicate warm smile 'Come, sit with me. Would you like a tea?'

'Right, yes'

Lily walked to the kitchen top and poured out a cup and returned to the table to sit opposite her.

'I'm sorry I left. I had to get back down to town. I did tell you. I'm not finished down there.'

'Neither are we. He's making up for lost time. Ron might not show it, but we did appreciate that you stayed here with us when Jackson made a human life for himself down there.'

'Did I have any choice? Sorry I don't mean it like that.'

'I know. We can only try to begin to understand what it must feel like for you and Jackson.'

'Even so, he had done the wrong thing. He won't easily recognise that.'

Lily stood and went to check on the stew as it simmered on the oven hops in the two large rattling pans. The smell was unbelievably satisfying and much like a Sunday roast Katherine now knew but wished she did not.

'Your friends can't go on, not after this.'

'Did you have to take the ones they knew?'

Lily simply stirred the stew around, added some torn pieces of fennel and coriander.

'Do they understand yet?'

'I think so. Some reluctance but...'

'Of course.'

Lily tasted the stew, licked the large ladle with a nod.

'Another hour or more I'd think' she said.

'I look forward to it' Katherine told her and walked back to her room. After a moment of gazing out of her window at the town she quietly stepped out to the hall and down the stairs to the door. She came out of the Briggar stone, Pete, and Samantha, Jackson's stone worshippers were approaching to pray there. They were shocked as she materialised through the stone casually. They fell to their knees, mouths open in awe and surprise, heads bowed.

'Hello again. You waiting for Jackson?' she said.

'We came to pray to the stone and to God' Pete uttered.

'Right, of course you did. I understand. It is not what you think' she told them.

Samantha stood 'Are you...a witch?'

Katherine let out a quiet laugh.

'He would like that but no. No more than he is' she replied.

'What is inside?' Pete asked, his head still bowed low.

'A home, a refuge' Katherine told him.

'Is God there, inside it or through it?' Samantha asked.

'Not yet, or if She is...she waits for the right time to intervene.'

'We've seen miracles' Pete told her.

'Not the kind the Lord makes, only imitations, tributes' Katherine replied.

'Then, you're wicked devils' Samantha stated 'Pete, move away. This is wrong, we've been wrong, tricked and fooled here' She tugged him to stand and move away with her, but he remained on his knees, his hand on the stone.

'Samantha, we're not devils we are...we're confused I'll give you that, we're angry, possibly abandoned or forgotten. Keep Her in your heart.'

'Curse you, to Hell with both of you' Samantha spat, and she walked away, tugged at the arm of Pete to follow her. He looked up at Katherine in wonder as he stood and was pulled away from her and the stone.

Jackson watched Mae as she stood in the kitchen of his house and put together the ingredients for a home-made soup beside the blender. This was his woman, the beautiful human woman he had decided would be his current companion and her mind had been tainted. He could not let her thoughts stray too far.

'She is a killer, your friend Katherine' he told her in a gentle tone 'It sounds unbelievable I know, and I didn't want to tell you like this, but it is true, and she needs professional help. Her parents hide her out of town, they protect her. Stay with me, keep away from her. She doesn't care about you or the others, she doesn't think like any of us. She is a threat to all of us.'

Mae could not easily decide. She didn't like being told what to do or how to think, even from Jackson her lover but her thoughts were clouded with the words of her friends, the scepticism and questions unanswered.

'Keep me safe, I trust you' she told him, and they kissed.

The bedroom was still as Jackson and Mae sat on the bed together naked. They breathed heavy, their sex set their blood rushing within them. He moved toward her as she sat legs apart, but she came up and spread his arms and turned away to face the wall.

'The other thing, I know you need to do it' she said quietly.

He held her arms gently and the long tendrils slithered out of his limbs and pierced her skin. They began to suck and feed on her energy with a steady pulse. She fell into a sleep. It lasted a few moments until he fell back, and the tendrils came away. He sat back and coughed, spat on the floor, heaved, and threw up bile to the floor with a look of shame and rage. He stood and punched the wall twice, his knuckles bled and split before he stormed away from the room. Mae privately did start to wonder about Jackson's life, when he came to town, why, his job and more, she was noticing some problems, things which did not make sense.

Once Jackson left her alone, she waited a while until she walked out alone to visit the Briggar stone on riverside. She knew Katherine had tried to tell her something about it, that there was some serious connected between her and it, but it was not obvious. Perhaps if she did meet Ron and Lily, they could tell her what they knew about it, if they would speak the truth. She was unsure where she would really hear that now. The barking came loud, each bark like a screamed word, a declaration. It felt wrong, a danger to avoid and so she rushed away, stumbled as she heard the call, the barking calls for Katherine. She fell into mud and brambles. As she looked up, she saw him. A man with a tall and stretched body with horse legs and dog torso. The face was someone familiar. The bark snapped out-

'Katherine!'

She got to her feet and ran through trees and dirt trails until she came back to the street where the house of Jackson stood. She fumbled

with her keys, fell inside behind the door, locked it, and fell to the floor.

In the night Jen stepped out into the back alley. She floated up arms stretched out, stopped near fifteen feet from the ground and floated into town over quiet streets just below clouds as bats and owls fluttered nearby. She was only half conscious of what she was doing. She enjoyed what she believed at first to be a very pleasant dream. She came to stop in the branches of an old tall tree which overlooked the high street. She took in homeless people in the doorways and corners of shop fronts below, foxes roamed for leftover takeaway scraps and the rippled joints of where the town had been folded and rearranged by Katherine recently.

Issy Sleepwalked out through the open flat backdoor naked into the back alley. She fell to her knees, stretched, and groaned as a changed came over her. Her arms snapped and took longer form, her legs loosened and moved inward. Her face took on an animal snout and fangs and eventually she appeared to resemble shocking large cat, her body coated in thick fur, hands and feet contained sharp claws where nails had been. She bounded out into town.

Jen fell down a moment later from her tree and flew back to the alley and stepped back inside her flat below. Soon she lay her head down in bed and slept until dawn. Neither saw each other in the night as they moved through the town in other forms.

Jackson approached the river, came toward Briggars Stone. He stepped close and around it. The light moved, the sight of it moved, folded the town behind him away and further out of his vision. The ground shook under him. He stood and faced the town as he blinked his eyes. He spun around.

'Hey Ron! Lily! Let me inside, come on now' he yelled at the stone. He smacked his palms against it, cursed and stepped back from it. The door opened inward, and he stepped in to meet them in his old familiar home. He sat at the table in the lounge of Briggars House. He carved into a skull as he waited and heard the dogs at the entrance down below, the barking and whimpering groans before footsteps. Ron and Lily came up and through into the room to meet him.

'Have you seen her?'

'She's down there, we know it.'

'I know it. Get back there and bring her home. Every hour, every day risks our home here, what I have and what you have and our lives as we know them. She should not have left us again at all.'

They left him to chew and suck on his stewed meat broth as they cleaned up in the kitchen together.

Lily spoke quietly first 'This could be too much, Ron, too much, too far. We're not Jackson or Katherine.'

'That's a good thing' Ron replied 'We saw them do all this, we stood back and watched their mistakes for generations. We know what to do better and how.'

'But one, 1608. He really was a sick fallen bastard with that, he lost control. We stopped him. What if we...'

'He'll be around. It's him and us. Three of us to put down new lore in this town, new fear, and superstition, our own this time.'

'Who were saints or sinners this time? Who were the martyrs and heathens? The suffering would show them. That bastard never appreciated what he had been blessed with when they had fallen.'

She nodded in agreement as they rejoined Jackson in the lounge.

'Look I must go; I have clients and meets to attend' he told them.

'Of course, such a life you leave' Ron scoffed.

Deep down within Briggar Ron sat among the display of body parts, blood splashed all over his legs and arms as he moved the pieces with anxious confusion.

'What do they tell us? Where's the life, that bastard soul always hides. Every one of them has what's needed inside, more than what we could hope for...' he muttered.

Lily shook her head 'Leave it, clean yourself. You're tired and they are doing what they've been allowed. That's all' she countered.

'But they lose sight. The gift, the temple and their duty and they go into town and forget it all.'

'She is right. I hear it. Too long we've listened to him, she has found her path once more.'

Jackson eyed her with sudden contempt and a simmering anger 'No. No, no...' he growled and quickly slammed down his fist on the table, eyes shut 'Father...Ron has helped you. You and Ron here'

'Oh, yes. Sorry. Ron and I have been cooking the meal. But we are a family Jackson, it can be comforting sometimes remember especially with how things are right now.'

'I know' he quickly added 'I understand it is me, my fault. He is watching, he may hear and see our mistakes easily enough. We don't wish to anger Him...' he remined them.

'Eat up the meal and enjoy, please. We're a good family. We talk and enjoy our company together at mealtimes. Discuss our days and keep a good house in order' he told them and watched them pick up the spoons.

'Do we, I don't think so. You might want that but it's not what happens' Ron muttered.

Jackson slapped his right hand flat against the table 'We've been away' he replied quietly.

'Yes, because things weren't right here.'

He stood and knocked his bowl off the table across the floor, the contents slopped out. Ron shook his head, Lily murmured nervously.

Lily stood and rushed out of the main room. Loud and pained howls were heard moments later. Ron stood and stepped to Jackson.

'Look what you've done. She's upset now. You don't think son, you need to think like...like a son and a man.'

'No, no father I don't. Sorry father'

Ron shook his head and walked away to find Lily down the narrow side corridor.

Katherine sipped her wine, looked up at Jackson.

'It never works. All the pretending and trying to be like others in here where it doesn't matter.'

'It matters to me, and it matters to Him, you know that. You going there alone when it wasn't right did not do us any good. You're lucky...'

'Am I? Why is that?' she asked 'You left us here. Me and them. You got your break, your chance. Mine wasn't done with.'

'He thinks otherwise. You know that. I told all of you. You heard it anyway.'

'We can't be sure, we can't.'

'If you go back, the hurt, the pain will be even greater, the response you'll receive.'

'I'm back here, aren't I?' she replied and finished her glass of wine. He sat and did the same before he stood and left the room.

She looked out of the window shortly after and saw him outside below with Ron as they appeared to be searching for Lily. She saw Ron collapse down and mutated to his dog form.

She went to her room and prepared herself.

PART 3 ISSY'S ENCOUNTER

Chapter Thirty

Both Jen and Issy had restless night of disturbed sleep. Fitful and tormenting nightmares rattled their subconscious minds through until dawn. They stumbled half-awake to the kitchen where Issy put together some toast, cereal with coffee and orange juice to wash it down.

Jen turned to face her as she held up a slice of burnt toast and sipped her black coffee 'So Jackson's in danger too as he's trying to protect Mae? But Katherine won't hurt either of them, will she? Will she?' Jen asked.

'We don't know that. The dogs, they talk to her, that's what she told us.'

'Yeah, and how insane does that sound?'

'As mad as her returning from the dead and acting like some phantom ghost in the shadows for the last week.'

'She needs time. She's holding things back, there's been trauma she can't easily speak about it even to us. She wants to, but it's not coming soon enough. We need to help her.'

'Until then death near you and near Mae, and what next...we could talk to her parents more, see what they suggest. I mean, they must have the best idea of what to do. Don't they understand her more than us?'

'No, no way. We know her relationship with them was kind of fucked in some ways even if we don't know the real ins and outs of it, it's pretty damn obvious. We can't just hand her over. There's some family abuse thing going on from them.'

'Really?'

'In some way, don't know how but yes. Come on, we know it. We do'

'Are we her friends or not?'

'She's different now, not the same as before, she's secretive and...'

'We have to hang in there, wait for her to be clear about it all. Until then just stall her parents and wait, listen to her when she is around. We tell them nothing. Or just not yet. Not until she's okay with that, if at all. Agreed?'

'Does she even know what she wants?'

'It's hard to tell I know but we'll help her with it, won't we?'

'Yes. But if she is really ill, mentally and an actual real danger to herself and maybe us...'

'Don't speak like Mae as well, please. We can't think that way. It's trauma, family shit, whatever and we will understand and help.'

Jen looked away 'What if she isn't innocent like we want her to be? Then what? People do things and don't realise sometimes, very bad things and have like mental block.'

'We'll get to know what the real truth of it is. We'll help'

Katherine had yet to make an appearance and Issy did still want to go to her shift at the youth community job if only to protect the teens and her fellow staff. Perhaps they would be safer without her but from what had happened to Mae and Jen at their jobs it seemed like the best thing to do was to go and stick with them. Jen decided to go to her own flat and continue to look over the collection of tattered poems and note pages they had retrieved from the house. With a couple of hours until her work shift, it was late morning and Issy was returning from the shops with groceries in her large bag when she saw Lily stood near her front doorstep. She almost wanted to grab hold of her, shake the life from her, scream and yell all the profanities she could think of right into her pale gloom filled face. Why the hell had She and Ron taken their good friend three years ago? Why did they let everyone think they had all died? Could she explain any of that in any kind of satisfactory way at all she wondered. Could Lily spit out whatever disgusting or improbably reasons for it all?

'Morning Issy dear. Getting a few things stocked up, are we?' Lily said with a pleasant smile, sun bleached the regret from her face.

'Yes, sorry I'm not on the trail of Katherine. But I guess you think I'm lying when I say I don't know where she is' Issy replied as she put a hand in her pocket to find her door keys.

'Are you?'

'Yes. Look, I have to put these things inside. Excuse me now' Issy said as she turned the key and opened the door inward.

'Can we talk, have a nice cup tea maybe?' Lily suggested. Issy looked and saw a kind of nervous desperation in the eyes. She nodded and let Lily follow her inside. She had the feeling that Katherine was not too far away and did not think she could refuse or stop Lily anyway. They stood in the kitchen, boiled the kettle, two teas on the kitchen top. Once Issy put away her groceries, they sat and looked at each other.

'Why did you all go?' Issy asked as she stirred her tea took a sip.

'Lily was looking down at the tabletop when she spoke. 'It was the time for it. We had lived in town long enough. Not entirely my idea, can't say I fully agreed but it was decided. We were happy elsewhere,'

Lily told her as she took a sip of tea, glanced around the kitchen and out of the window to town. It seemed as if she expected to see someone of something specific out there.

'You're content here, are you?' she asked Issy, who then straightened and tilted her head.

'This is how it must be right now. We can't all easily have a plush middle-class lifestyle, big, detached house, two cars in the drive and holidays in the Caribbean every few months. Maybe I don't even want or need most of that. Strange right?' Issy responded with a cynical frown.

'Sorry if I offended, not my intention. It just seems what most people want.'

'Doesn't mean it is the way to be. Temptation, right? Take that apple from the snake and all that' Issy suggested 'No, don't worry. I work with disadvantaged and the neglected on a daily basis, see people living with hardly a thing and in the most unbelievable conditions sometimes, living in fear of eviction, unemployment, hoping to have enough for food for the next day. I appreciate the basics that many take for granted far too often. So, you want to talk about Katherine? I don't have too long before I have to get out to work.'

'Yes, I see. That is very admirable. Katherine, yes. Let's get to her. She is very precious to me.

'Same here'

'She is so special-but dangerous. But you see, so am I. I don't wish to be, really, I do not.'

'Is that right? Where is your dog, with Ron? Are they around town looking for her?'

'That's right. Issy, are you scared?'

'Of your dog?'

'There are two of them. You know Katherine is more than just a confused young woman. Am I right?'

Issy drank up her tea and finished it quickly. 'We've been to your old house. We've seen enough. I know she is dangerous; I know things were hidden, changed and more. Your dogs are loyal but confused, aren't they?'

Lily began to sniff; a tear came down her right cheek from her eye. She gently rubbed it away, coughed quietly.

'We wanted to be a real part of the history of this town, this was our time you, see? How she has been, that was not our doing' Lily told her.

'No?'

'We were all to stay in the Briggar stone. He set the terms, always has. We're from him. He set the conditions, the terms of everything.

'Who is he?'

'Jackson, he is with your friend Mae. She is from Katherine also. You know that, yes?'

Issy clenched the mug in her hand, threw in down and they heard it shatter across the kitchen floor.

Lily gave a slight thin smile. 'We though, let her out. You can thank us, you can thank me,'

'Thank you so much Lily. Now I know, now I question my life, my decisions, my choices, my fucking free will...oh thank you so very much.'

'He's with Mae. He's had no idea about any of this, what Ron and I are doing, that I am talking with you now.'

Issy looked at her 'I do remember you; she does remember the past. She doesn't forget any of it now. She just needed our help.'

'Yes, I understand' Lily replied 'I know she needs all three of you but Ron well, he is confused and can't hold him back, not now. So, when you see her, be careful.'

'You too'

Lily stood and stumbled, fell across over onto the front door. Her arm reached up, hair covered, clawed talon fingers etched into the wall beside. Her back had hunched up muscular, her neck coated in quick grown fur, she stared back with canine wild eyes and jagged teeth, tongue snapped out around her cheek.

Lily 'My Rondalt is angry and very bitter. Feels we've missed out on a lot, wants his time and his own mark felt and remembered in this town. I know you protect Katherine; I understand that. That is how it would always be. Does it hurt though?'

'It...it's necessary.'

'But wasn't expected, was it? You've got your own life here, you're a good person, doing such selfless and kind things. I can offer more time, take her back in, like we've done before.'

Issy looked around her, at her flat. While she was not where she wanted or hope to be in life, she was at least proud of trying to live a righteous way how she could.

'I'll see you in town. I must get to work now' she replied.

'I...don't want...to harm you. You too can be this, you can be with me, be something different, free, and feared. Jen, Mae...I'll be with him' she slurred as she swung open the front door and bounded out into town and out of sight. Issy stood, her heart rattled, her hands trembled against the door, she shook as she clutched her shoulder bag and checked the time. Footsteps approached as Derek knocked at the front door, entered with his familiar warm smile.

'You look pale as a junkie, you alright pet?' he said as he dropped his satchel on the desk in the corner.

'Yeah. I'm fine. You?' she replied with a distance expression.

Mae stood by the window in the large front lounge of Jackson's house. She looked out to town where she thought she should be at that moment, with Jen and Issy.

'My friends have been messaging me. You know I said one of them, her work employee was found dead' Mae said.

'Oh right, bloody horrible, I mean sad of course. Are they checking on you?'

'The other one Issy, she's had the same thing.'

'One of her people at work gone like that?'

'Yes, pretty much. A real mess, out near the big park. She was with young people she works with and others.'

'God. What are the chances. You'll be okay. Don't go getting all paranoid. These things can be just horrible coincidences even deaths'

Jackson told her 'This is my house. It has the brand new, hugely expensive alarm system and cameras on front and back doors. We're safer here than anywhere. I mean, tell your friends to come on over here if you want but it seems they're very happy to go doing something else in the city.'

'They're looking into something together, might be related to the events.'

'Right. They'll call if they need advice or help. You could even track them over google, couldn't you? But let's stay here. Police would say the same' he suggested. He presented his familiar sympathetic and endearing handsome face. How often did she see that expression when she was telling him about her problems and dilemmas in life? How real and genuine was it toward her she wondered?

Jen phoned Mae as she walked away from the house with Issy beside her.

'Mae. Get with us. Katherine is around but at a distance for some reason. showing us something, leading us to a path or some truth to follow'

'What, I don't understand any of that.'

'It would make sense if you were with us here.'

'I'm with Jackson, at his house. Full expensive security. You should be inside somewhere. Police will look into all of it. You're not helping yourselves walking around doing weird shit.'

'We're figuring it out. It is weird but she is around us. Something important is happening. You wouldn't say that if you have seen how we're putting things together. You're seen her around you right?'

There was silent moment.

'Exactly. Be with us to be safe until it is sorted otherwise, he can't protect you with all the security invented. Nothing can except this, what we're doing right here.'

'Jen, what are you doing?'

'It is Katherine. It's her and more.'

'Listen to what you're saying. Stop it. It was not our fault. If you're not careful we'll end up like her'

'Not like how she is, that's for sure. I'll call back soon.'

'Jen don't...'

The line cut off.

'Shit' Mae said and slammed her fist on the wall beside her. A gleaming white face met her sight across the room. She cried and stumbled back; Jackson came into the room.

'You, okay? Come get a drink, even hot chocolate if you must hon' he suggested, arms out to her.

She hesitated.

'Yes, let me just freshen up in the bathroom. I'll meet you down in the kitchen soon' she told him.

'I'll wait for you there' he replied.

She walked alone downstairs, her thoughts consumed with who this deadly person was who was killing and stalking her and her friends. What had she ever done to anyone to deserve anything so horrible? She did not believe that she in any way deserved this kind of trauma or fear. Issy and Jen may have got in the way of something with her work and their restless curiosity which she knew well enough. That was not her. She designed clothes, she only wanted to be what she could be with that. There it was, the haggard female figure of Katherine along past their car, beyond the neat lawn and tall topiary.

'Why us, why here?' Mae asked quietly.

The other two did not have Jackson, they were single and paranoid, no one person in their lives who would do anything to protect them from any kind of danger, even something as unexplainable as this. She did see the woman roman out, the cryptic yet savage expression in her withered face. She feared what she might do to her, though it seemed she had let all three of the friends be free so far only to witness deaths and experience continual terrors ever since. For how long would it continue? How would it come to an end, how could it? She remembered what Jen and Issy had tried to explain to her. They seemed to believe they were onto something which could help stop this horrific woman. Could they be correct in their findings? Katherine, she thought. Their old college friend. The death at the time had not affected them too much as they enjoyed the final parties and pub crawls, the funeral a brief afternoon of sobering up until the next session together. It had been such extreme bad taste to suggest this was in some way connected to her. What were they thinking? There was a person killing around them, tormenting them without clear reason, not their neglected quiet friend. They were obviously grieving over a year later; most likely a combined hysterical fusion of regret or malaise affected their perception at the worse time. But then what they had been saying- a trail, the college, what they had each witnessed...its was specific, definite and it did all lead to Katherine she came to see. That really was true, she came to realise. It may not make entire sense; she may not even want to let her accept how any of it could be true, but it seemed that way. She flipped out her smartphone, dialled.

'Hey Issy, yes...listen I'm going to come meet you two. I see that it makes sense' she told her friend.

'Well great, be careful, like really fucking careful. We're not far from her home actually.'

'Who's home?'

'Katherine of course'

'Right'

'Remember where it was? It was hidden from us all this time. She has opened up the streets, unbuckled it all. Out behind the swimming pool and alongside the river. We went to her place sometimes in college days. Even that house party where we got Kyle together with Gary. God, we made a horrendous mess that time.'

'So, say around twenty or thirty minutes.'

Mae smiled in agreement 'I'll get a bus hopefully and a few minutes after I should find you. Speak soon'

Chapter Twenty-Six

Katherine stood and gazed out of the window down upon the town below them, over the fields beyond the rows of trees and rooftops. Right then streets had been changed, stretched as Ron and Lily had tricked and tormented, confused and killed people her closest friends knew and cared for sincerely. She had taken them to their fate, she knew it but for the most part her recollections her hidden behind a fog in her head, but it had begun to quickly dissipate and clear. She spoke while to looked out.

'I've seen prophets, miracles, real righteous miracles we should remember. You should know…you are imps, you are perverse.'

Ron gasped out 'You think I've done wrong, where is he?'

'He's busy, he looks after us' Lily remarked.

Ron shook his head and spat over the floor 'Bullshit. He left as well, wanted to be there in town just like us. Left us starving like…'

'Like dogs'

'Yes,' Katherine agreed 'If I come back, I'll bring him and we'll be how we should be, you can be what you want to be, not what is needed.'

'But is that your decision?'

'It can be,'

They looked at each other and then back at her.

Katherine blocked Jackson out of Briggar while they ate together, discussed the state of things. She left to find Jen and Issy, Mae; bring them to Briggar but Ron and Lily go out after, knowing Jackson thinks they are still searching for her. He soon realised she had been back, and they were not obeying him.

Before Katherine left Briggar again-cleaned the house with Lily, checked the holy sacraments of the temple within.

'There's been death around my friends down in town. Jackson, he is not right out there, we must bring him back. I understand what you're doing, why you feel the need to take these lives. You are not us; I know that. He and I know it. He's been pretending he is so human, stable but....he should not have left just as much as I.'

'We know. We did see some of it when we went out looking for you. A real shame'

'You have both been alright without us, you have been how you should haven't you?'

'No. Honestly, no we need the both of you, you know that.'

'But you came from...'

'Both of you'

Ron stepped in the doorway,

'Like old times, locals think witches and stone worship to hopefully see any glimmer of a helpful or forgiving God. Even in this professed independent secular land. Poor fools'

Katherine turned to see him 'You know, I just missed my friends, my sisters. I've brought it to them, the deaths and the fear...'

'No, it's part of their experience.'

'Will you help me get Jackson back inside this temple?'

'Why the hang up with being dogs this time?'

'He always had dogs outside Briggar through all the games, the troubles over the land and the town. They were loyal and dependable. He killed them, I saw that. I saw it.'

Ron stepped inside as he wiped his hands of fresh blood from the rooms below and he sat at the long table to drink some beer.

Lily placed a hand over that of Katherine 'We shouldn't let you leave now; we are all best inside here, really. We've been so worried, and we have missed you, you know that?'

'Us, your family. And isn't that more important?' Ron added.

'But that's pointless. Give up the parents and daughter thing.'

'Oh no, it is not. Think about all of what you and Jackson want, have hoped to see from Briggar House for so long' Lily suggested.

Ron nodded and let out a belch brough from his drinking 'We should be out more often. It is worth it. What you are, people don't believe in anymore. But us?' he looked at both 'We deserve to roam, to eat and be known, to be feared. We watched the town; we learn things and keep the people how they should be. Until the two of you are what you should be. They need us out there, isn't that, right?'

'I...I'm not so sure. More than anything we need those two back in here' Lily responded.

Katherine held up her hands 'So I'll get him. We can decide after that. I promise'

She walked to the stairs and left them to their deeds within.

'If only I had simply been a witch' Katherine sighed beside Briggar's stone, once outside. She left the stone to return to the town to gather Jen and Issy.

Jackson opened the front door of his house to see Ron look back with a smile as he looked down at him from above. He scuttled around the door frame and landed at the ground, his arms and legs displayed as some blend of insect and reptile.

'Good day to you my old friend. How's business in town?' he said with a chortle.

'Good enough. What's your problem Ron? I think your time is almost up. You've been to the old family house, is she there?'

Ron 'We...do you know where it is?' he said with quiet embarrassment.

Jackson widened his eyes as he viewed him 'I didn't need to know. It was your life, your family. So where is she?'

'We have seen her. We didn't want to scare her. You know how she can be. She's probably just keen to check in on people. She won't do any harm.'

'Will you?'

'Do you want us to?'

'Be careful. Be civil on your search.'

'The wandering is over with. She knows that. Listen, we've got the fog stored up in Briggar, plenty of it left. When you clouded her mind, you did good but didn't last. I wanted to make a strong batch but that's not my choice...'

'No, you can't. It would be easily done, we're not...it can't be done quickly. Damn it Ron, keep her back inside. Don't present yourself like this, it's bloody foolish. You're from me, you and Lily should be strong to do that without too much mess and disorder. Hear me?'

'Well, you've your business work to do, respected man about town. That is your focus. We will be expecting you for a meal soon enough' Ron said with a grin, and they parted ways.

Jackson clutched hold of his arm, pulled it close, his eyes wide with hunger. Ron pulled back; a lizard tongue snapped down on the hand quick, startled Jackson.

'You've your human life. You are a success; you don't need my old energy, do you?'

'I could give you more, I could offer you more time in town...'

'Oh, you could?'

'You know I could.'

Jackson reached out and tapped him on the shoulder. The tap became rhythmic, assuring. Ron watched him with cautious eyes, and it made sense. His move was not quick enough. The hand and arm of Jackson split open, fanned wide out like some dorsal fin. Ron offered a wide idiot grin as he simply watched the chest of Jackson tear open and he was pulled in with one forceful heft.

'Wait...hey, wait!' Ron stammered.

Jackson kept hold of him while Ron was submerged, halfway consumed. Inside the body of Jackson, Ron viewed the familiar gargantuan vista of that cosmic elsewhere, the thick deep skies of multi coloured landscapes uncharted for millennia. He felt the alteration and fever infect his own being. His perception and conscious awareness began to drift. In that moment Jackson wrenched Ron back out of him, dropped him down onto the grass, bile and indefinable energy aura smeared over his jeans and jacket.

'You took your time with that. Put us back in there and it's all on you. Back to doing it all yourself and that's so exhausting remember. Plus, it doesn't always work out, does it?'

'The country changed, the people came, science and technology. Had to be careful' Jackson argued.

'Right, yes. Always good to look upon those distant shores. Feel better?'

Jackson simply wiped his hands and straightened himself.

'We'll see you soon, you heavenly bastard. Come find me in town. Good luck with your human problems until then.' Ron said with a sneer. He could feel the energy taken from him. He cursed under his breath as he stumbled away into town down a narrow side street.

Lily roamed outside of the town, among the trees, scratched around, coughed as she mutated to human form with anguished pain. She walked to town to where she saw Ricky collect his sausage bacon wrap at his regular café before he made his way to his community service reparation work. She watched his scrolling on his smartphone, chucking at some TikTok videos as he waited for his food and hot drink.

She stepped inside beside him by the window.

'Good to have a decent sarnie like that to keep you going through the day I think' she commented 'Keeps a young man fit and strong, ready for anything,'

'Huh?' he managed before he glanced up and gave her a wide grin, taken back by her beauty 'Oh yeah, right. I love a good buttie, like. What you having?'

'Bacon and lettuce, the usual I think' she said as she presented one from the chiller to the person on the counter with a tap of her bank card as he picked up his own order.

'Haven't seen you here before, have I?' he said with a hope to sound smooth.

'I'm from town, just been away a while. You're off to a hard day's work now, are you?'

'Yeah, that's it. Sort of. Gotta do what you gotta do innit?' he said with a sly smirk. 'See you around I hope,'

'There's a change. I know Issy' she replied.

'Miss Issy? Shit, I mean...' he blurted out. 'How's that?'

They walked down the street together.

'She knows my daughter. They grew up together, went to the same college, the one up the road there, know the one?'

'Yeah, I know it. That's…interesting. So, what's miss like in real life?'

'Mostly the same but like all of us, hide a few secrets.'

'Like what?'

'Well Ricky, I'm not sure I can really say. Maybe you'll find out. There is a chance of that.'

'Does she have a record of something?'

'Ricky, do you know the history of this town, the old legends specific to us?'

'Not too much. Like what exactly?'

'The one about the dogs, really big dogs like people?'

'What? Nah' he responded with a laugh.

'How about the one about the people who were killed by angels, hung up and burnt to a crisp as an offering, said those townsfolk were witches but were sacrificed while innocent. They were bad people though.'

'Don't know that one. That really happened here, in this town?'

'It was forgotten but yes, a very long time ago. Barely recorded at all, it will be known more widely soon.'

'Oh right,' that was when he was suddenly less keen to talk to her and get on his way to work.

'In fact, the great, great ancestors of your miss Issy were involved in those murders believed to pacify an angry God and rid us of witchcraft. She knows about it. You can ask her.'

'Really?'

'Think she'll probably deny it but yes. So don't annoy her will you. She knows the witchcraft past.'

'Right. Shit, that's crazy. Do you want to meet again?'

'Keep getting those bacon and sausage sarnies and you'll find out.'

He responded with an over enthusiastic laugh. As car horns bleared beside them, he looked to the traffic build up. She was gone from sight when he turned back, her lips and lingered in his mind.

Chapter Twenty-Seven

The locals of the town moved through the day as casual and carefree as usual when Jackson came out and found Ron and Lily in the quite side north of town, beside the church and Mosque.

'Here to pray, are you?' he asked with a smile and raised eyebrows.

'It could be we don't to' Lily replied.

'But there's tradition and superstition. I must tell you that I think I will lend my experience and intuition to your activities if the offer is still open.'

Ron patted him on the shoulder 'Finally. It's my show, I'm proud of our efforts but...good, come help us.'

'But then...the matter of our dear Katherine'

'We know where and what she is doing. Right Lily?'

Lily looked back at him and attempted to erase any doubt which may have danced across her face.

'Plus, Mae is with you so she's out of luck, isn't she?'

Jackson gave a nod 'That is true. Lead the way, Ron. What are we up to now?'

They walked together, Ron confident but paranoid pf anyone seeing them.

'Another favourite, think back to the year 1608. Think I gave some advice on that one, didn't I?'

Jackson smiled with an expression of fond remembrance 'My broken angels burning for Hell...you may have Ron, you may have.'

They walked on as Ron led the way with a loud chuckle. They led him around to view the youth work building.

'Issy works here. There'll be a few fresh young ones to take later, should be memorable, very satisfying don't you think?'

'Could be. The ones so far, they've gone well have they, no problems?'

'What makes you say that?'

'Ron, I know you both have been watching, listening and admiring my work all this time but have not really have the experience...'

'You think we've been messing it up do you?'

'Mae has heard things from the other two I think.'

'That doesn't matter, doesn't mean anything.'

'Doesn't it? Where is Katherine now?'

'Oh, she's lost, confused, and tired. She'll be back at Briggar by now. Really, she will. Lily's going to cook for her like always. You know she cannot resist that.'

'You remember how you prefer it on the outside? And that's all it took, Lily's splendid culinary expertise? just remember the humans made to appear angelic with their sufferings. Wings for their troubles, for their sins, fires to welcome them down to the place they forget too often. Sights and sounds they'll know for an eternity' Jackson said.

'Assuming they are headed for that place. Surprising how many are...we can even lead them out to Briggar if you like...' Ron suggested.

'No, no need. Simply put on a show as best you can. One day left to get Katherine back inside Briggar, or you both go back inside me. I have a business to run like other of the more successful humans this town has to offer.'

He glared at Ron as he turned and marched away to the street where his business was situated. He made it halfway before he turned and made for the river instead. Minutes later under a cool pale grey sky he kneeled by the stone at the riverside, head bowed.

'Hear me Beniah, she is out. I thought I did not care but she is confused, going against the plan. Take her back in, give her what she needs. I will help this to happen, I will try my best. My dogs are out looking. I will act in the old ways if it is necessary, you have my promise. I will not enter until I have restored balance. In your name' he spoke quietly.

He looked around him, over his shoulder and stood, walked to town with the clouds over him beginning to sour and darken.

Chapter Twenty-Eight

As the afternoon continued Lily walked fast and found Annekia in a coffeeshop. She bought a drink quickly and sat in the booth next to her. With a smile she leaned over.

'Hello there. I think you know my friend Issy?'

'Hi, yes. I'm working for her. I...did something I shouldn't have and I'm making up for it with her. I know what I did was wrong, I was led on by others, not exactly real friends. I' not proud of it but learning to see things better and do things better.'

'She's helping you understand things in different ways?'

'You know her?'

'She is a friend, yes. She is helping you a lot you think?'

'I'm not a bad person. It was a mistake. She doesn't judge me, she's good like that. How do you know her?'

'I'm sorry, I didn't mean to suggest you're a bad person. I can see you seem kind at heart. Yes, she does look to bring the best out of young people, listens and shows a better path. You are seeing her soon?'

'Later today, for another session. It's been good. With someone else it might have been a real chore but she really nice and a decent adult to hung with. Even though it's her job to be with us.'

'Annekia, will you watch her, keep an eye on her. She's been a little stressed lately, overwhelmed recently. If you can tell her what good work she does and how the town needs people like her to stick around that would be so good of you.'

'Is she okay?'

'Yes, it will simply help for her to hear this right now, I think. I should be on my way. Nice to chat'

'Wait, my name, how...?'

Lily was gone as customers moved further inside the coffee shop. She walked down and around narrow back alleys of town to find Ron alone by the overgrown trees where the park opened out. They walked deep in together to the most secluded part deep at the back and transformed to their dog beast selves.

Ron jumped out within the trees of the woods howled, his body half dog with goat legs and Lily watched him from a distance, hesitant to transform.

'No miracle stone, fools...' he snarled.

'Look...at...us' Lily cried and jumped at Ron, they tore in at each other, wild and aggressive. Snarled at Issy.

'What, people...things?'

'Things Katherine knows about...not parents...' Lily looked at him.

'We are...no...we're...not them...not even devils' she wept as she bit into Ron who clawed at her, held onto her. They gripped each other, as they clawed and let their blood flow.

Katherine wandered in among the trees and found them.

'You're not dogs, stop it' she yelled at Ron and Lily as she looked on at their confused forms before her.

'You want us to be, and him. You need us to be' Ron argued.

'Sometimes but it's your choice. Not a command from him. It can be different.'

'You need us to be this and do this. So does he. It's 1608 and I'll do it right, those angels can burn without offerings. You do like adore them so.'

She shot furious eyes at him, released a slow breath.

'The chase is over, is it?' Katherine asked Ron.

'Feed us! Feed us, it's what you do!' Ron cried out.

'It's what he does. I have to stop. Stop wanting it. Get them yourself, play by the rules he made if you play at all, if you respect the past' she returned.

'But it's the way, please' Lily said.

'I'm out, you can be, should be. The order can change, it really can.'

'We shouldn't have released her' Lily said and looked across to Ron. They both slumped down to all fours and took on the full dog form as they headed to the riverside.

Katherine walked ahead of one, behind the other dog, unafraid but unsure of their intentions. She had no fear of them as they were, not of their size, their teeth or snarling or barking. The truth of Ron behind the fur and fangs, did make her shiver. His dog with that black stipe of fur down his face. She held it together, remained strong knowing she had reached her old friends and knew it was possible they would be with her at the right time soon and do what was needed. The Ron dog behind her barked out, snarled and she turned to look at it, the face of it almost at level with her chest.

'Oh, you desperate thing, put the fangs away, we're heading to the riverside, aren't we?' she said.

It looked at her, sniffed and all three of them continued, the barking done with.

The town behind was folded, bent out of regular sight, the per-spective shrunk down on the horizon. She noticed and had expected it. They could only do so much in their canine form so she believed she could return without much more effort than necessary and retain most of her own energy.

Only a few yards away from the riverside the tallest dog ahead of her leaned over where it stood, growled as if a mouth full of stones, and began to stretch out human words fell from within the jaws as they grew and buckled movement by movement as the legs stretched, became even longer, thicker, the hair receded, as the neck thickened and turned as the long tongue swirled and flicked between the fangs while it spoke.

'We...we're... tog...ether...again' it stammered as it mutated into a taller and more human form though. It finally became Ron as it stood naked. She stepped close, touched the elongated man-wolf face, the human arms with their claws and fur.

'So, kill me or lead me back inside. I hope the fire is warm and a good meal is waiting for us' she suggested.

Ron dog shook his head, snarled and the Lily dog behind her barked and they walked together on to the riverbank. They came to Briggar stone, and the daylight view snapped and shifted, the door in the stone opened inward and Katherine moved in, Ron and the Lily dog followed behind. Katherine tried to keep in mind the hours which passed as Jen and Issy were somewhere back in town making their own decisions.

They moved inside Briggar together quietly. Ron led the dog away down a side corridor as Katherine stepped forward up the row of steps and into the lounge up ahead. She walked to the wide window across the room, looked out over the town below them. It was a view only they could see from inside the building. No others knew of it or had ever looked down with that perspective for centuries. She turned and saw the fire was out, the house cold and dark. There were piles of rotten carcasses and bones forgotten scattered to the corners of the room.

'I knew this would happen. His old games, his old folklore forgotten out on the streets. To be expected I suppose. Couldn't you keep things in order?' she said aloud. She moved to sit at the table as Ron and Lily came into the room from opposite doorways of the lounge. They sat to either side of her, gave her satisfied smiles, held her hands on the table before them.

'Look at the disorder, the mess in here. Will it be cleaned away?' Katherine asked. She spoke as if they were the children and she the parent.

'Of course it will, you know it will' Ron quickly responded, touching his jaw as it slipped apart, the flesh only just reformed, the fangs visible, dog hair on his arms and hands shedding thick hair over clawed fingers on the table.

'We're sorry' Lily added.

'Don't think it will be my doing alone, don't think that' Katherine told them.

'We see you're upset. Jackson will feel the same, we know.'

'You want a meal tonight; you do have what is needed now don't you?' Katherine said.

They looked at each other and Ron replied 'We do. Hung and prepared, fresh, and ripe'

'Yes, thank you. You've spoilt us, you have' Lily said.

There were two bodies hung in the silent kitchen, a few flies starting to navigate around them. She unhooked them, using the chains at the side wall and with the selection of well sharpened utensils in the chambers began skinning and separating the limbs as could do well with her many decades of practice.

From behind her, Katherine came in to join her as the cutting and preparation began.

'You remember how we do this, yes?' Lily said as she cast down into the flesh with the razor-sharp gutting knife.

'Yes. Lily, I have to be back there in town, bring them here. I appreciate what you're doing. I see they would come down on you.'

Lily simply continued to slice and rip at the pieces needed for the stew, placed them in a heap in the tray.

'I scared Mae, but she is with Jackson. I mean, for the love of...' Katherine sighed.

'Yes, who'd have guessed. You gave your own better lives, gave them love and hope. What did Ron and I get?'

'I'm sorry. I could not remember, the poison he fed me...'

'We...I am sorry. You remember what I used to tell you of the other ones from other stones?'

'I think it is still there in my mind. Remind me'

Lily stopped her work and look around at her.

'The old books tell me of the others like us when the castles fell, the stairway came down from somewhere, we fell through,' Lily stated 'In hills across the land we waited, we haunted dreams, blessed, and witnessed, hunted in fields and forests for centuries. We influenced the people, the changes, the faith, the industries, the kings and queens, rebels, and seers. We exist under lands, some like us also wait, they pray, they change forms and fly and borrow and wait. Some are ill or angry like Jackson and Ron. We should be careful if we want to meet and reconnect with these others and to know truths. The old fables, parables and proverbs teach us to walk out strong, to transform, be proud and thankful. Never mind what Jackson and Ron say, they will understand, they must eventually let times change. Remember Katherine-sister Gullmesh and her days of vision bleeding, Nishal Mah and somewhere in Black country when he cast out demons on the hilltops before the councilmen and traders Silmah Mee as she rounded up the lost sheep and goats in their form and put the trolls in their place and was shot down from the skies as she tried to return home'

'It is returning to me now.'

'Silmah is dead, but Nishal and sister Gull Mesh may be waiting in stones elsewhere across the land like us here.'

'I know you believe that.'

'Don't you? Tell me you do.'

'I want to see you happy, see your hope as reality. I want that for you' Katherine answered.

'Then take yourself and find them.'

She sat and watched the Ron and Lily move about the house, moved furniture, spoke cryptic prayers, and chanted the ancient names they knew so well and had placed so much hope and faith in for all their years.

Katherine fed the dogs to keep them satisfied and distracted. She knew she felt necessarily tired and weak but needed to hold the folds of land and dimensions tight and locked outside in the day until she was gone.

Chapter Twenty-Nine

Lily appeared at the front entrance to the community centre as the teens were working and wasting time equally. She smiled over to Issy who noticed her instantly.

'You have seen my daughter? I know you. She knew you. Where is she?' she said.

'Oh hi, Katherine's mum, right? I'm Issy'

'Yes, hello Issy. We're searching for her. She is in town but lost, confused.'

'I knew it. She's not. I mean, she doesn't want to go back to where she has been.'

'She told you this, you've seen her?'

'Yes. She wanted to come back. You and her father, with respect, you shouldn't hold her back. She wants a life, her own life here and much more. She wanted to be an artist. You know that right? She still can be. She needs help and support; she wants her own space to do that.'

'Where did she go, where is she?'

'I don't know. She disappeared. I saw her yesterday. At first, I actually wasn't sure it was real, she seemed like a ghost or something.'

'You've no idea where she is now?' You haven't seen her yet?'

'Hard to say. Possibly. Think my friends already have. We're all good friends you see. If she is around, we'll stick by her' Issy told her. 'I don't think she wants to see either of you right now. Maybe give her space for a few days or so.'

'No, that's not the way' Lily spat out 'Good loyal friends are special, that is respectable. She is ill though. She will return to our new home, she must be with us, it is for the best.'

'Is it, we're not too sure. Look, I'm busy at work here, I'll phone you if Katherine tells me she agrees with you on that.'

Lily cursed quietly, tugged at her hair, tapped her dried lips, and moved her shoulders in a strange manner.

'Your name is Issy Portsheild, yes?'

'Lily, don't start your head game with me. You or Ron, I couldn't give a shit about the past, I live in the here and now.'

'You're here and now was shaped by your poor, tragic past, by others who meddled in it. Specifically, Katherine'

Issy stood and stared at her 'I have work to do. Good night' she turned away.

'Angels were in this town, real heavenly angels but they played with the lives of good families, tortured them, ruined their livelihoods. You know what Katherine has been up to all this time, why she must come back with us?'

'I know my friend; I trust her and will help her how I can.'

'She will not help you, or Mae or Jennifer. Far from it. After the fires and broken wings, you will be gone, I warn you now.'

'Good night, Lily. Leave or I'm calling the police right now. No bluff'

Lily stepped back as she continued to stare at her 'After fires and broken wings...' she repeated as she walked away to town, one last ice-cold glance.

The buzz of her smartphone took her attention and Issy answered it when she recognised the name.

'Hello, this is Issy Portshield. How can I help?' she stated.

'Hello Issy. This is Collin Grating of the department of council's budget, I spoke to you and your colleagues last week' he told her.

'Right, yes. Everything is going well with the discussions, is it?'

'I can tell you that, this is not official in writing yet but of the record we have decided to grant your team and council the amount requested for the new equipment and on top of that funding for new premises for future work. We were extremely impressed with the dedication and enthusiasm of your team and especially yourself. Congratulations. You will see this all in emails soon and we will have an official meet in the next couple of weeks.'

'That is such good news. Thank you so much, really. We will be so pleased to know we can look ahead to the ideas we put forward to keep doing our work in supporting the local young people.'

'That's great to hear. Speak soon. Goodbye'

She turned around with a satisfied yet still troubled smile over her face. The news was so good, but she knew to put it to the back of her mind for the next couple of days. She could not think about it while they were helping Katherine.

While she checked in the utility cupboards for extra paint and brushes Issy took a casual glance out of the window as the person behind the shop counter was quietly preparing the orders, frying up fish and sausages. The main thug guy outside on the roadside was standing by two cars waving his arms with two other guys. She recognised them as some of the familiar abusive and possibly dangerous adolescent young men who often vandalised buildings, started fires or stole bikes in the area. The bastards she tried her hardest to keep her own young offenders away from constantly. They looked over at the coffeeshop nodding and Issy felt her heart thump repeatedly, her pulse began racing. She clutched her smart phone tight, ready to film anything or call police. The fog out on the street swirled and moved around. From within stepped Ron. Issy gasped as she watched him follow the two thugs walk across the road toward them. One was pointing and laughing, one looked angry and enraged. She heard them laugh and taunt him as he moved closer to them casually. He held out his arms from under a tatter old coat and long strange claws came out which he directed at them. They clamped onto the loud young men, pulled them in fast, shook them before him as he smiled. He shook and snapped back his head, tore his lower jaw away. The other came up to the chip shop as he took hold of him. Issy was the only person to see how his arms were snapped back, watched him fall to his knees and his head crushed, tongue pulled out and thrown to the road. Ron threw him up against the window of the chip shop. He looked back at her, gave a wink, and carried them away down a side alley. She heard the horrific screams and sounds like chopping and grinding of wood and stone until a definite silence arrived. She let out a long breath, turned back around eventually to see Ricky and Annekia painting the railings in quiet bored manner.

'So...we...we're going out to the town hall railings next, finish the job from earlier this week. Okay?'

'Yeah, got to, haven't we? Don't want you getting all angry with us. Terrifying that was' Ricky commented.

Jackson parked his car at the riverside. He got out and opened the boot, pulled out the two bodies one at a time and stared down at them. He placed a hand upon each and the eyes fluttered open after a moment.

'You have more time; you've been blessed with a divine purpose. The stone provides. Come up and I have work for you. You must honour the stone' he told them. They stepped onto the riverbank sodden, their clothes smeared with mud, weeds, filth but their faces quiet joy and thankfulness.

'We will do what should be done. Lead us to our tasks' Peter said to him.

Jackson stepped back, avoided the nauseating odour of river filth and human decay which drifted from them.

'What are we? I don't feel the same as before' Samantha asked.

'You are what you need to be, what you should be. Don't question the blessing of the stone. Now come'

Their faces were sickly grey with veins prominent, eyes swollen bloodshot, some teeth had fallen out of both mouths, fingernails gone, as were some fingers and clumps of swollen and gangrenous flesh of their hands, arms, and faces. He gave them their orders and left them by the Briggar stone as the rain came down over them.

Chapter Thirty

Issy stood over her teens by the long fence of the town hall and made sure they painted just as well as she did this time.

'I'm totally counting down the days, hours, and minutes until this is over with. Got things to do, hustle and better jobs waiting, you should too, hear me?' Ricky said loud and boastful to Annekia as they painted in the afternoon sun.

'We know, you've told us all enough times. We all have better things we'd rather do. We made our mistakes. We're learning stuff. Miss here is a good teacher be honest' Annekia replied as she put on another lick of paint. They finished painting and moved back to where they were cleaning up the area, the refuse which needed to be moved.

Annekia needed to stop responding to his loud agitated outbursts and simply do the reparation work they had been given. Only a couple of session left, and they could get back to their own casual personal activities, only without breaking windows or vandalising buildings in future. She did like being around Issy, hearing her views on things, getting advice on ways to act in the world, careers to aspire toward, seeing her own value and spotting people who try to use you. That was what got her doing this work in the first place. She knew better know. They saw Issy look dissatisfied as she looked at her phone.

'So, are we dumping all this crap on the motorway or in the church carpark miss?' Ricky called out. She looked up.

'Hmm? Oh, hilarious Ricky. I'm checking my colleagues are around. I told you; we're loading it up into the truck next and we'll sort it at the building, check for reusable things and the rest to the landfill recycle processing plant.'

'You do look a bit worried, miss' Annekia commented.

'Just some issue with Gwen and Derek, they've got Abdul and Suze but not replying to me. They are bit quiet, probably tidying up where they are that's all. You two get doing what you've been doing well. I'm proud, I honestly am' Issy told them.

They continued with the loading of the truck of furniture and discarded waste as the evening sun came down outside.

The phoneline broke up when Derek did eventually call Issy. She knew the other reparation youth workers Gwen and Derek and had appreciated their support and guidance while she had been training in the job over the last year and a half. She did not want them to think less of her.

'In town...different...barking...street looks...leave...Abdul and...come...' she heard.

'What? What do you mean? I can't hear you properly. Message me Derek' Issy responded.

A few minutes later a broken message did arrive on her phone, just as puzzling as his broken-up speech.

'What the hell does he mean? Silly old sod' Issy sighed. She turned to look at Ricky and Annekia.

'Okay look, you two, better come with me to find Derek and Abdul. He's got the keys for the other truck. We'll drop you off at home then.

We'll be maybe ten minutes or fifteen. Not more than half an hour I promise.'

'Yeah, this is doing my balls in anyway, sweet' Ricky told her.

As she stepped outside with them and they started up the street she saw Jackson sat on a bench, looked around the main high street in town and down at some new buildings.

'Oh, hello Jackson, is Mae, okay? I haven't heard from her in a couple of days' she said.

'She is safe and well. How are you?' he asked as he stood and stepped along with them.

'I'm working right now, got to meet my colleagues. Got these teens with me so got to get moving. See you around anyway, bye' she told him and prompted Ricky and Annekia to moved fasted with her up the next street.

Jackson nodded to himself and turned back to walk along in another direction. As he walked through and up Coulter Lane and around to Wendel Road the view ahead did not seem the way it usual would. He was certain now at this point. Ron appeared beside him a moment later. He wiped his hands with a long rag, some torn shirt sleeve as he tried to wipe away dark filth and muck from his nails and forearms. He was excited, jabbered, and tongue-tied.

'Things are moving, changing. Old times are back, opened out and about around. You have to go see it all' he urged.

'Come here Ron, you've done so well. I am sorry I doubted you and your talent' he said and pulled him close for a hug. Tears formed and Ron gave a sigh as he moved close. The grip was powerful and tight. Jackson wrapped his quick spread membrane energy wings around and bit in deep, sucked and fed with aggression, as he looked at the town, he had grown too much respect for in recent decades. Ron moaned, whimpered, and fell to his knees but smiled as he did so.

'Sixteen hundred and eight, you bastard...' Jackson whispered as he walked out into a part of town which was familiar but different at the same time. Some buildings were missing, others new and street names changed or gone. He noticed a statue to an unknown local heroic quarry owner and archaic symbols etched into the stones of the cobbles underfoot. He looked in dismay and fury at the unbuckled chaos of hidden ancient streets and buildings of town opened out and overlaid in places. Some had formed over or on top of existing roads and modern streets and structures, some even climbed up, rose through into the high sky defying physics and logic up to the heavens. He cried out at what he saw, walls and rooms levitating and connecting to cracks of ethereal light.

'No, not right...not time for it. Shit Ron, fuck, you fool Ron' he called out. The cursed game was on around them but could not be played as centuries before. He knew he had less control and rushed to feed while he still barely had the chance.

Jackson fell back as he saw Lily walk casually down the road outside his apartment, flames around and between her, her wings burnt to almost nothing, her face, arms, legs charred. Her hair was down to brittle tufts, face was a dark black ashen injury, smoke came up from her as some light rain spotted down from above.

'Sixteen oh eight, burning angels for Hell. Stop this. I want it but should not...we shouldn't' he called out to her.

'Oh, no? But you must relish and enjoy it, we all should, like it never ended all that time ago' Ron said from across to his left on the street.

'Where are the offerings? You're not an angel Ron. Neither is Lily'

'No, we should be, we fucking should be. Look at what we do. We never let up; we sat back all this time. You and I, we're the best fallen bastards on this cursed island.'

'No, just me' Jackson replied.

They struggled but Ron escaped down some side streets. Out of sight of Jackson he changed and into a new disgusting and undecided form of hulking animal parts. His head was close to that of a lion, torso like some bear, legs of goat with feet of man as he ran and loped through the streets to oversee the wickedness of the ancient game set out on the returned streets.

Mae stood in the apartment alone and regretted her bitter words with Issy and Jen. Even if she wanted to stop Jackson and find Katherine, she believed that time had passed. She finished the bottle of wine, placed it on the kitchen counter and pulled out the next one from the lower shelves. The figure stood out in the garden and tapped on the window. She looked and saw Lily and after a silent moment of glancing at each other she opened the back door to her.

Mae Jackson on her phone from the bedroom and what he heard did not please him 'Jackson, the big dogs are out, near me. They howl but they talk too. That sounds crazy I know. I've seen Katherine. I'm heading to the Briggar stone, on the riverside, okay?'

'No wait' his line was faulty, crackling and it broke up.

Mae stood and rattled the lock on the door to the bedroom for the third time, but it was no use. She knew Jackson was protecting her, but she wanted to have the choice. Did she need to see Katharine once more? She fell back onto the bed behind her and let out a sigh. Before the wall to her right the air shimmered and a quake came, and a slip emerged and from within a large portal hole Lily stepped out and took hold of her hand.

'You should be out. Come with me. She needs you. They all do' Lily told her.

'Things are changing. I'm not sure of everything I knew' Mae said.

'That is fine. Don't be afraid but do come out. He will hurt you eventually, probably soon and he'll do it to them too.'

'But Katherine...she...I think she has murdered.'

'No, she didn't know, was sleepwalking, in a trace. Only took them to Briggar stone.'

'I know the stone.'

'You must come there. For her and for Jen and Issy' Lily urged.

'...yes' Mae replied and followed her out in the ceaseless rainfall.

'Join me. This is not right, you know it' she said. Mae stood and followed her through as the dimension hole sealed up behind them.

The betrayal obvious to him, Jackson took his phone and flicked through the live feed of hidden cameras set up around his house. He could not see Mae in any of them. It was clear she had gone to find her friends. He called her immediately, unsure of where she was but he hoped she had not met Katherine yet. She did not answer his call. Jackson rushed out ahead, each street and next turn offered up a different contortion of the town he knew. He knew where she was heading, he knew what he had caused when he screwed over Katherine three years earlier. His memories were perfectly clear, even if he wanted to scrub them right out forever. He could not. How brittle and naïve she had bee he thought. Did he think Issy and Jen would be there to pick her up once he was with Mae when they all left college for good?

Chapter Thirty-One

Issy brought the car up beside the town hall and she let Ricky and Annekia unload the tins of paint and bags of brushes and equipment inside the back entrance.

'Stay by me, we're out there for a short while that's all. If you see Derek or Gwen, tell me immediately, okay?' Issy instructed as they left the community depot together and crossed the main road toward the library.

'I hear Derek...' Ricky yelled and rushed out and turned a corner.

'Oh god damnit...' Issy sighed.

'Town looks weird, maybe it's the evening light, sundown' Annekia stated as she stood beside Issy.

'Don't go anywhere' Issy told her.

Issy confronted Ricky and Annekia as they walked through town.

'Listen, there are histories to our town you don't know. We all have been brough up with ideas about our past which have shaped our outlook or who we are and what we. Don't let that limit you. I might someone or something I don't agree with, but you go for what you can be proud about, be someone who lives beyond what we've been told to fear or avoid.'

'Are you okay miss?' Ricky asked.

'I think I understand you, miss' Annekia said.

'Does town look different tonight, how's that? Not just me, is it?' Ricky blurted.

'Maybe, look did you hear Derek near here?'

'Look up that street...' Annekia said and pointed. Issy waved her attention away.

'We're going the other direction. Come, follow me. You'll get more credit this way, they're waiting for us.'

She led them away from what looked unusual and unexplainable.

'I hear dogs. I don't like dogs when they're off their leads by themselves' Annekia said.

'Let's keep moving. They'll be with their owners, I'm sure. Keep moving now.'

She received a message from Jen-

'Issy I've been with Katherine. She knows we got to the old house. She knows more now, like we do. She is sorry for our truth but needs us.'

'I've got my teens with me now' Issy messaged back.

'We need to be there with her at the Briggar stone.'

'Okay. I'm in town. I think Ron and Lily are doing something tho.'

'Can u get ur teens away safe and meet me?'

The sound of the dog barking became a cry or wail of anger. Some argument behind it. The street they walked quaked underfoot.

'I'll try to do that. Meet u soon' She messaged.

Issy had seen the dogs, those unnatural things- they were not simply wild or mongrels. These things were exactly what Katherine had described in her strange dream fantasy stories in college times. After the gang abuse near the chip shop the fog, the dogs are heard...Katherine is hidden but Issy and Jen see her in the streets...

'Hey, miss Issy, aren't we going to go back and finish the painting?' Annekia asked.

'We will. We'll meet Derek and Gwen soon, but I need us to go across to the community hall just until then. Follow me both of you' Issy told them.

'Ricky scoffed 'I'm not afraid of dogs, even big ones or staffies. I know how to handle 'em. Besides, don't sound like the real mad ones, they're just excited and loud that's all.'

'Well listen, I've seen these ones recently and they're different. We actually should be careful and get moving. I think they're dangerous and you're both under my orders right now anyway so let's move, okay?'

'Because you'll get a proper bollocking from your boss if we're attacked by mad dogs, but you really don't give a shit?' he suggested.

'No, because I care about both of you even though you're a bit of an arse. Let's move out. Come on'

They did as she said, Ricky huffed and groaned audibly while they crossed the roads together and moved across town. They made it a few streets on before Issy stopped and decided the plan should change. The dogs could still be heard and so to continue toward the community hall seemed too great a risk.

'New plan now, my place. It's not far from here. I'll think of something from there.'

The few streets ahead were quiet and the fog was clearing out as the moved. They reached her apartment as they stepped in Ricky noticed the sky shift in the most strange sudden way and he rubbed his eyes in disbelieve.

'Fucking weird out there' he muttered.

Annekia turned and looked at the street behind them. She was sure the houses had appeared different; half the block had been shops or takeaways. It must have been quick rush across town with the fog dispersing and the nervous rush of adrenaline with the dogs confusing them she thought.

'Here we are. This is my place. Wouldn't usually invite my work clients in but this is a safety issues tonight and we're still on the clock anyway. Get inside, sit yourself down. Don't anything unless I say so, or you'll have another two weeks service you hear?'

'Miss, yeah. Relax' Ricky said and dropped down onto a bean bag by the window while Annekia sat on the sofa near the bookshelf.

'Those dogs are out there. How do we get home? Do we call for an uber and get in real fast?' Annekia asked.

Issy sighed 'Well look, if it comes down to it, you both can stay here the night. I've a futon and the sofa. Ricky would be on the sofa of course'

'What? They'll be gone soon in a bit. I mean, I don't mind crashing here. We can watch a movie and order a pizza innit.'

Issy looked at Annekia and the rolled their eyes together.

They peered down out of the window. It was hard to tell if the dogs were right below the building on the street or further away. The barking came every minute or so still, but it sounded strange, almost like shouted words or calls to them.

The question on the mind of Issy was how could Katherine get rid of them, if she could? It was now apparent that she had some relation to them, with them. No fear or not like any other person but some understanding. These beastly mutated things which did try to disguise themselves as shabby mongrel dogs of outlandish size wanted things only, she knew. The talk with Jen about their purpose and nature, the prey they sought was mostly futile other than remembering and discussing the old tales then before she had disappeared. Each had spoken to her, asked her to explain why she had come back, how, and why the wild dog creatures were around them and her. She only decided to tell them vague pieces of truth as if she was ashamed or uncomfortable revealing all of what she knew. There was obviously hurt and pain her, gnawing at her, struggling, and making it difficult for her to be truthful to her old and closest friends which is what she most desperately wanted and needed.

She messaged Jen.

'Is Katherine with you?'

'She was but I think she was going to find you.'

'Shit. The dogs are near my place, and I've got two of my teens with me now.'

'Will she stop them?'

'Her parents must be near, they'll stop the dogs, it's their dogs, I think. Only they'll do it.'

'It's not that. The story of the giant dogs and the stone kennel. The whistling woman, the angry god of the rivers in the water'

'Right, Katherine's story in college. We didn't clear that up, didn't get to the truth of that one, where it came from and what it means.'

'It's her and them don't you see it? I mean that's sounds nuts I know but...you see it don't you?'

She looked back blank.

'It's her parents, they're the dogs. She wasn't messing around. Wasn't making us the stories or telling us old legends and folklore. She was telling us what she knows. Ron and Lily, call them out. I can come over and help if you want.'

'Call them, the dogs?'

'By name. Tell them Katherine is watching and helping us. She's angry with them.'

'Okay well, no look, wait for Katherine to show and maybe you can bring her.'

Jen and Issy came together on the unfamiliar rearranged town streets as they looked around with shock and awe at the way buildings were stacked, broken, rebuild or half-formed ahead and around them with the dark purple and black clouds which cracked with thunder overhead.

'I got my teens away and to near their homes. They're not messaging back. I don't think they got home' Jen told Issy.

'They must have. Wait...'

she meets Katherine.

'Have my teens from work got back to their homes safely?' she asked.

'No guarantee. Sorry. All the reason to give yourself to the stone with me' Katherine replied.

Fog drifted in from the left gentle but devious and distracting. She turned and turned, the shape and movement of it confusing and misleading her attention. Her eyes eventually came to stop on Ron who stood hunched against a wall with a grimace as he rubbed his misshapen arms and hands, his fingers like long claws or pincers.

'Issy my dear, hello. Found my Katherine yet? Or are you going to tell me another white lie?' Ron sneered as he stepped casually out before her. There was something wrong with his stance and his face. His face was a sickly blue and grey, he moved with a hunched limp toward her, and she stepped back with caution.

'What's up with you?' she asked.

'Been out here all week looking for my Katherine, haven't I? I'm fucking tired now. I'm exhausted. Feel I might collapse...' he slurred.

He did appear weak she thought. There was barking somewhere out to her left or was it around on the right or all around her?

Annekia was gone she suddenly noticed.

'Oh fuck, Annekia...hey?' she called and walked out ahead. She turned to scowl back at Ron, but he had moved on already.

Chapter Thirty-Two

New narrow streets and roads came up before Annekia. She was struck by how they appeared to look unusual, they had some old and almost medieval or Victorian style around the roofs, the arches of windows and doors. Had these streets always been in the town? From behind some strange statue erected to some person she did not recognise, Lily stepped to her with a smile.

'Hello. Do you know these streets?' she asked.

'I...no I thought I did. What part of town is this?'

'It's old but new to many now. You know Issy don't you?'

'Yes, she's my guardian sort of. She's...not far.'

Lily 'Has been good for you? Has she inspired you?'

'I suppose. Actually yes. I don't know many adult women like her. She cares about me and my not getting into real trouble. She forgives as well.'

'Forgiveness is good. Does she love?'

'Love me? I...'

Lily levitated up from the ground a few inches, not much but enough to cause Annekia to stand mouth open in awe. She watched as

Lily floated up the narrow alley and she followed behind, fascinated. She continued behind her until some loud crack and roar came from behind her, around her elsewhere. When she looked back Lily was gone.

'Hello?' Annekia called.

Ricky shuffled along around a corner as he chewed gum and mumbled to himself. He looked up and stood confused.

'Where's this?' he said as he took in the unexpected view, the new street, and unexpected buildings ahead of him. He spun around to see more of the same behind him. Some of the walls were cracked and crumbled, disjointed, and seemed stacked up high apart from the structures of the foundations of the buildings they came from. It looked unsafe and illogical.

'Where's Bailey Road and…Greenarch street?' he said. He spat out his gum as hands rushed out from the behind and pulled him away into folding shadows and unfolding buildings behind, a loud crazed laughter hit his ears.

Down on a street in town which only appeared half familiar Issy fell to her knees and began to wretch. She vomited over the cobblestones, her sight blurred, and she ambled ahead on her knees. In seconds she blacked out. Time passed; she could not be sure just how much when she opened her eyes. She stretched out her limbs and felt different. Her hands moved in some unusual manner; her legs felt longer. She pushed herself up from the ground and stumbled up to her feet. With a turn toward a shop window on her right she took in a breath at the thing which looked back at her. The feline creature moved its jaw silently, a quiet meow released.

'Oh…my word…' she said. Her hands her paws, soft but with claws and her body, when she glanced down was still female but coated in fur with long clawed feet. A tail curled around her right thigh.

'This is it. This...is a dream. This is our answer' she stated. She bounded ahead; necessary instinct thrust her forward. It took only moments in the streets ahead for locals to scream and gasp, run, and fall as she appeared and moved between and past them on her journey.

'Ricky? Annekia?' she called. She realised it would be better to not do this and simply protect them. Her nose took in the scents, so many but the ones she needed did come eventually. She moved on, prowled with stealth and focus.

Katherine walked on toward the first dog creature. It stood five foot tall or more in height, its eyes red and vibrant stared hard before it rushed to her and latched down on her right arm. She looked at the creature as it bit down, spittle flew out from its sharp teeth which dug into flesh though it seemed to cause hardly any pain or reaction from her. She was not hysterical or in severe pain. It was a brief annoyance, a frustration.

'I did not fall, I was held, as I am held now' she told the dog creature plainly as she looked down to it and took hold of the savage beast as it wrestled and held her arm, her flesh pierced. She took it by the mouth and prised it away, threw it down and stared at it.

'Turn, this is wrong. It is not the way to be. These ones should not hurt like us, know that' she said.

The dog creature shook, shivered on the ground. The legs quivered.

It spoke to her 'You left us. You get this.'

'Hurt me, not these people or my friends, this town.'

'This does not hurt you' a voice called from their side left. The other large dog creature roamed out toward them as the first was convulsing and changing shape and returning to human form before Katherine. It became her father Ron, naked but displeased.

'Lily, not this. No suffering for these ones. It is no offering as it should be' Katherine told her.

'Oh, you see that? That's all we wanted' Lily replied.

'You're no...saint...yet' the one changing stammered as it became the familiar aged form of Ron, naked and wounded. He had sprouted horns from his head and ridiculous long and cracking forked tail from above his arsehole. As the other came nearer she was clothed by rushing leaves, branches, and grass which wove together wildly to become a long coat form around him.

'You've hurt them, your teenage friends. See what you've done coming back now. It is not the thing to do.'

The other dog came up before Kathrine and spoke 'We...told y ou...this would...be...your price...for it' it snarled, and it fell while it morphed back into the human form of her mother Lily. Leaves and branches quickly came wrapped her it a coat like form like that which Ron stood wearing.

'I will return. You can stop all of this now. You will, yes?' Katherine asked.

Both her parents looked at each other and back to her.

C hapter Thirty-Three

Above the rooftops some strange unfinished constructions had risen, broken and incomplete walls and floors of buildings. Logic and reason to local reality was disrupted when Jen looked out as the town spread apart and Briggar stone came right into view, all else was pushed to either side of her vision. It seemed to move toward her silently, sought her to enter inside.

Ron and Lily stood back down a narrow alley to watch the escalating confusion.

He smirked as he spoke. 'We get them knowing fear and helplessness, they want human life, don't they?'

'But Ron...' Lily responded quietly, eyes cast away from the town which had steadily begun to reform, transfigure around them from their united moments of touching the ground and praying, whispering, and chanting.

'Not Rondalt, not Leighleth. We're things, we're from them and they used us. Not now, this is our time, and we'll have Briggar's and the town how we need it to be. Like all the lore and legends that last, the ones misunderstood and made up. Better than all that, that'll be us'

Lily remained unsure, walked away, and shaped into dog form to rush away through the trees.

Jackson stepped out on the high street amazed and awed by what he and Ron had released. His decades, even centuries of denial were fractured now by what he saw. He felt shame and guilt. He blamed Katherine. What kind of sister would let him forget his destiny? He levitated up before Derek who was chained to a doorway upon a floating town building in the sky twenty foot or so up. Jackson met with Ron at a distance, ashamed and feeling the guilt of his own desire to take charge of the killings and murder.

'Well done, Ron. I applaud your reproduction of what we carried out in town. Some of my favourite games the people feared and somehow forgot. I see both of you are useful and very skilled. I cannot deny that. Where is Katherine? Is she helping you with these acts?'

'You would like that?'

'It would not be a bad thing I think.'

Ron gave a slow smile as he thought about the notion.

'You do not understand this. I do, I forgot. She let me forget. I used to test you, question you. We were left here. We could not easily understand that. I took hold of this town for judgement, I did that' he declared.

Derek cried and pissed through his jeans onto the door behind. Jackson held onto his quivering pale face.

'You sin, you burn' he said with calm decision and drifted back from him as the flames burst and snapped into life around Derek.

Jackson peered down to examine the cavernous howling shifts of fatal suffering cast over the face. Gwen and Derek screamed as they ignited where they were held and chained in place on other doorways upon town shop fronts. Jackson moved back and chased Ron who limped through town the backstreets, he cheered and wailed as he slashed and swiped out at people who screamed and tried to escape his grasp and get to safety.

'Hey, hey Ron you shit! You've made mistakes. You've done it wrong. Come here, let us do it together. Ron, stop there' Jackson shouted as he flew along the back street toward him. Ron dropped a terrified victim and swivelled his head around to look at him.

'I am a mess. What...what did you make me? Why?' he asked.

'Come, let us do this together tonight' Jackson offered. They walked back where they had come from. Jackson stopped and looked at the floating buildings, the buckled, unfolded old streets which had been hidden and erased long ago. His flesh opened out, his wings snapped out, chest opened as he snatched hold of Ron and pulled at him, sucked him within. Ron was gone, and Jackson turned to head out to reach Briggar alone. Jackson made his way out of town and could easily view the river and Briggar stone no matter what street or road he walked.

The local betting shop they clung to, overturned, unfolded. A juddering eruption of concrete and mud blasted through the broken and warped walls and doors behind them. This sight of incredible surreal geographic change made Ricky fall back into Annekia beside him.

'It's that legend, it's the local thing, a witch...erm...she burned people she chained to doors after...'

Annekia agreed. 'After the plague or civil war thing'

'Fuck, look that is...no, that's wild. This is acting, it's like for a film or something right? Yeah?' Ricky said. He rushed around one street with warped shop fronts and doors upon doors to see Derek chained up and bleeding. Ron loped out ahead, muttered out of the shadows, his horned and hunched silhouette cast large and exaggerated across the buildings across from them.

'Her young sinners. See and say, tell your children, this is the fear now, this is the lore of the land here' he told them.

Ricky stood mouth open and pointed. He could not believe or comprehend what spoke to them. Ron was some mutated ungodly abomination. The thing that was Ron reached for him but fell and crawled on the ground like some preying predator, gnashing teeth as its goat legs behind clawed the road beneath as it moved toward them. Phil pulled Ricky away, shoved Annekia too.

'Go, forget it, go on just run' he yelled 'Where is Issy?'

'Back in the other street, where we came from' Ricky replied.

Jackson moved out and took hold of Phil and knocked him down. A fleshy spike shot out from his palm and Phil was pulled away. Annekia gasped as Ricky tugged her arm and they began to run away from the nightmare scene back to where they had left Issy. She was gone.

'Hello Issy? Miss?' Annekia called out.

'Town is different, Ricky's right. Are we safe here miss?' Annekia asked.

'You will be. I must meet my friend. I've played my part. I am ready now' Issy told them.

'I don't understand.'

'What's she chatting 'bout?' Ricky snorted.

There were cries and yelled screams from another street. They saw the buildings risen into the night sky, floated and not of modern times as if the past had been ripped from below. Ron fell out at the top alley, threw up where he was. He saw them down the low end and chuckled.

'See me...I am more...folk more' he spat and crawled along the road.

Issy pushed Annekia away 'You and Ricky go.'

The phone Issy held buzzed.

'Where are u? Meet me come on' It was Jen.

'On my way now' Issy responded.

Chapter Thirty-Four

In that moment Jen walked out around a corner into a street which she had never seen in her life. It should not be possible, but she understood to think differently and expect anything now. While the town rumbled and shook around her, she collapsed onto her back. She gave out a moan and pulled away her jeans and jacket, jumper and tights, underwear. She lay naked on the cold stone ground while her body became the other thing, she thought she had only dreamed of before. Her arms snapped, stretched, and shook. Her legs kicked and tensed, and she sat up while her back hunched and took on another position and the wings spread out wide. In only seconds more Jen was the bird creature and up into the sky. She stumbled and perched on a rooftop on the shops to her right where she sat for a moment and looked down over the town as it became a patchwork of new and old streets and monuments all around. She heard the barking and howls easily from some direction below and she jumped away and glided out.

The faces looked up and she caught their fear, awe, reverence and more as she flew over them. With her beak and long beautiful wings she hoped they could perceive what she tried to make a peaceful smile toward them. She noticed the phones held up, footage being immediately recorded and uploaded to local news and among the people of the town and elsewhere. Further away, most would not believe what they saw but the locals had already been told to expect this visit and to be prepared. Katherine had approached a few of them in the last couple of days and to the ones who would listen she urged them to leave out offerings of toasted bread soaked in oil and mugs of wine. When Jen flew down and set foot on the street, people stepped back from her speechless. She held out her wings behind her and stalked around them as she noticed how the streets had shifted, reformed. She tried to keep her barring and understand where familiar buildings and places she knew should be with luck if they had not shifted too far or worse. Down by her long-clawed feet she noticed the offering of bread and wine in a shop doorway and the owner stood by head bowed as she moved close.

'Thank you. This is new to you and me' she spoke as she knelt, ate, and drank. The barking and erupting voice of familiar anger echoed nearby. She stood straight and thrust up to the sky once more.

The people below on the street stood back silent and grateful for her presence.

The clouds came close toward as Jen glided higher above the town, the thrill and exhilaration of her transformation something she found hard to contain or put aside. Her thoughts her confused and collided inside her head. Focus was difficult but some instinct moved her on. As she passed through the lower side of clouds something emerge ahead which caused her to parabola and fall back momentarily. A split, a hole in the sky appeared ahead of her, some organic orifice where a figure stood inside and looked out at her.

'What...who...?' Jen gasped as she struggled to balance in the air.

The figure on the doorway in the sky spoke to her.

'Held her, down there, give yourself' it spoke.

'...yes, I...yes' Jen replied and she turned and flew back down in among the streets of the town.

She came down and saw Lily walked quietly through a narrow street alone.

'Wait!' Jen called out and Lily spun around. Shock and hesitation appeared over her face.

'Where is Katherine?'

'You...from her?'

'Yes'

'It is Ron and Jackson you must confront. This is not my wish, the town in this state' Lily told her.

Jen as bird creature stalked away from her up the street and turned a corner. If she could not find Katherine, she knew she must try to stop the ones who had abused her. The movement below knocked her balance as she walked on. She took sustenance from another offering by a doorstep. The next turn ahead brought him into view.

She rested down upon a roof of the old library as the barking grew louder and the voice was one of a sly bastard, she knew must be slowed down in what he was attempting.

Ron moved along, his body contorted between that of dog and human with hunched wide back to her as he mumbled and laughed to himself. She rushed at him as he approached Ricky unaware bedside the doorway of a record store. When she saw Ron stood laughing as he swaggered along and touched a tall post in the street, she swooped down on him. He felt the breezed behind but was too slow to react. She knocked him down as she let out a piercing cry of fury, her claws scratched his face. Knocked to his knees, Ron twisted and howled out. He spun around and jumped at her, eyes wide with shock but quick to attempt to lash into her with his fanged mouth and clawed hands.

She swiped her right wing down against him, deflected his attack and pushed Ricky further back.

'Run now, find safety' she cried and turned back to Ron.

While Ricky stumbled away from them away down a back alley, Ron moved toward her cackling and barked out in her face.

'What a freak you are' he snarled 'Come from our Katherine did you?'

'Better a freak than an abomination' she retorted and kicked out at him. They came together, claws interlocked as they pushed and pulled, their faces inches apart. The tension lasted until he buckled and fell to one knee. She released him and returned to the sky above. He watched her leave and spat down at the ground.

This was something else, a different time, a new moment in the history of the town. Truths and facts and lore and legends of the past could not apply too easily now. There was no time to think about any of that but to only trust in what Katherine had led her and Issy to find in the old family house. The stories and poems, the paintings and dreams had been gentle preparation for this time she understood. Jen flew over the streets she knew well and those she did not. She could not see Ricky or Annekia and so continued to cut through the sky.

Katherine saw burning Lily with her withering angel wings come up through the town side streets, weak but proud.

'Have mercy, I pray on her soul' she whispered and ran to her. Her own wings torn open her shirt and jacket, sprung up high and wide. They wrapped around. She could not reach her, the crowds of locals were out, shocked, and afraid but smartphones out recording and sending images.

Lily fell and ran burnt and broken to the river and away. They saw Katherine risen in the air, four feet from the ground, wings out and a shimmer of blessed golden energy around her. That was what Lily had been praying to see for centuries. She looked up at her and wept as she fled through the enveloping dark and whispers of the night.

C hapter Thirty-Five

'Ricky, you jerk, where are you?' Issy shouted out as she walked on alone. The howls were there somewhere around her. She moved to where she believed them to come from and noticed a local down by a tree on the street making some strange arrangement.

'What are you doing there?' she asked.

The woman turned and looked up at her 'This will sound stupid but a woman, a very sick looking woman told me to lay this down tonight. She was off the ground; I was scared but she told me of something much more terrible to fear. To avoid it she said we should do this. It doesn't make sense but sometimes not everything does.'

Issy looked down closer to see the arrangement of stones and roses and carnations laid together. There was blood upon the small stones below them. She had a sudden flash of memory. Events from her childhood. She had been taken, pulled away from helping another young girl who drowned when they were picking flowers. The stones by the river splashed with blood when the girl fell, hit her head, and drowned.

Issy coughed, fell, and shook on the ground before the woman. The clothes Issy wore brunt up instantly and her body transformed, mutated, and became feline, remade as a cat and she stood on her back legs. She took up the flowers, touched the stones and looked at the woman.

'Thank you' Issy purred. She rushed away through a side street when she heard the voice of Annekia. A long procession of local towns people stood on either side of the next street. Some held wine and bread offerings, others the flowers and stones. They saw her and watched in silence, bowed their heads while they held out what they had with them.

Feline Issy moved on ahead through them, gave a quiet and gracious thank you to some as she came to the end of the street. She turned to face them.

'There are two men out here who wish to torture some of you tonight, they change and erase the town we know and love. See them and defend this town how you can. With my sisters I will do the same' she told them and left them where they stood, candlelight illuminated their silent nodding faces.

Streets away Ron cursed and spat out in rage as he watched the torture walls rise and contort. He spun around and watched with hesitation and anger aware of these new beast things out to disturb and disrupt his plans.

'Lily! Where the fuck are you?' he shouted. He looked up at the moon overhead as it came out transparent yet enormous. He stood alone and frustrated as he knew time was ticking away. He would twist and change the town to something none of them knew and he would take it for his own.

Jen came down beside the sports club building, her body drained and her head light. She could only think to move people away from

Ron and find Katherine, but her body felt heavy and slow. Shuddered and once she fell her body returned to her familiar human form. Katherine came up behind her, clothed her, poured water between her lips. Her tendrils sunk into the arms and neck and fed from Jen.

Locals came out in two long rows, all held out burning torches as they confronted Ron and Lily in their dog forms. They back away, barked and howl. The Lily dog rushed away and left Ron as he stood on his hind legs and snarled out at the townsfolk.

'It changes....your town, you people. Know us, fear us' he told them. They moved toward him once they noticed the Issy cat creature in the opening of the alley right behind him. Ron stumbled back, snarled, and ran out as he was burned and hit with the torches. The cat creature moved away into darkness somewhere as the townsfolk stood together, flames crackled and protected them as the Jen bird creature swooped and arched overhead.

Chapter Thirty-Six

The manic screams of ecstatic joy burst from the lungs of Ron as he danced on his goat legs with dog features and moved from street to street to inspect and admire the contortions of the landscape of the town centre around him, the buildings which had cracked, rebuilt themselves from hidden potential unlocked up into the sour blue night sky above.

'What have you been offered? What has she told you?'

They did not answer, simply tried to continue their attack. He smacked the cat thing down and grasped hold of the bird creature once it pecked into his forehead. He shook and swung it until the cat creature return to bite and claw his legs. He fell to his knees but aimed a punch to the head of it, knocked it back to the ground where the other came to find it.

Jackson stumbled up, looked up the great high lore torture structure until he rushed away to find Ron.

Ron found himself lost and confused by streets he had contorted and disturbed into new directions.

'Damn you Katherine, wasting my time! Your bitch siblings ruining my time!' he cried out and lurched toward a local woman who cowered low near a bench. He clutched at her hair and tugged her to her feet.

'You people in this town, you don't appreciate what has shaped you all, you must remember me this time...' he told her.

Someone clutched his own wrist. He turned to see Katherine at his side. She was haggard, pale, decomposing but held a crazed anger in her eyes.

'Too far. Too much, far too much' she told him quietly.

'Get off me!' he spat and tugged to no avail. A weakness shook his bones, shivered in his veins as he stumbled back, shook his head, eyes winced shut.

'You don't feel quite right do you?' she said.

'Fuck off, fuck...' he muttered as he fell back, stumbled, and let go of the woman who instantly ran from the scene.

'Goodbye you greedy bastard' she said, and pushed him to the ground, his teeth cracked and splintered on the cobblestones.

She walked away back down a side alley and a moment later Jackson found him in a heap.

'You tragic fucking mess. Come here' he said and pulled him close.

'See it all Jackson? You hear them down on the streets? They'll remember all of this. Pass it down just like they did with your games. Fucking spoken and streamed for a century to come and more!' Ron cried out as he heard the casual footsteps close by on cobblestone.

There was panic and fear within Jackson, but he held it back with the greatest effort as he moved toward his lying devious offspring.

'You're falling to pieces, your poor bastard. You're unstable' he commented as they observed the crooked and towering structures risen between the streets, above rooftops.

Ron took a bow and displayed and foul smile 'I am their nightmare, my friend. I'll be right inside their minds, gnawing at their subconscious for lifetimes from now, not you!'

'You're a mess dear Rondalt.'

'We do what we were made to do, you know that is the way!' Ron spat out; an unhinged laughter tumbled from his thin lips. 'Yes, you've been doing such a good job. Always have, haven't you?'

'No, do not lie to me' Jackson yelled and clutched a hold of Ron by his neck. The devil tail snapped and cracked the hand of Jackson quick. He fell to the ground and stumbled back to the nearest alleyway opening. Jackson moved after him as the street rumbled and continued to warp and buckled around them, shadows collapsed and folded his view. Ron ran fast and confused, shifted through various forms as he moved desperate to be remembered and feared like nothing before as Jackson stalked the streets nearby to find him. Jackson watched Ron when he found him, watched him suffer, unable to control or contain such transformative energy. He watched him bleed and fall apart, desperate to control his form, his myth and lore to be. Jackson took hold and cradled him, looked into the manic wide eyes.

'Ron, hold steady. Focus yourself' he suggested. It did not help as Ron continued to shake, judder, cry and mutated in his grip. From goat to dog, boar to chimera beast the body would not remain one form. Jackson took him by the head, stared into his eyes.

'Time is up. I understand, I had my adventures, my own depraved games in my desperation to see God come down to us, to burn us, break us or cradle us. I see your games, your lore. Well done my child' he told him in a soft gentle voice before his torso split and writhed, shimmered and Ron lowered his head with some degree of pride and gratitude in his contorted features as he was pushed back deep inside Jackson who sealed up in seconds and buttoned up his long jacket, brushed down his shirt and trousers, pushed back his hair from his forehead.

Ron howled as Lily jumped up and sunk her fangs into the arm of Jackson. He screamed and shook her from him. Ron instantly knocked him down, held him by the side and bit into his face. Jackson closed his eyes, held out his arms as they attacked and began to rise from the ground.

'This is not my wish. Do not make me do this. My love for you is there, always has been' he told them.

They tore at him, Lily as dog opened his chest, Ron fumbled for any delicate parts he could pull forth and release. Jackson moaned, eyes to the sky above as blood wept out of him over them. He shook and throbbed as Lily gnawed his chest, clasped onto his left arm as Ron pulled himself up and drew back a fist, punched down into Jackson, smashed his jaw. The act was extremely satisfying but his fist was soon stuck. He pulled and twisted but no release came easy. He grinned and his eyes widened as he realised what could be happening.

As he realised what could be happening.

'Lily...' he gasped. He fell against Jackson when the chest opened wide like a fly trap, tongue-like tendrils snapped out and wrapped around him, pulled him tight. One shot out and wrapped around the neck of Lily unaware, she yelped but could not escape.

The Issy cat creature launched out and pounced onto Jackson as he and Ron stood and looked up at the new sadistic lore game construction up above them raised on stone and wood. Jackson fell back, arms out to pushed her away but she was at him, clawing and biting instantly. He stumbled and knocked her away.

'Who...what...Ron?' he cried and turned to see Ron with mouth open simply pointing at it.

'Fucking lore...one of them, has to be! She's done this, Katherine!'
he yelled and fell back as he began to mutate and attempt to reform
his body to his own beast preference. It was a slow to occur, stutter-
ing and troubled. He was too weak for it to continue. He spat and
pushed Jackson toward the creature. Jackson gabbed him in a rage. As
they began to fight, the Jen bird creature flew down and hit them. It
screeched and clawed along with the other, both eager to inflict pain
and suffering upon them. Jackson waved his arm over his head as he
pulled Ron who fell to his knees before he ran down an alley to the
left.

Jackson peered up to the bird creature while the other came at him
again. He knocked the cat thing back and yelled up.

Soon Lily appeared to find only Jackson on the street. They stood
and looked at each other.

'Your Mae went looking. Went to Briggar stone. We should help
her' she told him.

'Yes, let us do that.'

She stood at the other end of the street. They saw each other and
she beckoned him to follow.

'Katherine is heading to Briggar, she had taken your Mae there' she
called back to him.

'Wait, Lily, I need you. Ron is back inside now; you should be too
for your own safety' he called not at all convincingly.

The townsfolk came in toward him from to opening of the street
where he stood. He saw their many blazing torches aflame and their
defiant faces as they stood in tight formation close together. He threw
back his gaze but saw Lily gone.

'God damn...' he uttered and looked around him. He rose from
the ground, moved ahead slowly and the line of townsfolk gradually
backed away, hesitant fear in their eyes.

'That's right, part and let me pass. For your survival' he told them. They did so, only a few thrust their flaming torches to him which he instantly knocked back and smacked down as he glided through them to the next street.

Chapter Thirty-Seven

Moments later Issy rounded up the teens away from the large Lily dog. They ran away from her, and she stood still as she heard the bark, the howl from behind. Issy stopped when she saw Lily come out into the road on fire. She did not look as though she felt any pain and large arched wings came up from her back blazed and crisped in the snapped and bright flames. She walked near with purpose.

'Jesus...' Issy gasped.

'No, but he'd be proud.'

Lily walked out before Issy and she stepped back from her, cautious and fearful.

'I have Mae in Briggar, she is weak. They are unaware. Katherine must be with all of you. If not...'

Lily fell as she twisted, tired she shifted and growled. She bounded away through the streets.

Jen came forward with Ricky and Annekia

'See who I found' she said and turned to them 'Go now, in the car, to Issy's place.'

Issy gave her keys to them and sent Ricky and Annekia them away.

'She is calling us' Jen told Issy as they looked out down the quiet street together.

'Where have the large dogs gone?' Issy asked.

'They're away, separate. Katherine has time to intervene. She still needs us,'

'Needs us as creatures?'

'No. That was amazing, but she needs us inside. At Briggar'

Katherine came and caught up with Issy and Jen as they trudged out of town in the direction of Briggar on the riverside. They had gradually receded from their creature forms back to the human and while they looked dejected, they pushed on ignoring bruises and bleeding.

There were two people moving in some unusual manner toward them as they pushed on.

'Who are they? They look ill' Issy stated as they walked together.

'No idea'

They came to stand before them, and the man lurched forward.

'Witch women. Stay back from the stone' the man announced and moved at Issy, his arms straight out, hands clawed.

'Hey, stop' she responded but he took ahold of her.

Jen clutched his arms as the woman figure came to join them.

'Whores of the stone. Devil women, keep back now. He tells us it is wrong.'

She made to grab at Jen who instantly smacked her away.

She stood with Issy as they looked down at the aggressive strangers.

'What is wrong with these two?' Issy asked.

'I don't know. Let's get to the stone, come on' Jen replied, and they moved on quick. In seconds, the two strangers got to their feet and started to follow them.

'Run now, come on' Jen suggested, and they start just as the woman clutched at the jacket of Issy who struggled with her and fell, kicked at her and the woman moaned and reached out and cursed in a dazed voice.

'Get off me bitch!' Issy yelled. The man was back at Jen, and she poked at his eyes, hit his nose, snapped it successfully. He fell back with a cry and the woman held on with desperation to Jen.

'Witch, witch defying our God, our stone, keep...back witch' she garbled.

From above them Katherine glided down and took the woman by the head, gave a violent twist and it turned all the way around. The woman dropped to the ground, mouth still moving, muttering curses. As Jen stood speechless, Katherine turned and grabbed the man, snapped his arms, and knocked him down, stamped on his legs and he lay broken before them. She looked to her friends with urgency.

Katherine descended low before them. They watched her float down to them and take their hands.

'Fucking hell, Katherine' Jen gasped. Issy found no words.

'Thank you both for helping back there. You were spectacular. Just as I remembered' Katherine told them.

'Wait, we've been like that before?' Issy asked.

'We have' Jen said, 'I feel now, I know that's true.'

'That's right. Listen, you must enter within, before he gets near' Katherine said.

'We're almost there, I see it up ahead' Issy said and pointed to the Briggar stone.

'Katherine shook her head and pointed to her chest 'Within' she said, and her body peeled and split open like an enormous wildflower of flesh and sinew. The sight was disgusting yet alluring and magnificent.

Jen bowed her head 'Katherine, take what you need. I understand, I see our lives weren't our own.'

'Oh, they were, and I hope you have felt and experience what you should and what you wanted to in that time.'

She wrapped her energy winged arms around her and the pincers within drained energy from Issy quietly until she fell, weakened into the arms of Katherine.

Issy staggered back as she watched Jen pulled deep within, into the mysterious cosmic place. Some part of her wanted it, desired to be in there. Her nipples hardened and her breathing quickened. She was of the town but that was the past, a false past given to her. Her parents, her identity created not by her, not to be hers forever.

'I don't know...we're leaving the way we were in town, our own selves. I...can't we stay or come back?' she asked.

'You will return, as will Jen and Mae.'

'And you?'

'Enter, please. For the town, for me, for us'

Katherine came forward and showed a curious expression. Issy wonder if it was suggesting sorrow or suffering or even apology?

'Why are we who we are?' Issy asked 'We came here, you led us. We found your letters, the painting, all those stories you told us and things you showed us. We are other things. We know it. We understand our past. Who do we fear-that or you?'

Katherine hunched low, to her knees. She looked up at Issy silently and the face seemed to change. It could have been the moonlight or the flesh and bone of the body, but Issy could see the face of Kathrine before her. Her old friend Katherine was crying. Issy walked up closer to her.

'I am sorry, we all are so sorry for what happened. We were awful, real bitches. We regret how we were. We offer ourselves to you' Issy asked as she leaned down and investigated the face of her old friend. Katherine held out a delicate hand and touched her face.

'We accept the past. We know you are suffering and greet our own to save others' Issy said.

Issy looked back and thought she saw a male figure walk up on the horizon at the edge of the town streets. In that moment, Katherine grasped her by the neck and pushed her down inside her, the flesh petals recoiled back together, the sinew and muscles wove together and sealed up. Katherine glided up from the ground and flew quick to Briggar.

As she reached Briggar, the door opened to her, and she entered within. Back out on the misty field by the riverside Jackson walked up and came to find the broken and twisted bodies of his resurrected Peter and Samantha.

'It was worth a try I suppose' he said as he noticed their injuries, the blood and eyes looking to him, their mouths quietly muttering questions of why and words of mercy and hate.

'Thank you anyway' he said as he knelt and touched each one. In a moment they set on fire, flames rose and snapped and twisted in the air as he moved on toward the Briggar stone.

Chapter Thirty-Eight

Before Jackson arrived at Briggar, Katherine had all three friends down on the riverside below concussed. She pulled each one in and blessed them, baptised each, each time blood flowed from them, from her and back into them. Mae struggled, screamed, Jen unsure, Issy gave herself obediently, wilfully, seemed to speak on tongues.

From inside Briggar Katherine looked down across the field she saw Jackson walking quick across the grass. The offerings were there on the grass by the riverside he saw and shook his head as he continued. He saw her with them up at the window. She gave a smile.

'Katherine, no,' he exclaimed as he began to walk faster.

The window opened, she pushed each of them out one after the other, lifeless but saved from their torment. They fell into the river, their bones snapped and cracked against the rocks and riverbed as the water splashed out and around and over them.

'Our family has changed Katherine' he called to her across the wide lounge room as she stood beside the window.

'I know, you are right,' she replied.

Jackson lumbered on over the thick grass and mud, across the moonlit wide field to the riverside and he saw the familiar shape ahead. She knelt and he heard the crying. He stepped to Lily, held her face in his large hand.

'You think it is her time?' he asked.

'Remember all of your destruction and deceit and see Ron has tried his best to go beyond even that' she said as she looked up at him, tears down her cheeks.

'I was finding the way to be human, to know them, to know the reasons they are made to feel joy, pain, life, and death. I have watched it closer than ever before, studied the moments, over and over.'

'Where has it got you?'

He arched his back, his jacket billowed, and shirt tore open along with his chest, the layers of flesh exposed the cosmic depth, and she recognised her time.

'Be with her. Let Ka-ta-raheen guide you.'

He clutched her and threw her inside him, his sides sealed and submerged her screams as she disappeared within. He fell back, threw up onto the grass. A shake of his head and he looked ahead to see the Briggar stone greet him, the moon risen behind it.

Moments later he came up to Briggar stone and waved his hand for the door open to him. He stepped inside and up the stairs wasted no time in his mission to confront his betrayers. His established human life back in town could not be ruined by their petty jealousy and grievances toward him and their own shortcomings.

Jackson was lured upstairs inside past the dining room, the table with bread and wine, the old trophies of skulls, historical relics of centuries before, various old Bibles and books of faith, crosses all around. He saw Mae out on the window ledge. He stepped to her, she is beyond in the folded buckle of time and space of town, in the past version of Briggar while Katherine has placed the current version between them.

Katherine 'We've got a responsibility.'

Jackson stumbled and coughed as he moved toward her 'Do we? It's never really worked in all this time.'

'Open your outlook. Which of us was really ill? We should be ashamed of ourselves. We've let the others down.'

Jackson 'Ron and his stupid tales. We're freaks, we're a secret minority. You're not stable, I've got a place as a man in the world. I look out for us. I told you that.'

'Ron and Lily, my friends, my sisters- from us. We made them, we need to be accountable. Who fucking does that? Those from the blessed garden'

'We've never found any of them, so we do what we do in this town.'

'They hide and wait; they perform small acts of kindness and shift the world in good ways.'

'You don't know that. Speculation. You and your hopeful dreaming. Do your dreaming back in Briggar.'

Jackson 'We shouldn't have left.'

Katherine 'No, you shouldn't have. It comes down to the town. We don't even know us. All this time, generations of them. We wait, still wait at Briggar.'

'Look what we made. A family for us' he said.

'No, we're sick, ill ever since. We shouldn't have done it. It's not our thing, our way. We don't create, we lead, we show.'

'Not for the longest time if we believe what they say. We're forgotten. Centuries have passed Ka-tu-raheen.'

'We are not forgotten.'

'Oh, fuck off.'

He scowled and stormed away.

'Where is Mae? Mae I'm here. We'll go back. This isn't the place for us' he called out as he stormed further inside Briggar. Straight ahead through the lounge room he saw Mae who stood silently before the large window and looked back at him.

'I am here for you. Don't be afraid of anything...' he stuttered as he spat blood and bile over the floor and fell to his knees. He landed on his side and bile coughed out from his mouth. Unable to continue, all energy ebbed from him, the mind fogged by the poison he lay still while Katherine came and pulled him across the room. She took up his weak body and threw him into a narrow doorway on the far left. Once she had slammed the door, she took the bar and locked it, hammed it shut and cast a spell to seal it shut. She sunk down to her knees, head low and breathed heavy, exhausted let out a sigh. She stood and walked back to the centre of the lounge. Around her she saw the faces of Jen, Issy and Mae look back at her from the large, mounted mirrors on each wall around her. They smiled back at her, and she did the same in return.

Her face changed to each of theirs one moment at a time, part of her, inside her as she held them within her.

'I was always jealous of you. Like he was of Ron and Lily, me with the three of you' Katherine spoke as she glanced at the faces of Mae, Issy and Jen in the three large mirrors around the lounge room which looked back at her.

'What comes next?' the voice of Mae asked inside her head.

'We wait in here as we used to. We watch the town, we held them' she responded.

'Do we go back down there?' the voice of Jen asked.

'I do not know.'

'There is something outside the stone' the voice of Issy stated and Katherine wandered to the large window and saw the doorway in the sky directly ahead open and the figure which shimmered and shined looked back at them. It stepped through the sky to the window and walked through then entered Briggar to be with them.

'Have you always been here?' it asked.

'We think so. Where have come from? We've been waiting' she replied.

'My name of Oriella. Where my stone stands, we need some help. Can you join us?'

Katherine looked back at the sealed and locked door which trapped Jackson.

'We will join you, yes.' she replied, and she followed the shimmering figure out of Briggar through the wall, across the sky and into the doorway in the clouds above.

END.

EPILOGUE

In the days that followed, Katherine continued to feed Jackson the mind fog soup in the dungeon room. She opened herself and released Mae, Issy and Jen who walked back to town, to set up the new lore, clean up the ruins and mess created by Ron. They quietly visited their old families who could not see them, knew them no longer as any part of their lives or having been so. They seemed content and safe which matter more than any selfish connect. The streets were brought back into shape, buildings shrunken back to their previous state, locals lost all memory of the events and only kept in mind the possible sighting of the cat woman, the bird beast, wolf woman, all of whom seemed to protect and nurture the town. Sacraments and offerings were left by the stone every month after.

Acknowledgments

This book was the last of the three books I started writing during the covid lockdown times. The other two I self-published as an experiment and with this last book I decided to go with a small independent publisher as it was something more unusual and they often will take more chances than the big well known and established publishers. The other two books were intended as straight horror tales where I focused on suspense and chills. This last book however was intended as a bridge from my straight horror and some projects ahead which I hoped to explore and push the boundaries of the genre with more unusual, fantastical horror. I have taken things only so far here while keeping the story largely horror themed but it may test and challenge some readers.

I want to thank Tony at Anuci Press for taking an interest and having it as one of his books for 2024. I also want to thank authors such as Catherine McCarthy, Keanlan Patrick Burke, Tim Lebbon,

Adam Hulse, Adam Nevill among others for advice, encouragement and inspiration as I finished this book.

About The Author

James Parsons currently lives in Manchester, UK but was born and grew up in Newcastle where he studied art & design, followed by film production & animation. After working in that field and writing screenplays he turned to writing fiction over a decade ago. He has had two science fiction novels published, more than a dozen short horror tales, followed by three horror novels.

In any spare time not writing he is still a regular film nerd, attempts to learn guitar, paint and work on art projects, see live music of many kinds. There are more fiction tales in the works as you read this. James can be found on X/Twitter- ParsonsFiction, Instagram- ParsonsFiction, Facebook- James E Parsons, BSky.